Born in Lincolnshire educated in Sussex before entering the University of London where he gained an LL B with honours in 1937.

He joined the Royal Horse Artillery during World War II, and served in Europe and North Africa, where he was captured and imprisoned – an experience recalled in Death in Captivity. After the war he worked in a law firm as a solicitor, and in 1952 he became partner.

Gilbert was a founding member of the British Crime Writers Association, and in 1988 was named a *Grand Master* by the Mystery Writers of America – an achievement many thought long overdue. He won the *Life Achievement Anthony Award* at the 1990 Boucheron in London, and in 1980 was made a Commander of the Order of the British Empire. Gilbert made his debut in 1947 with *Close Quarters*, and has become recognized as one of the most versatile British mystery writers.

BY THE SAME AUTHOR
ALL PUBLISHED BY HOUSE OF STRATUS

MICHAEL
GILBERT

SKY HIGH

HOUSE OF
STRATUS

This edition published in 2011 by House of Stratus, an imprint of
Stratus Books Ltd., Lisandra House, Fore Street,
Looe, Cornwall, PL13 1AD, U.K.

www.houseofstratus.com

Typeset by House of Stratus.

A catalogue record for this book is available from the British Library
and the Library of Congress.

ISBN 0-7551-0511-7

ARMADO:
The sweet war-man is dead and rotten: Sweet chucks, beat not the bones of the buried: when he breathed he was a man. But I will forward with my device.

The choir rehearses and the quiet life of Brimberly village goes on. Yet sinister undercurrents simmer beneath the surface. It starts to emerge that the respectable choir members may not have been entirely honest about their pasts. The usual peace and tranquillity of the village is threatened. The rifling of the church poor-box may not be unprecedented, but then there is an explosion . . .

Chapter One

THE CHOIR REHEARSES

BOYET: *'The trumpet sounds: be mask'd; the maskers come'*

'Christ,' said Mrs. Artside pleasantly. 'Not Kerr-rist.'

'I'm sorry, Mrs. Artside.'

'That's all right, Lucy. It's a difficult word to sing. Jesus is much better, and, of course, Jesu is easiest of all, but we've got to take what the hymnographers give us. Let's do it again from the beginning.'

She sat down at the bench, which protested a little under her weight, and laid her thick, wrinkled fingers on the keys of the portable harmonium. The choir once more attacked Charles Wesley's great morning hymn.

'That's not bad,' said Mrs. Artside at the finish. 'Not bad at all. There's no need to look quite so down in the mouth, Maurice, when you're singing "dark and cheerless is the morn". I'm all in favour of expression, but you needn't act it. That covers the hymns for the next two weeks, so now—'

'What's the last hymn next Sunday, Mrs. Artside?'

'Hundred and sixty-six. Old Hundredth. You all know *that*. We'll have the treble descant for verse three. "O enter then His Courts with praise." All right, Rupert?'

Rupert Cleeve nodded sombrely. Beside the three Hedges boys, thought Mrs. Artside, he looked like a greyhound puppy in a litter of collies. Where they were slow, shaggy-brown, and already thickening

1

out into small replicas of their huge father, Rupert was thin, pale, and a bundle of controlled nerves. Dress him in a frilly collar and a satin suit and he would take the shine out of any Hollywood Fauntleroy. Even in a plain flannel suit he looked good enough to eat.

'All right, then.'

'What about the psalms?'

'Plantagenet, Llandudno and Snagge,' said Mrs. Artside rapidly. 'It's no good getting ambitious if we're to make time for an anthem. After all, it's the first one we've done since the Christmas before last. Hand the sheets round would you, Tim?'

The thick young man in flannel jacket and corduroy trousers distributed the anthems and the choir, from Ellen, the youngest Hedges girl to big Jim Hedges himself, in his best black, stared with dutiful curiosity at the symbols spread out before them, symbols which their unstinting efforts had but three weeks to turn into a river of liquid harmony.

Only Major MacMorris, the Cantoris tenor, seemed unperturbed. He glanced in quick, professional manner, through the score and bent across to say something to Sue Palling, the Cantoris Alto.

Tim Artside noticed the movement but did nothing about it. There was five yards of vestry floor between them, and in church and directly under his mother's eye was not the best place to start a fight.

'"Come, ye thankful people, come",' said Mrs. Artside. 'We can't run to first and second trebles, so I think, on the whole, we'll stick to first. The tenor solo – that'll be safe enough—'

Major MacMorris exposed his white teeth in a smile. He assumed, correctly, that the compliment was being paid to him. Tim Artside chalked that one up, too.

'I'd better do the bass voluntary – "ere the winter storms begin" – unless—' she looked politely at Jim Hedges, who grinned and said that on the whole he thought Mrs. Artside would do it better than him.

'There's no alto solo—'

'Thank heavens,' said Sue Palling and Lucy Mallory in most perfect unison.

'I suggest we take it straight through. Start on the tenth beat – like this—' She sketched the introduction nimbly on the harmonium, and at the appropriate moment burst out with the word 'COME' in her resonant bass.

'All right – once more then – I want you all to come in this time – plenty of attack. Da dum diddy dee—dum dum—dum dum—COME—yes, what is it?'

'May I leave the room?'

'I should have thought you could have lasted four pages of music without—all right, all right—we won't argue about it. You ought to know.'

Rupert walked sedately from the vestry and closed the door behind him. All his movements were composed and unselfconsciously neat.

'Whilst we're waiting for Rupert we might run through the treble part. All ready? On the down beat. "Come ye thankful people come. Raise the song of Harvest Home." Oh dear. That wasn't very good, was it?'

It was evident that the trebles leaned on Rupert.

'Try it once more. Well. That's a little better. Perhaps if the altos backed you up this time—'

'Come to God's own temple come. Raise the song of Harvest Home.'

The thin wailing drew to a close.

'Wouldn't raise the price of beer,' said Jim Hedges. He spoke with the authority of one who was not only the father of five-sixths of the trebles, but also owned and drove the only taxi in Brimberley.

'It hasn't got much attack,' agreed Mrs. Artside. 'It'll get better with practice, I expect. Here's Rupert, at last. Try it once more.'

It went better this time. The bass, which consisted for the most part of a repetition of the words 'Harvest Home, Harvest Home' was safe enough in the hands of Jim Hedges who, in forty years, had sung every part in Brimberley choir from treble and wobbling alto through green-stick tenor down to the comfortable depths of bass. Major MacMorris made child's play of the tenor, rebelliously followed by Tim Artside, who was reliable if he had someone to help him start but had no idea of striking the initial note. Lucy Mallory and Sue Palling were, at best, moderate altos.

'I think we shall make out,' said Mrs. Artside at last. 'We've got two more Tuesdays before the big day, and I'd like one private run with the trebles. Friday? No, that's Institute Night. Next Monday then. It'll save opening the church up if you can come to my house.'

On behalf of five of the trebles, Jim Hedges agreed that Monday was as good an evening as any. Rupert said he would find out.

'Come to that I can ask your father to-night,' said Mrs. Artside. 'He's driving over to collect you. Thank you, Lucy. If you'd just put the psalters back in the choir stalls. You'll want them all on Sunday. I'll take the anthems home with me for next Monday. Would you lock up, Tim? I've got to hurry back home and put the coffee on. Are you going to be in this evening? The key goes back to the Vicar. If he isn't in you can put it through his letter box, but I think he must be in, it's Confirmation Class.'

'All right,' said Tim.

'You know there isn't a key for the inner vestry—'

'I've locked up this church at least twelve times,' said Tim. 'You go and get the coffee ready. And reverting to your last remark but three, I don't expect I shall be joining you, but if I do I am capable of getting out another cup. And who's taking Rupert home?'

'He can come on the back of my motor-cycle,' said Mrs. Artside. 'Would you like that, Rupert?'

'All right,' said Rupert. Even the thought of riding pillion to Mrs. Artside did not seem to stir his remarkable soul.

Left to himself, Tim bolted the outside door of the vestry, fastened the window, and locked the anthem cupboard. He could hear the sounds of the choir dispersing; the dominant note was the squeal of the Hedges children, who seemed to recover full voice the moment they got outside the church. He grinned as he heard the eldest boy, Maurice, chanting 'Kerr-rist, Kerr-rist, Kerr-rist'. The deep roar of his mother's motor-cycle, rising as she changed gear for the corner, diminishing as she swung into the road, and muttering away into the distance. Heavy footsteps on the gravel – Jim Hedges, he judged – and the rattle of Lucy Mallory's voice.

He stepped out into the body of the church, shut the heavy inner door of the vestry, and made his way slowly through the choir into the aisle. All around him, in the quiet dimness was the church smell of hassocks and coconut matting and lamp oil and holiness.

Out in the porch he could still hear voices. One was MacMorris. He would have recognised anywhere those amazingly gentlemanly cadences. The other was young Sue. She was laughing.

MacMorris said, 'But you don't do that sort of thing at Blackpool.' She laughed again.

Tim stepped through, shut the wicket door, and turned the key. He could see Sue now, white against the dusk, perched on the railing of the porch. MacMorris was standing beside her.

'Oh, hullo Artside,' said MacMorris. 'Turned cold hasn't it?'

'Seasonable for the time of year,' said Tim. 'You walking home, Sue?'

'I promised Major MacMorris I'd go with him.'

'You promised me first.'

'Did I?' said Sue. She sounded genuinely surprised.

'Well, old boy,' said MacMorris judicially, 'why don't we all go together.'

'Because, old boy,' said Tim, 'I've got something I want to tell Miss Palling, and I don't particularly want it broadcast over half of Brimberley.'

A brittle silence impended.

'I may be wrong, but that sounded to me rather offensive.'

'It wasn't meant to be particularly offensive, or non-offensive, for that matter. It was just a thought. Are you coming, Sue?'

'When you've apologised to Major MacMorris.'

'Apologised,' said Tim blandly. 'But for what?'

'For behaving like a silly little schoolboy.'

'If I'm behaving like a silly little schoolboy, might I suggest that MacMorris – I beg his pardon, *Major* MacMorris – was behaving like a silly little grown-up.'

'Really, Artside.'

'What do you mean?'

'Possibly I misunderstood you. I thought he was offering to walk home in the gloaming with—'

'Oh,' said Sue. 'What a stinking thing to say—I—really—'

She looked at MacMorris. There was a pause in the proceedings, broken only by Tim, who was whistling quietly through his teeth.

MacMorris seemed to appreciate that the next step was with him. He cleared his throat.

'I think,' he said, 'that we're both behaving stupidly.' He turned to Sue. 'If my offer offended you—'

'Of *course* it didn't.'

'Then I'm sorry it should have been misunderstood. Perhaps you'll both excuse me. Good night.'

The dapper little figure swung away down the path. Tim and Sue watched in silence until the wicket gate clicked and he was gone.

'Yellow, too, for all his high C's,' said Tim.

Sue said nothing.

'Let's get going.'

He saw that she was shaking.

'You're cold,' he said. 'If we walk quickly, you'll get your circulation back.'

'Don't let me stop you.'

'What do you mean?'

'Walking quickly. In any direction you fancy.'

It was rage, not cold.

'But look here,' said Tim. 'What's up? I'm sorry if that little twerp upset you, but—'

'Are you going? If not, I am.'

'You're not going home alone.'

'It's a free country,' said Sue. 'You're bigger than me. I can't stop you using the public roads, if you feel like it.'

She set off up the path and out into the road. Tim padded along beside her. Offended dignity kept him quiet for a hundred yards; then he said again, rather feebly, 'What's it all about?'

'I think,' said Sue clearly, 'that that was about the most oafish performance I've ever listened to in my life.'

'Why?'

'Threatening a man who is half your size and twice your age, and then crowing like a silly little bully because he has enough gumption on you.'

'He shouldn't have—'

'And of all excuses for forcing a quarrel on him, you had to pick on suggesting filthy things about him, because he offered to walk home with me – which he has done umpteen times before, without your permission – seeing that he lives in Melliker Lane only two houses away from us.'

'I never—'

'It was so silly it ought to have made me laugh – if it hadn't made me sick. And now'—she swung round at the top of a dark lane leading off the main road, among the pine trees—'will you go home. I can actually see my front gate. Are you satisfied?'

'It's a bit dark,' said Tim obstinately. 'I'd better come down with you. Or are you afraid to trust me?'

'Afraid of you?' said Sue. She looked at him speculatively. 'You great big war hero. I shouldn't think that little girls are your strong point, are they? At least, I've never heard about it, and we hear so much about you, I feel sure anything like that would have cropped up by now. Prancing round with soot on your face – yes. Sticking knives into people, small people, I should imagine, on tonight's form.'

'Now you're being silly,' said Tim. 'And anyway, I never stuck a knife into anyone.'

'Wouldn't they turn their backs on you?' said Sue. 'How tactless of them.'

'You're being stupid.'

'If you don't want to listen, you know what you can do with yourself.'

At this point both disputants realised, with embarrassment, that they were not alone.

Standing quietly in the shadow, under one of the trees, was a tall figure in cape and helmet.

'Good night,' said Sue with tremendous emphasis.

She stalked away up the road, and turned in at the white gate, visible at the far end. The gate swung shut with a click. The door opened, a light came on in the front room. Tim watched. The cloaked figure watched.

'Turning cold,' said Tim, at last.

'Afraid it is, sir,' said Constable Queen, stepping out on to the road. He was a big, blond, red-faced, serious young man.

Tim pulled out a cigarette, lit it and, after a moment's thought, offered one to Constable Queen, who took it, said, 'Thank you, sir,' in a noncommittal way, and put it away in his top pocket.

'Nice and quiet round here.'

'It certainly is, sir.'

'You wouldn't describe Brimberley as a hot-bed of crime.'

Constable Queen laughed tolerantly. 'Dogs without licences, and bicycles without lights,' he said. 'That's our main excitement. Still and all, you never know.'

'I hope you're not expecting trouble.'

'What I've found about trouble,' said Constable Queen after a pause for thought, 'is that you never do expect it – until after it's happened – if you see what I mean.'

'I couldn't agree with you more,' said Tim.

The constable seemed to be in no hurry to move on. Probably he would smoke the cigarette as soon as he was alone.

'Well, good night.'

'Good night, sir.'

Tim turned on his heel, and walked up to the corner. A right-hand turn would have taken him back along the main road, towards his mother's house.

He turned to the left and strode off into the darkness.

II

General Sir Hubert Palling, G.C.B., G.C.M.G., D.S.O., T.D., a member of the Honourable Corps of Gentlemen at Arms, Colonel Commandant of the Deeside Light Infantry, and grandfather of Sue, was over eighty, but hardly looked more than sixty. He had kept his figure and his wits and had every intention of living to ninety or beyond.

Longevity, in his view, belonged to a soldier as of right. There was no such thing as dying in middle age. You might die young, either in some operation of war or in one of those violent sports which are part of the preparation of an officer for war. Or you might survive this period of active service and still more active sport, in which case you were practically booked for a long and useful old age.

Despite the honour of knighthood and the gold braid on his ceremonial uniform, General Palling kept no car and no full-time servant, inside or outside his house. He drank little, and smoked not at all. And whilst he weeded his own flower-beds or helped with the washing-up in the evening, or walked in the rain to the bus stop, he did sometimes chuckle to himself over the comforting thought that he still had his wind and his waistline; whilst his contemporaries and his juniors, more opulent and more sedentary, had long since gone to their account – at seventy – at sixty – at fifty.

Why, good heavens, he had read in the papers of a business man of forty-five who had collapsed and died in his office, apparently as the result of walking up two flights of steps. At forty-five a man should be in the very prime of his life, ready to spend fifteen hours in the saddle and a night, in his greatcoat, under the stars.

Naturally he never voiced these opinions, even to a close friend, like Liz Artside, in whose drawing-room he was at the moment sitting. It would have sounded like complacency. But the thought was there.

Sad to say, as Mrs. Artside bustled in and out with her coffee making and the General sat perched in the wheel-back chair with padded arms beside the fire, they were bickering; about poetry.

The General could see no good thing beyond Tennyson. Mrs. Artside had more catholic tastes.

'Well, then, what about Columbus?'

'Did he write something called Columbus? Move the atlas and I'll put the tray on the table beside you.'

'Were you at Salamanca? No? We fronted there the learning of all Spain. All their cosmogonies, their astronomies. Guesswork, they guessed it; but the

9

golden guess is morning-star to the full round of truth! Isn't that splendid. Browning and better.'

'Browning and water.'

'Trust a woman to be wise after the event. If I'd said it was Browning you'd have gone into ecstasies.'

'I never go into ecstasies,' said Mrs. Artside, standing a full coffee-pot carefully down on the Benares tray. 'I agree that it sounds a little better than his usual drip. Birds in the high hall garden when twilight was falling, Maud, Maud, Maud, Maud, Maud crying and calling.'

'I like that too,' said the General loyally, 'but this is scientific, if you follow me. *"The compass, like an old friend, false at last"*. That's terrifically true. Whenever you really get lost, the first thing you begin to blame is your compass. I remember once, in South Africa, leading a column of all arms. Don't know why I was leading it. Probably the junior officer available – he usually got told off for that sort of job. I suddenly looked at my compass and—are you worried about something?'

'No. Not really. Go on.'

'Something on your mind. I'll tell you the rest of that story another time. It's rather a good one. What's up?'

'Lots of little things,' said Mrs. Artside. 'Tim, chiefly.'

'Hmp,' said the General. 'Yes. Kittle cattle, grown-up sons.'

One of the pleasures of talking to Liz Artside was that there was no need for suppression or reticence. He could talk to her about grown-up sons without the fearful suspicion that she was being sorry for him because he had lost both of his own. The elder had died in France, in 1917, on the eve of his 21st birthday; the younger, having lost his own wife, Sue's mother, in an air-raid in 1940, had pulled sufficient strings to get himself sent to North Africa where he had gone to his account in the messy fighting round Medjz-el-Bab, accompanied by a satisfactory number of Germans. Sue had been six at the time.

'What's Tim up to now?'

'That's one of the things I'd like to know,' said Mrs. Artside. 'He goes up to London every day, but I've no more idea than the man in the moon what he does when he gets there.'

'What's his job?'

'That's just it, I don't know.'

The General looked surprised.

'With a war record like his,' he said at last, 'I should have thought he ought to be able to step into almost any job.'

'Do you really think that?'

'Of course he ought.'

'I mean, Hubert,' said Mrs. Artside gently, 'do you really mean that you think he had a good war record.'

'Got two M.C.'s. What more do you want?'

'You're evading the question.'

If the General had had enough spare blood in his arteries, he would have blushed. He managed to look ruffled.

'What a damned sharp woman you are. Did I sound sarcastic?'

'A little.'

'I must watch out for it. One of my prejudices. As you get older you collect prejudices. Like barnacles. Yes. All right. I have always been opposed to the idea of a corps d'élite. Special terms of service and special pay. That sort of thing. Of course, you can't prevent some men being braver than others. Like dogs. It's biological. But you don't want to segregate the brave men and dress them up. Bad for them, and bad for the rest of the Army as well. You want to keep them in the regiment. In the Peninsula,' (the General spoke exactly as if it had been one of his earlier campaigns), 'we had picked men in every regiment. Light Companies, we called them – men who could be trusted out on their own to hold a strong point or make up a forlorn hope. You'd band them together, you see, for a job like that. But after it was over they went back to their regiments.'

'In short,' said Liz, 'you don't approve of Special Service Units.'

'Nothing against them personally. Very good chaps. It's the idea I don't like. The hardest job in war is done by the Infantry holding the line. No way out of it. Mud and frost and trench mortars and trench feet—'

'I don't think this last war was quite like that.'

'Bound to have been. All wars are like that if you're in the Infantry. That's why I don't think it's right to take men out of it, and give 'em

11

a lot of publicity and train 'em up for – for bag-snatching expeditions behind the lines. Just a point of view.'

'Do you mean,' said Mrs. Artside, 'that you object to the idea of Special Service because it cheapens the rest of the Infantry, or because it doesn't achieve its object or because it's bad for the men in it.'

'That's what I like about you, Liz,' said the General. 'You're the only woman I know who thinks like a man. First and second reasons – not the third. I don't think it turns 'em into crooks.'

'Well, thank goodness for that. Have another cup of coffee. I'll have to make some more for Bob anyway.'

'You didn't tell me Cleeve was coming.'

'I wasn't sure myself. You know what Bob's like. He usually comes to collect Rupert on choir nights, if he isn't too busy.'

'He's a worker,' said the General. 'Always had the reputation for it. Even in his Army days. I'm only sorry he won't be performing for us much longer.'

'What's up?'

'Nothing's up. But he's sixty-four. As soon as anyone tumbles to it – always supposing they've got someone capable of counting up to sixty-four – they'll be looking round for a bright young nincompoop to take his place.' The General paused to consider the peculiar ways of county councils, and then added, 'extraordinary how he's grown on everybody. You'll hear 'em all saying *now* that he's the best bet the county's ever had – and so he might be. But that wasn't the tune when he was elected seven – eight – years ago.'

'He's been Chairman for nine years.'

'Nine, is it? How time goes past.'

'It wasn't exactly a popular appointment, was it?'

'It certainly wasn't,' said the General. '"No experience". "Brainless army has-been". "Jobs for the boys". So much balderdash. If anyone had taken the trouble to look up his record, they might have saved themselves blowing off a lot of hot air they had to swallow back afterwards.'

'I don't see that anyone could call Bob exactly inexperienced,' agreed Mrs. Artside. 'After all, he had a top Q job in the Rhine Army at Cologne when he was only—let me see—he can't have been more than twenty-nine. He was sharing a house with Tom and me when—'

'Yes, I remember.'

Again something was left unsaid.

After a pause the General added, 'I'd like to see some of his critics trying to do Q to an Army group.'

'Then when he retired from the War Office – he was Deputy Chief Constable in Liverpool – and he did that security job for the Home Office in this last war.'

'I know,' said the General. 'I know. But the fact is, poor old Bob looks almost too like a soldier, and that prejudices people.'

'No doubt about it,' said Liz, 'his face is his misfortune. If he was brown, with a hatchet jaw – or white faced, with keen grey eyes – everyone would realise what a tremendous person he was. As it is, he blows out that silly moustache at you, gives you a popping look from his great button eyes, and says "Hrrrmph" – and how can you help thinking, blimp in person! Wasn't that the bell? I have to answer my own door to-night. Anna's at the cinema.'

The General sat and listened. He heard the front door open, and Mrs. Artside's voice, and a man's voice in reply; and something about Rupert, and 'Sam can look after him', and then the drawing-room door opened and Liz came back, followed by the Chairman of the county council.

'Evening, General. It's turned cold, hasn't it.' Then to Liz. 'If the car takes Rupert home and comes back, you'll have to put up with me for an hour. Do you think you can stand it? I'm in need of decent company. I've been spending the last two hours with a lot of old women who call themselves a committee. Is that for me? Thank you very much.'

Bob Cleeve accepted the armchair and the coffee cup; lowered himself into the former and lifted the latter to his lips; drank and put it down.

'Hrrrmph,' he said genially.

13

Chapter Two

ANDANTE

BEROWNE:
'And I, forsooth, in love,
I that have been Love's whip?
A very beadle to a humorous sigh,
A critic, nay, a night watch constable.'

'In theory,' said Cleeve, 'only policemen should be made Chief Constables. After all, they know how the British police system works. They've been in it since boyhood. It no longer has power to annoy them. So they're the obvious choice.'

'Then why not choose them,' said Liz.

'It's a sore point. Shortage of suitable candidates.'

'No officer class,' said the General.

'It would depend on what you meant by officers. In one sense all policemen are officers—'

'I always call a policeman "officer" when I don't know what else to call him,' agreed Liz. 'If I see he's got three stripes, then I promote him to sergeant.'

'You know perfectly well what I mean by an officer,' said the General crossly.

'In our case,' said Cleeve, 'no question arises. We've got a good one, who happens to be a policeman. I had dinner with him this evening.'

'Tom Pearce is all right,' agreed the General. 'Does he run you, or

14

do you run him?'

'It's a moot point,' said Cleeve. 'As Chairman of the county council, I'm automatically head of the Standing Joint Committee, and in theory the Standing Joint Committee superintends the county police. Actually all we do is appoint a good Chief Constable and let him rip.'

'And Tom is a good one?' asked Liz.

'Yes,' said Cleeve simply. 'I think so. He's unusually co-operative, I should say. And he's not above asking for advice. When he's got anything really in his hair he comes round to a meal and talks about it.'

'And what is it in his hair just now?'

Cleeve looked startled. Liz said, 'Deduction. You told us he came to dinner with you to-night.'

'Our chief headache at the moment,' said Cleeve solemnly, 'is grocers.'

'Grocers generally?'

'Well, grocers who happen to be county councillors. He's got a big shop in Bramshott. Mind you, I've nothing against grocers. I know some very nice ones. But this one's a particularly—a particularly grocerish sort of grocer.'

'He keeps a lady in a cage, most cruelly all day, and makes her count and calls her Miss, until she fades away,' suggested Liz.

'What? Yes, that sort of thing. Well, this one's moving heaven and earth to get the police to divert the traffic out of the Market Square, down a side street, and back along South Street. A sort of one-way traffic system. Every time we meet he's got a fresh reason for it. Overcrowding, parking offences, congestion of pavements. This time he'd managed to tie it up with immorality amongst shop assistants.'

'He sounds a persistent type,' said Liz. 'I suppose he's got some reason for it.'

'Of course he's got a reason. His shop's in South Street. His chief rival's in the Market Square.'

'Why don't you make it plain that you've spotted what he's up to and tell him to go to the devil?'

'My dear Liz! That comes of living all your life in nice clean Army

15

circles. I've no doubt that Bill, rest his soul, would have upped and kicked him in the pants. But this is the age of democracy. You can't kick grocers in the pants anymore.'

'Bill was the most reasonable person who ever lived,' said Liz.

'Of course he was. That was what made him an autocrat. Real autocrats are always reasonable.'

'What nonsense you do talk,' said Liz dreamily. (It was the real test, she thought. If people who had known and liked Bill talked about him she felt warm and happy. There was no twinge of the old pain. If any other sort of people discussed him, she felt edgy straight away.)

'—war's to blame for most things,' she heard the General saying.

'Such as which things?'

'Crime. Violence. Read in the papers the other day, two youths, armed with knuckledusters, attacked an old lady of seventy. Robbed her of her life's savings. Over two hundred pounds in notes. Kept them under her mattress.'

'I hold no brief for youths with knuckledusters,' said Liz, 'but I can't help feeling that some of the trouble is caused by the old ladies themselves. Why must they keep their life's savings under their mattresses? I keep mine in the bank.'

'I don't agree that there's been such an increase in crime since the war,' said Cleeve. 'Immediately after, perhaps. Bit of disorganisation then. But we've got over that. It isn't a case of *more* crime. It's *different* crime.'

'Advance of science.'

'No. I didn't quite mean that. Crooks get more scientific. So do the police. That cancels itself out. I meant fashions in crime. Before the war it was all gangs. Robbery and violence and intimidation. A sort of backwash from across the Atlantic.'

'I'm glad gangs have gone out,' said Liz. 'I never really cared for gangs. What is it now?'

Cleeve paused for a moment before answering, and looked unusually serious. 'I should say,' he said, 'that it's the age of the solitary criminal. The one-man army. I'm not talking about murder. Murder's always a solitary job. I mean, real criminals. Blackmailers, burglars, forgers, receivers and larcenists of all sorts from men who blow safes to men who live on handfuls of coppers extracted from telephone boxes—'

'And you mean,' said Liz, 'that all these people work on their own.'

'Not all. But increasingly more.'

'I shouldn't have thought that it was easy to break open a safe single-handed,' said Liz.

'That's because you're not an expert,' said Cleeve with a grin. 'Well, no. Perhaps safe-breaking isn't a good example. Safe breakers usually work in threes. But take your country house burglar. There's your crown prince of criminals.'

'The trouble with you, Bob,' said the General, 'Is that you're really half in sympathy with all these blackguards.'

'Not really,' said Cleeve seriously. 'Most of them are sad nuisances. But just an occasional genius. Do you remember Feder? Or Barry, as he called himself. Outwardly a respectable average adjuster in the city. And no nonsense. It was a real business. If you had an average to adjust, he'd adjust it for you. Only it didn't quite support his flat in Albany and his house near Leatherhead and his three cars and his strings of racehorses and girlfriends. Those had to be paid for out of his homework.'

'Homework?'

'Not very often – so far as one can judge, not more than two or three times in a year – at about eleven o'clock at night he'd leave his country house. No guests that weekend. A conveniently deaf butler and a cook who slept in the far wing. He'd roll his car quietly out of the garage and drive off fast into the night. He'd be back before morning. Old man Reynard, lolloping home to his earth, with a big grin on his face and a tuft of feathers in the corner of his mouth. And sure enough, you'd read in your paper that the country house gang – when in doubt the papers always call it a gang – had broken into the Earl of Mudshire's residence near Sunningdale and had removed the gold plate from the dining-room, the intaglios from the Long Gallery and the Countess' own hundred diamond matching necklace (which was of the highest sentimental value to her Ladyship) and the insurers had been informed. Only it wasn't a gang. It was clever Mr. Feder, who was known to the county as Barry. Who had taken the trouble to teach himself – at an age when most young men are training to cut out an appendix or draw up a will – to pick a lock, dislocate a burglar alarm, silence a dog, and cut a precious stone or a throat in a neat, quiet, gentlemanly way. All his jobs were surgical operations. Long, slow, careful planning, followed by quick, ruthless execution.'

'I should have thought,' said Liz, 'that when he got back to his roost with the loot his troubles were only just starting. How on earth did he turn it into cash?'

'Well, that's always a snag. He overcame it by patience. He concentrated on jewellery and precious metals. As I said, he could cut a diamond as well as most experts. And he made his own settings. Lovely work, some of them. But the real thing was that he was able to wait. Years, if necessary. And, of course, when he did come to dispose of anything, his position in life was a help. He wasn't a hole-and-corner sort of person. He lived a straightforward ordinary life and had lots of rich friends. If he offered a well-known jeweller a pair of pendeloque-cut diamond earrings set in platinum filigree, the jeweller was hardly likely to approach the transaction in a suspicious frame of mind. But suppose, as a matter of precaution, he checked through his latest numbers of "Hue & Cry" and the "Pawnbrokers List." He wasn't going to find anything. The diamonds were probably a pair of reshaped marquise-cut stones which had been stolen three years before. And anyway, why should he be suspicious? He knew Mr. Barry well. A very nice gentleman indeed, who had bought a gold cigarette case from him only a month before.'

'Clever that,' said the General. 'I suppose you'd say that his greatest risk was being seen actually on the job.'

'A risk for him,' said Cleeve soberly. 'But, by the Lord, a very much greater risk for the person who happened to see him.'

'A killer?' A look of interest flickered into the General's frosty eye. Killers, he understood. He had encountered a lot of them in his time, two-legged and four-legged.

'Not by nature, perhaps,' said Cleeve. 'But a man like that would kill to preserve his identity. There aren't many of them about at one time, and the police have got a short list of suspects. I don't know just how the list is compiled, but you can take it it's there.'

'And you mean,' said Liz, 'that if some absolutely independent witness – a servant or a guest or the householder himself – happened to meet your man actually on the job, then he'd have to be killed.'

'That's right,' said Cleeve. 'Otherwise the police would be round next day to show him a bunch of photographs and – respectable Mr. Barry, businessman and churchwarden, would be marched off to the clink, and no one more surprised than the Vicar.' He paused. 'I didn't tell you how Feder was caught. It was just before the war. He had broken into a house at Great Missenden – after diamonds, as usual. Only this time, for various reasons he went in whilst the family was at dinner. What he didn't know was that the son and heir, a bright young chap aged eleven, was hiding in a cupboard in his mother's bedroom. Why he should have been doing that, I don't know. There's no accounting for children. He watched Feder walk in, break open the dressing table, force the wall-safe, remove the jewel cases, and so on. Took him about twenty minutes.'

'Was he wearing a mask?'

'Not on your life. He wore gloves, but never any form of disguise. Reckoned it was safer that way. If he was seen at a distance he calculated on being mistaken for a guest or servant. It would have spoilt the effect if he'd been wearing a hood or a false beard. When Feder had finished, the boy thought he would jump out and say Boo! – just to see what happened.'

'But he didn't,' said Liz, whose throat was unaccountably dry.

'By the grace of God, no. At the last moment discretion got the better of valour. Of course, that's why the boy's alive today.'

'And he identified Feder—Barry?'

'Without hesitation. Made a splendid witness, too, I believe. Completely unshakeable.'

'Bob, you're making my flesh creep,' said Liz.

'Sorry. Unforgiveable. And I'm doing more than that, I'm keeping you out of bed.'

'I must be getting along too,' said the General, regretfully.

'Give you a lift?'

'That's very good of you. Don't know why Liz puts up with us. Come along here, drink her coffee, talk our heads off. Bore her stiff.'

'It's her own fault,' said Cleeve. 'She listens too well.'

'I can assure you, poppets,' said Liz, 'that whatever else you do, you don't bore me.'

She was getting past the age when she cared for a lot of sleep. When her guests had gone she took out the coffee cups, and washed and dried and stacked them. Then she threw a handful of fir cones on the economical early-autumn fire, and settled down to read.

Eleven o'clock had struck faintly from the church tower up the road when she heard the sound that half her mind had been waiting for; the click of a key in the lock.

Footsteps, which paused in the hall. Sometimes Tim went straight up to bed. Sometimes he didn't. Tonight after a moment of hesitation, the footsteps came on.

'There you are,' said Liz. 'I'd been wondering what had become of you.'

'There I am,' agreed Tim.

'You've missed Bob and the General.'

'Had they got anything interesting to say?'

'I always think Bob's interesting. He was talking about how Chief Constables get appointed – and about country house burglars.'

'Sounds fascinating,' said Tim.

He threw himself back into an armchair, which twanged softly. He was not tall, but thick and solid. 'What had Bob got to say about country house burglars?'

'He was telling us about one who used to operate before the war. His name was Feder, but he called himself Barry.'

'Oh. Before the war.' Tim seemed to lose interest. He lay slouched in the chair, his shoulders hunched, his arms hanging down so that the knuckles brushed the carpet.

'You look as if you'd got the grumps,' said Liz.

'That's right,' said Tim. 'I've got the grumps. And don't tell me that all I need is a dose of salts. It goes deeper than salts.'

Mrs. Artside was not sure if her son wanted to talk or not. If he did, she was very willing to listen. If she said the wrong word he would dry up and go to bed.

'Who have you been terrorising this evening?' she asked.

'First, it was the Vicar.'

'Not worth powder and shot.'

'He's a silly little man,' agreed Tim. 'Really, a silly little man I happened to meet him on my way down to choir practice. We started talking about politics.'

'Oh, dear. And him a timid, pale-pink radical.'

'Not about *his* politics. About politics in general. I said, what a pity it was we hadn't got a system of free election in the church. Then parishioners would have a say in electing their own vicar. He said, terribly solemnly, "You ignore the spiritual values, Artside." I'm sorry to say I laughed.'

'That wasn't terribly tactful.'

'Spiritual values my foot. A four-figure living and only two hundred parishioners to look after. He's on to a soft job here, and he knows it.'

'It's certainly well-paid, as livings go,' said Mrs. Artside. There isn't much connection between work and stipend in the church nowadays. Probably never has been. Still, you mustn't go around quarrelling with the Vicar.'

She did not say this with any conviction. She was not greatly attached to the Reverend Hallibone. 'Who did you fight with next?'

'After choir practice,' said Tim sombrely, 'I had words with our phoney Major.'

'Oh, dear.'

'He's such a little snurge.'

'Even if he is a snurge,' said Liz, 'and it's not a term I'm familiar with, that's surely no reason for quarrelling with him.'

'But he's so bogus.'

'He's the best tenor in Brimberley, Bramshott or Alderham.'

'You and your choir. Do you know, I don't believe he ever was in

21

the Army at all.'

'He must have been, or he couldn't be called Major. Unless he was in the Salvation Army.'

'If you ask me, he's made the whole thing up. Do you know, I saw him once, at a tennis party, *saluting* one of the lady guests – wearing flannel trousers and a blazer, and he gave a natty little salute, and I thought, I bet he's seen some chap do that on the stage and thought how good it looked, and he'd try it out some time.'

'It still doesn't prove he wasn't in the Army.'

'I don't believe that anyone who had ever been in the Army would salute anyone else whilst he was wearing white flannel trousers and a blazer. Besides, he talks about the K.R.R.C. when he means the 60th – and the Provost Corps – and the Royal Field Artillery.'

'Perhaps he was in the last war.'

'Not old enough.'

'Well, anyhow,' said Liz. 'Suppose you're right. Lots of people call themselves things. I knew a man who called himself Commander *and* wore a yachting cap, and he'd never been further from the coast than the end of Blackpool Pier.'

'I wouldn't mind him calling himself a Field Marshal, if he'd keep his hands off Sue.'

'If he'd do *what?*

Tim realised that he had told his mother a good deal more than he meant to.

'He offered to walk home with her.'

'He lives in the same road.'

'He's a nasty little man,' said Tim. 'I can tell by the way he looks at her.'

'Is that all you've got to go by?'

'It's enough, isn't it?'

'Certainly not,' said Liz. She spoke with surprising firmness. 'You can't go round accusing people of that sort of thing without evidence. It's just not done.'

'All right,' said Tim, 'that makes two of you.'

'Two?'

'Sue said much the same sort of thing, only rather more pointedly. I had a stand-up fight with her, too.'

'Lord love us,' said his mother mildly, 'Is there anyone you haven't been scrapping with tonight?'

Tim ignored this. His heavy body was relaxed in the chair, but his curious green-brown eyes were wide open, staring up at the ceiling.

'I don't know what's come over Sue,' he said at last. 'I used to think she was rather keen on me. I don't mean anything serious. After all, she's only seventeen. Hardly out of school, really. Do you remember the first time she came round to tea here, when I'd just got back from Palestine. She must have been twelve or thirteen – all legs and tennis rackets. And that's the way she stayed in my mind ever since – until last month – at the staff college dance. I saw her dancing with some old buffer and thought – she looks rather good.'

Mrs. Artside, who was suffering from a series of complicated emotions, decided that it was safer to say nothing at all. Chiefly, she was filled with amazement that any man of over thirty could know so little about women. Good heavens, she thought, he's talking about this thing as though it had never happened before in the history of the world; as though, every day, some gangling schoolgirl with all her defences down didn't turn into a stickly, prickly bundle of complicated young womanhood.

'Then this evening,' Tim spoke in such a tone of pained forgiveness that his mother was hard put to it not to laugh, 'just because I put that snurge in his place, what must she do but fly off the handle, although I don't believe,' he added magnanimously, 'that she can have meant half the things she said—'

'Don't you?'

'—and she'll probably be sorry about them later, but the fact that she could say them at all was a shock. She actually implied that I went round stabbing people in the back—'

'Lots of people I should like to do that to,' said Liz. 'Look here, I'm not worried about you and Sue – I mean,' she added hastily, 'it's very upsetting but, as you say, it'll probably be all right in the morning – but I don't like the idea of your being rude to MacMorris.'

'Oh?' With an obvious effort Tim removed his mind from the puzzling problem of sex.

'I don't expect anyone overheard you, and MacMorris is sensible enough to keep quiet about it, but we're living in a village, and I've lived in villages long enough to know that everything you do leads to something else – usually something you didn't expect – and ends in feuds, and people who live next to each other not talking to each other, and that sort of silliness.'

'What do you want me to do?'

'That's up to you.'

'You think I ought to apologise to him?'

'It wouldn't do any harm.'

'But he's such a—oh, all right. If you think so. I shan't have time until tomorrow evening. Busy day tomorrow.'

'I should think that would do very nicely. You'll both have cooled off by then. And as for Sue – you say she was really annoyed?'

'She didn't pull her punches.'

'You can take that as a good sign. When a girl's really finished with a man she laughs at him.'

'She certainly didn't laugh.'

'I'm going to bed. You won't forget to—'

'Stoke the boiler, put the dogs out, bolt the front door and turn out *all* the lights.'

'So long as you do it,' said Liz.

When she had gone, Tim lay for a long time, quite relaxed now. He had a gift for keeping still which a professional burglar might have envied. Only his eyes moved with his thoughts.

The telephone bell brought him to his feet.

'Hullo – yes? Oh. Well, I think she's in her bath. Can I take a message?'

The telephone said something querulous.

'I didn't quite get that.'

'Who is it?' said Liz from the top of the stairs.

'Oh, here is Mother. Hold on a second.' He put his hand over the mouthpiece.

'It's the Vicar. He's upset about something and it's making him squeak. I can't understand it all. Something about a key.'

'I'll deal with him.'

Liz sailed down the stairs, majestic in a flame-coloured dressing-gown.

Her arrival seemed to have a soothing effect on the Vicar, whose voice came down two semitones at once. Liz listened carefully and without interruption.

'I'll find out what Tim did with the key,' she said at last. 'We can't do much tonight. I'll ring you again in the morning. No, no. Of course not. Quite right to telephone me at once—'

She rang off, and said to Tim, '*Have* you still got the church key?'

'Oh, Lord. Yes. I believe I have. I dropped it into my mackintosh pocket. I meant to give it back, but that business with Sue—'

'Are you sure you shut the church door?'

'Yes, certain.'

'And locked it?'

'Yes, I'm pretty sure I locked it. What's it all about?'

'The offertory box has been broken open. Hallibone found out when he went up to the church about an hour ago. He's got his own key, of course. The one you've got's the only other one.'

'I see,' said Tim rather blankly. 'How much does he reckon he's lost?'

'The box hadn't been cleared for a week. It might have been as much as two pounds.'

'Crime,' said Tim, 'comes to Brimberley.'

Chapter Three

ACCELERANDO E FORTISSIMO

PRINCESS : *'Fair payment for foul words is more than due.'*

Liz always knew, at the moment she woke in the morning, whether anything unpleasant stood unresolved from the night before. She had no need to think about it consciously.

This faculty dated from the bad time, now more than thirty years past, when Bill had gone, and the world had been shaken and her life turned upside down.

Apart from it she was not, at this stage in her life, a particularly sensitive or apprehensive person. By the time she had got up and got dressed and started helping Anna with the breakfast her intellect would be back in command. Nevertheless, although it could be banished, the weakness was there; something in her make-up, which she would take along with her until she lost all sense and feeling; like a patch left by a clumsy surgical operation.

That morning her subconscious had no lack of material. One voice said menacingly, 'the Vicar', and another, like one of Tennyson's irritating birds, cried Tim, Tim, Tim.'

Liz dismissed both voices by heaving herself out of bed.

On the way downstairs, she knocked at her son's bedroom door. There was no answer. She knocked again, then opened the door and poked her head round. There was no one in the room. The bed looked as if it had been slept in with some violence.

She went on downstairs, had a word with Anna, the Austrian girl, who had come as a temporary help in 1939 and had been there ever since; and then went into the dining-room where she got a second surprise.

A plate and cup had already been used. She went back to the kitchen.

'That's right,' said Anna. 'He come down early and gets his own. I'm just up when he finishes.'

'Did he say why?'

'He said he catches an early train. Lots of work to do today. I make some more coffee for you now?'

'Thank you,' said Liz.

It did not sound like Tim at all. He usually caught the nine o'clock train, and when he missed that he had been known to fall back, quite complacently, upon the nine-forty-five.

Perhaps he really was working harder. Liz might have been able to make a more intelligent guess about that if she had had the least idea of what it was he did when he got up to London. He had never told her, and, after one rebuff, she had ceased to ask about it.

At ten o'clock came the Vicar.

'What an unpleasant business!'

'It's not nice,' said Liz. 'Tell me what happened.'

'It started,' said the Vicar solemnly, 'because I happened to be polishing my spectacles last night, in my study, and I polished rather—er—vigorously and broke the bridge. Most provoking. Then I remembered that I had left my only other pair of reading glasses on the ledge inside the pulpit.'

'What time was that?'

'Let me see, it must have been about half-past nine. Yes. I walked up to the church and let myself in by the wicket door—'

'Was it locked?'

'Yes. Luckily I had brought my own key with me – there only are the two, mine, and the one I lend you for choir practices. Then, as I went past the offertory box I noticed'—having reached his climax the

27

Vicar paused for a moment (it was one of the oratorical tricks with which, Liz reflected, he often embellished a poorly thought-out sermon)—'that the lid was very slightly raised. Someone had been tampering with it.'

'And it was empty?'

'Quite empty.'

'What did you do about it?'

'I was so upset, I forgot even to collect my glasses. I walked straight round to Constable Queen's cottage.'

'I don't suppose he was very helpful.'

'He was out – on a patrol, I understand. His wife was there and she let me use her telephone. I spoke to Sergeant Gattie at Bramshott.'

'Yes. I should think you might get some service there. What did you do then?'

'Then I telephoned you.'

'It was half-past nine when you went to the church, and it was quite half-past eleven when you telephoned me. You must have lost some time somewhere.'

The Vicar looked somewhat taken aback at this ruthless analysis. Then he said, 'I was very upset. I spent some time in reflection before I telephoned you.'

'Just general reflection, on the dishonesty of human beings, or something more in particular?'

The Vicar compressed his already thin lips.

'I was troubled as to what to do for the best. I was up at the church myself at six o'clock yesterday evening and the offertory box was undisturbed then.'

'I see,' said Mrs. Artside, slowly, as some of the implications of this sank in. 'You're quite sure about that?'

'Quite certain. The reason I went up to the church at that time – one of the reasons – was to put an offering into the box from an American lady who had been staying with us. I could not have failed to notice if there had been anything amiss.'

'Yes, I suppose that's right. The church was open to the public at that time.'

'The west wicket door was open. I closed it and locked it when I left.'

'And we start our choir practice about half-past seven.'

'That is so.'

'It doesn't leave a lot of time, does it?'

'It doesn't really,' agreed the Vicar politely.

Liz felt there was more to it than that. She was right. The Vicar compressed his lips once more and said, 'Did your son give you the keys after he had locked up?'

'Yes. I'm sorry about that, I told him to drop them in at the Vicarage, but he forgot. He gave them to me last night when he got in. I rather fancy—why, yes. There they are on the mantelshelf.'

The Vicar got up, retrieved the keys, and said, 'Thank you'. There were three of them, two large and one small. He stood for a moment swinging them by the ring which joined them.

'It passes my comprehension,' he said at last, 'how anyone could get into the church when it is locked.'

Liz thought of Brimberley Church, with its narrow windows, further darkened by wire netting on the outer side, its thick walls and its massive doors.

'I don't believe they could,' she agreed.

'Then how—'

'Since you ask me,' said Liz slowly, 'I can only think that the thief must have slipped in when we were busy singing in the vestry – the wicket door would be standing open at that time, of course – and rifled the box. We were making enough noise with our singing not to have heard anything.'

'Yes, I suppose it might have been that.' The way he said it made it plain that it didn't fit in with his preconceived ideas on the subject.

'Well, when else could it have been?' asked Liz, the beginnings of a note of belligerence in her voice. 'I opened the church myself. Most of the choir were waiting in the porch when I got there and we all went straight in together. Anyway, I don't suppose you suspect them.'

'No, no. Of course not.'

'Then after the service, as you know, Tim locked up.'

'Yes.'

For the first time in the interview she realised what the Vicar was driving at. Being a woman of exceptional balance she did not fly off the handle. She simply left the next move to him.

'Do you suppose,' said the Vicar at last, 'that your son may have let the keys out of his possession at any time yesterday evening and some—er, dishonest person got hold of them?'

'I don't see how they could. The keys were in his raincoat pocket when he got back here just after eleven.'

'Did he tell you where he had been in the interim?'

'The interim is, I fear, for the moment a closed book.'

'Oh.'

'However, I can easily ask about it when Tim gets home this evening. If it should turn out that he entrusted the keys for a couple of hours to a well-known church robber I'll let you know.'

'That's very good of you.'

'Not at all.'

'Stinking little rat,' she added furiously to herself, as she wheeled out her motor-cycle for the run to Bramshott and the day's shopping.

At half-past eleven she was seated in one of the ingles of the Inglenook Cafe.

She was sharing her table with a pleasant, pig-faced woman. She had been introduced to her at several fêtes and socials, and never having grasped her name was now reduced to referring to her as Mrs. Um.

'And how is the Harvest Festival Anthem coming along?' asked Mrs. Um.

'Not so badly,' said Liz. 'I wish they'd put a little more coffee in the coffee here. What we need is one really reliable alto.'

'*We* are doing the Kyrie from Bach's Mass in B Minor,' said Mrs. Um. It was now clear just why she had introduced the topic.

'Rather gloomy for a Harvest Festival.'

'Surely, Mrs. Artside, great music can never be gloomy.'

'It depends how you sing it. Talk of the devil. There are both my much-maligned altos. Hullo Sue. Lucy!'

There was only one empty chair at the table. Liz dexterously hooked a fourth from under a small man who was hesitating about sitting down.

'What a morning,' said Lucy. She deposited a bursting shopping bag in the gangway, where it would be certain to trip up the next passer-by. 'The shops are getting more and more crowded.'

'Oh for the old days,' said Liz, 'when you *rang up* the butcher.'

'You never.'

'Certainly you did. And bullied him about last week's joint. Butchers expected it in those days.'

'Well,' said Sue. 'You were spoilt. I can't remember any time when shopping was any different, and it seems quite natural this way to me.'

'I don't remember a great deal about before the war,' said Lucy defiantly. 'I was quite young.'

'I was practically non-existent,' said Sue. 'Who's meant to be serving today?'

'It's the Second and Third Witch,' said Liz. 'You must have seen Lady Macbeth as you came in. She's doing the home-made cakes.'

Seeing Mrs. Um looking puzzled Liz explained. 'We've come to the conclusion that everyone who works here is a character out of Shakespeare. I think it was Ophelia who started it. That pale girl with long blonde hair who used to bring your coffee with two biscuits and a far-away look.'

'She went off with a soldier,' said Lucy. 'We never heard whether she committed suicide.'

'And Caliban. You must remember Caliban. He used to work in the back kitchen and leer at the girls.'

Mrs. Um still looked puzzled.

'You mean they are actors and actresses,' she said.

'Just a joke,' said Liz.

'Talking about jokes,' said Sue hastily, 'or rather, not talking about jokes at all, rather the contrary, what's all this about someone robbing the Vicar?'

'I heard about that,' said Lucy. 'I couldn't make out what it was all about. He seems to be making out that it was something to do with the choir.'

Mrs. Um, still looking baffled, gathered up her parcels. What a curious village Brimberley was! The choir robbing the Vicar! She left her money on the table and departed.

'Poor woman,' said Sue. 'Fancy having a face like that and no sense of humour either. Now, Liz, what's all this about—?'

The three ladies drew their chairs closer together whilst Liz expounded.

'—and practically accused Tim of stealing the money.'

'What nonsense,' said Sue. 'I was in the porch with Major MacMorris and nobody could have broken open the box without us hearing. Quite impossible.'

'As if he'd do such a thing anyway,' said Lucy warmly; so warmly that Sue glanced at her reflectively.

'As a matter of fact,' said Liz, 'I gather that the box wasn't actually *broken* open at all. The lock had been picked. Rather carefully picked. I'm not an expert on picking locks, but it sounds like a job that could have taken some time.'

'The idea being, I suppose,' said Sue, 'that whilst we were blasting away at the Old Hundredth some joker walked in and rifled the box. A neat idea, really. How much did he get?'

'No one knows. The Vicar reckons it may have been two pounds.'

'Not big league stuff.'

'A hundred years ago,' said Lucy, 'you could be hanged for stealing forty shillings.'

'Two hundred years ago you could be burned for witchcraft,' said Sue. 'Talking of which, here she comes at last. Two cups please. And a plate of biscuits.'

II

'Ah, Artside,' said MacMorris cautiously.

He was standing inside his front door, blocking the entrance.

'Could I come in a moment?'

'What? Oh, yes. Come in.' He backed off and Tim walked past him into the hall.

After a moment's hesitation MacMorris closed the front door and said in his soft, almost feminine, voice: 'We can't very well talk in the hall. Perhaps you'd like to come into my snuggery.'

'What I've got to say won't take a minute,' said Tim. 'Still – it's very good of you. All right.'

They passed from the hall into the snuggery, which turned out to be quite an ordinary sitting-room, rather dimly lit, or rather, thought Tim, not exactly dimly lit, but oddly lit. None of the electric bulbs, of which there were quite a number, seemed designed actually to illuminate anything. Two of them, in bowls, threw their lights up on to the ceiling, and three more, from such incongruous perches as a Chelsea flower girl, a dimpled whisky bottle and the crows-nest of a ship in full sail, cast their respective lights on limited portions of the walls and floor.

In spite of this unusual arrangement, Tim managed to pick out a number of interesting regimental groups and one undeniable photograph over the sideboard of MacMorris himself, some years younger, smiling in the uniform of a second lieutenant. Then he found himself reclining in a shabby leather armchair, the seat of which was tilted at such an angle that he could see practically nothing but the ceiling.

'As I expect you've guessed,' he said, 'I've called to apologise. I'm afraid I made rather an ass of myself last night. The fact is, I was rather worried – things up in London—'

'My dear chap, not another word. I quite understand. Business worries. They're the very deuce. Even a poor old retired warrior like myself knows that.'

He got up, and for an awful moment Tim thought he was going to come over and shake hands, but he moved instead to the sideboard.

'Well, that's really all there is to it,' said Tim, canting himself into an upright position, like a patient coming out of the dentist's chair. 'I must be getting along, I've got—'

'You'll have a drop before you go, I hope.'

MacMorris had deftly deployed two glasses, a syphon and a promising-looking bottle.

'Well—'

'That's the style, old man. Soda or water? I think you'll like it. It's pre-war stock.' He stood for a moment with the bottle in his hand and said, 'As a matter of fact, I've often wanted to have a word with you. Tell me now, you were in the Commandos during the war, weren't you?'

'Not actually the Commandos. Special Service.'

'But that was the same sort of thing?'

'The same sort of thing, but a lot easier. We used to fool round the Aegean in dhows and land at unlikely spots and—oh—blow things up, and that sort of nonsense.'

'I expect they taught you all about unarmed combat, and ju-jitsu and so on.'

'All the assassin's trade,' said Tim. 'Why? Do you happen to be in need of a reliable murderer? They're rather a drug on the market at the moment.' There was a shade of bitterness in his voice.

'No, but I might need a reliable bodyguard.'

'Come again?'

'I didn't really mean to tell anyone,' said MacMorris. 'It's a stupid thing, and I expect a chap like you would laugh at it – but, well, someone's been threatening my life.'

'Threatening your life?'

'I've been getting letters. I thought, at first, it was a joke, and of course, it still may be. Only – I'm not a man of violence myself, and it was getting me worried.'

Refraining from any inquiry as to why he should have joined the Army if he eschewed violence, Tim said, 'I suppose you kept them.'

'I've got the last one. It came yesterday.'

He went across to the desk in the corner, which was the largest piece of furniture in the room; rolled back the top, unlocked a drawer and brought out a sheet of white paper. There were letters pasted on in the form of words which said simply: 'GET OUT AND STAY OUT THIS IS FINAL NOTICE.'

'Short and to the point,' said Tim.

'What would you do in my place?'

'Go to the police,' said Tim promptly. 'Even if they don't find out who's sending the letters they'll trample round and make such a fuss that ten to one they'll scare this joker off.'

'Do you think so?'

'I'm sure that's right. I don't know that I should bother Constable Queen about it. Chicken roosts and bicycle lamps are about his mark. But why not have a word with Gattie at Bramshott?'

'Sergeant Gattie?'

'Yes. He's a good man. As a matter of fact, I know him personally. He was a sergeant in the Gendarmerie in Palestine – that was the Special Force they raised after the war to try and cope with the Irgun boys. I was seconded to them for a brief period. A short life, on the whole, but merry.'

Then perhaps you could have a word with him?'

'Well, I could do that. If you're sure you want me to. If you'd like to lend me that letter—?'

MacMorris hesitated. 'I'd better hang on to it,' he said. 'It'll be quite safe in that desk. I always keep the inner drawer locked. But if you could just explain the thing to him, since you know him. Then I expect he'll want to come over and look at the letter.'

'All right. We'll do it that way,' said Tim. 'But it can't be till Saturday. I'm afraid—'

The word died. MacMorris was not even pretending to listen. He was staring up at the ceiling. There was silence for a count of five.

'What is it?' said Tim at last.

MacMorris tilted his head forward and Tim saw his eyes.

'What is it?' he asked again, softly.

'Didn't you hear anything?'

'I'm not sure,' said Tim. 'As a matter of fact, whilst I was talking, I did think, for a moment – but it might have been anything.'

'It was someone moving.'

'Someone or something,' said Tim, as lightly as he could. 'Do you keep a cat?'

'I hate cats,' whispered MacMorris.

Outside on the main road, at the end of the avenue of trees, a car slowed, accelerated and passed on. The noise died and the silence folded back again.

'Look here,' said Tim at last, 'if you're really—I mean, if you think there's some funny business going on, why don't we go up and have a look? Two pairs of hands are better than one.'

'I'd be very grateful.'

'Don't whisper. If anyone is listening that'll give the game straight away. I'll help myself to a stick out of your hall-stand. Let's try and make it sound as if you're showing me upstairs to the lavatory or something. And there's one other precaution I'd like to take before we start. I'm sure you'll forgive me mentioning it, but I'd prefer to leave that thing behind.'

'What thing?' MacMorris showed his teeth for a moment.

'The one in your jacket pocket. If we're going to do some brawling in the dark it would be a damned sight more dangerous to our side than six burglars.'

'I—'

'Go along. Put it in the desk. It'll be quite safe there.'

It was a little, black, lady's gun. MacMorris dropped it into the desk, shut down the lid, and turned the key.

'You may be right,' he said. 'I think I'll take a stick myself.'

'That's the boy. Now I take it this switch works the upstairs passage light. Splendid. We'll just have the hall light off and the passage light on. Up we go.'

The first floor – MacMorris' own bedroom, a spare bedroom hardly furnished, a third room, not furnished at all, a bathroom and a linen cupboard – were all empty and in order.

Tim looked speculatively at the narrow stairs which ran up, almost ladderlike in their pitch, to the attic storey.

'What's up them?'

'Nothing to speak of,' said MacMorris. 'A box room on one side – it's got a window – I believe you can get out on to the roof from it.'

'Can you, though?' said Tim. 'Sounds promising.'

He went up the stairs, which hardly creaked under his solid weight, and pushed the door of the box room ajar with the knob of his stick. 'Is there a light?'

'The switch is just inside the door.'

The box room had nothing more sinister in it than three suit-cases and a tailor's dummy.

Tim looked inquiringly at MacMorris, who blushed and said, 'Not mine. It must have belonged to the lady who had the house before me. I've never had the nerve to throw it away.'

'It is rather luscious,' agreed Tim. 'This window doesn't look as if it's been opened for a long time.'

It was jammed with disuse and covered with cobwebs. Exerting all his strength Tim raised the sash an inch and a fat spider ran out and looked at him.

'All old inhabitants here,' said Tim. 'What about the other room?'

He opened the door. There was no light switch. Tim stood absorbing the peculiar mixtures of sound and smell. In the darkness water hissed and gurgled into a dimly seen tank. All around was the flat, choking smell of dust and rust and a sharper smell, which was something like metal polish, but was more probably the verdigris on brass joints.

'Nothing much to attract a burglar here,' said Tim. 'Unless he's come to steal the ball-cock.'

He shut the door softly and they walked downstairs to the hall.

'I guess it was a cat,' said Tim. He went back into the sitting-room, picked up his drink and finished it. Holding the empty glass in his hand he wandered, as casually as he could manage, towards the sideboard and set it down on top of it. What he wanted was a quick look at the photograph that hung there.

He couldn't make much of it. The room lighting was against him. It was a younger MacMorris. The picture might have been taken ten or fifteen years ago. He was wearing the ordinary service dress of a British officer. The cypher on the buttons was indistinct and there were no identifying badges, but a single ribbon was visible and it looked suspiciously like the ribbon of the Military Cross. The only other detail that appeared was that the photographer was a person called Ardee, who worked at 233, Charing Cross Road.

'I must be off,' said Tim. 'I'll try to see Gattie on Saturday. I shouldn't worry too much, if I were you. Most people who send letters like that are cowardly little squirts, who wither up and die of panic if they are forced out into the open.'

'I hope you're right.'

The last glimpse Tim had, as he stood on the step, was MacMorris' face, white but curiously composed.

Outside in the road he stood for a moment letting his eyes get used to the darkness. It was an automatic gesture.

Two houses further down the road there was an upstairs window lit up.

Tim loafed along, under the trees, until he was nearly opposite to it. He had his hands in his raincoat pocket and was whistling soundlessly to himself.

A few minutes passed, then a shadow started moving behind the lighted window; a gentle rhythmic gesture. Someone was brushing their hair. He watched, entranced.

A minute later the shadow shifted again and the General appeared. He was in pyjamas and, staring squarely out of the window, he took the first of the dozen deep breaths which were part of his ritual before bed.

Tim turned about and walked fast for the main road; so fast that he nearly bumped into someone who was standing under the tree.

'Sorry,' said Tim. And then, 'Oh, it's you is it, Queen?'

'That's right, sir.'

'Lovely night, isn't it?'

'It is that, sir. Might be spring.'

'Yes. I suppose it might. Well – good night.'

'Good night, sir.'

Curse the man. Could he have seen him? Might be spring! Could he even be laughing at him?

When he got home his mother was reading. She put the book

down and said, 'How did it go?'

'Like wildfire,' said Tim. 'We're terrific pals now. In fact, I'm not sure I've not been elected official bodyguard.'

'What does he want a bodyguard for?'

Tim told her.

When he had finished his mother did not smile. She said, unusually seriously, 'What did you make of it?'

'I'm not sure,' said Tim. 'At the time, I was for it. He's got quite a way with him, has little Bogus. You go there intending to be all terse and stand-offish, and before you know where you are you're having a drink and listening to his life story. Come to think of it, he's fairly accomplished actor.'

'Actor?'

'I don't mean a professional. But he registers emotions so hard that you can't miss them, even if you happen to have your back turned.'

Then you think he was making it all up?'

'I didn't at the time. No. Now, I'm not sure. When he was talking about the letter he started by saying, "I didn't really mean to tell you" – or words to that effect. But as a matter of fact he led up to it quite cold-bloodedly, by asking if it was true I had been in the Commandos, and then saying he might need a bodyguard himself – and so on.'

'And the noise in the house?'

'It was him who heard it. Not me.'

'I thought you heard something too.'

'I thought I might have done. But that may merely have been the way he put the act on. Or there may even have been a noise. A door banging, or the water tank gurgling, or something.'

'But he *had* got a gun.'

'Yes. That was right enough,' said Tim thoughtfully. 'That bit wasn't put on. And he wouldn't have produced it unless I'd insisted. I don't know.'

'Can you think of any reason for him putting on an act?'

'People do things like that,' said Tim. 'I told you about the chap in our unit who was always sending himself the most extraordinary telegrams from girls—'

The window was wide open and from where she was sitting Mrs. Artside could look straight out of it. Tim was standing behind her, and so they both had a good view.

A truncated cone of flame, squat and orange coloured; an obscene firework, throwing the tree tops into silhouette.

Then the curtains puffed gently inwards and the house seemed to be rocking with the noise. 'God in Heaven!' said Tim. 'Are we at war?' When his mother did not answer, he looked round. She was on the floor in a heap.

Chapter Four

ECHOES

SIR NATHANIEL: *'When in the World I lived, I was the World's Commander.'*

'Mummy. For God's sake. Mummy.'

Tim dropped down on to his knees beside her. She was breathing deeply and jerkily and her face was a bad colour.

What was the first thing? Get her off the floor. Make her comfortable.

Strong though he was, he doubted whether he could lift her dead weight. He pulled a cushion off the chair and put it under her head.

The words 'burnt feathers' flitted into his mind. Even at such a moment Tim almost smiled at the bare possibility of his mother having hysteria. Perhaps it was a stroke. Then he ought to get the doctor, and quickly. As he started to his feet his mother opened her eyes, looked blindly out of them and said, quite clearly, 'Bill.' Then her eyes cleared as her senses returned and she said, 'Tim. What's happened?'

'You passed out. Do you think you could get up on to the sofa?'

'Of course I can get up on to the sofa.'

'Take it easy,' said Tim. 'You may not be quite as spry as you imagine. You hit your head an awful smack as you went down. That's right. I'll put my arm under your shoulders. Up we come.'

'It's the first time I've ever done that in my life.' Liz sounded cross.

'There's a first time for everything. How's that? I'll get you a drop of brandy.'

41

'Tim,' said Mrs. Artside, '*was* there an explosion?'

'There certainly was. A whopper.'

'I thought that might have been in the dream, too. What was it?'

'No idea. It looked like a ten-tonne bomb. Probably the gas-works blowing up. We shall know soon enough. Have a shot of this.'

Ugh,' said Liz. 'Urrrh. I don't know why people always rush round giving people brandy in a crisis. What a revolting taste. Take it away.'

'Pity to waste it,' said Tim, and tipped up the glass.

In the hall the telephone began to jangle.

Tim darted out, snatched off the receiver, and said, 'Yes?'

'Palling here,' said the voice at the other end. 'Is Mrs. Artside – oh, it's you, Tim. Good. Now listen, I think you'd better come over here quickly. Don't alarm your mother.'

The General's voice was modulated to the deliberately casual tone that he used in moments of real crisis. There were staff officers still living who would have recognised it uneasily.

'What is it, sir?'

'There's been an explosion down the road.'

'MacMorris?'

'Yes.'

'Are you all right?'

'We're all right. Lost a bit of glass. The house next door caught the brunt. Lucky it's empty.'

'And is Sue—?'

'Yes, yes. She's all right. Now jump on to a bicycle or something and get over here as quick as you can.'

'Of course,' said Tim.

He went back into the drawing-room. His mother was on her feet and looked fairly steady.

'Are you all right if I—?'

'Yes. Go along,' she said. 'That was Hubert, wasn't it? I thought it sounded as if it came from that direction.'

'It was MacMorris.'

His mother looked at him but said nothing.

Tim ran to the garage, got out his bicycle, and pedalled off down the road. A soft full moon had come up over the edge of the trees. As he swung off the main road into Melliker Lane, the sharp smell of high explosive and death hit him. It was not new to him. MacMorris' house was the farthest down the lane. Next to it was the empty house. Then the Pallings and then three others. All the latter were blazing with light.

There was a little knot of people in the road; the General, Sue, and Constable Queen amongst them.

The shell of the MacMorris house was still smoking gently. It was as if someone had torn the top half roughly away, lifted it into the air, and dropped it back sideways on to the bottom half. The soft moonlight made it look somehow even more horrible.

The General said, 'Here's Artside. I asked him to come along.' He sounded like a host putting a late guest at ease. 'I'd like you to talk to Queen.'

'Talk?'

'Tell him he mustn't go into that house yet.'

Constable Queen said obstinately, 'It isn't a matter of talk. It's a matter of duty. The man may still be alive.'

'My duty as a magistrate,' said the General, 'is to save any further loss of life. Tim, will you talk sense to him?'

Tim looked at the house.

'There's no one alive in there,' he said. 'The blast alone would kill instantly; even if nothing else hit him.'

The little crowd had fallen silent as Tim spoke. Nobody answered him directly. They were ready to help, if wanted, but were not going to put themselves forward. Tim could not help reflecting that most of them must have seen that sort of thing before in the last fifteen years.

'I've sent for the fire brigade,' said the General, and as he spoke a squeal of tyres on the main road brought all heads round together.

A big car cornered sharply and came to a halt. A dapper, black-haired man climbed out from behind the wheel, and Constable Queen went forward, relief evident in every line of his figure.

'Good evening, Sergeant,' said the General.

'Good evening, sir,' said Sergeant Gattie. 'Would someone mind telling me what's been happening?'

The General looked at his watch.

'It happened just over fifteen minutes ago,' he said. 'I doubt if anyone can tell you much more than that.'

'How many people inside?'

'Only one, as far as we know. Major MacMorris. The next house is empty.'

'Bit of luck there,' agreed the sergeant. He caught sight of Tim and moved across.

'Did you see it happen?'

'More or less,' said Tim. 'My mother and I were both looking out of the window, and we got a good view, even if we were a bit far away. I don't think it was a gas explosion, if that's in your mind. Much too heavy. If it hadn't been so impossible, I should have said a solid charge of H.E. And detonated.'

'Would have made a good deal more sense in Tel Aviv,' said the sergeant softly.

'I agree,' said Tim.

They had reached the back of the house, out of sight of the others. The damage here seemed less extensive.

They looked at each other.

'If it hasn't come down by now, it'll probably stay put,' agreed Tim.

'That's right,' said Gattie. 'I've often noticed that. It's the first ten minutes you want to watch – whilst it's still rocking. Have you got a torch?'

'I've got my bicycle lamp. Better not let the others see. The General practically put Queen under arrest when he wanted to dash in.'

'Quite right,' said Gattie with a grin. His strong teeth showed white under his line of black moustache. 'Can't waste trained constables.'

There was no need to open a window. The whole casement, frame and all, was slewed outwards, sagging drunkenly on a single upright.

Inside the dust still hung in choking clouds.

Tim barely recognised the sitting-room he had been in two hours before. The word 'snuggery' came unbidden into his mind.

The light from Gattie's torch was swivelling round the floor, along the rubble of plaster on the carpet, under the table, where a space showed, clear and black; a heap in the corner.

The sergeant squatted and probed gently. It was nothing more sinister than a tapestry stool, which some freak of the explosion had covered with the tablecloth and then buried in debris.

'I think he'd be upstairs,' croaked Tim. He was speaking through the handkerchief that he had tied over his mouth and nose.

Sergeant Gattie nodded. He also was wearing a handkerchief and it was impossible to make out much of his expression.

Tim slid gently out into the hall. The door was immovably shut, but it was no longer completely filling the doorway. The bottom half of the staircase was quite intact, the stair carpet and even the rods in position. The top half had disappeared.

Tim got as high as he could and felt above him. There was a ledge of broken joists. It was awkward, because he had to hold the bicycle lamp in one hand, but so far as he could feel it was tolerably secure.

After a moment's thought, he put the lamp away. There was a dim radiance over everything, and he looked up and saw the moonlight shining through the space where the roof had been.

He pulled himself up, got one knee on the jagged edge, grabbed at something solid looking, found that it was a pile of loose slates, and started to slip.

The hand of Sergeant Gattie came up from below, grabbed his foot, and steered it into a hold.

This time it was easier. Another pull, a quick wriggle, and he was up.

If the bottom rooms were a mess, the top storey was naked Bedlam. The blast had been more direct and more wilful. It was almost impossible to tell where passage ended and room began.

If there's any of him anywhere, thought Tim, he'll be in his bedroom.

Immediately in front of him, turned on its side and almost completely blocking the passageway was a mountain of twisted metal which Tim tentatively identified, after stubbing his toes on it, as the cold water tank.

He edged round to the right of it, and a crunch of broken china suggested that he was now where the bathroom had been.

A few steps further and he sensed he was in the bedroom.

He got his lamp out again and flashed it around.

The explosion had played its usual tricks. Three of the walls were more or less intact. A picture, its glass unbroken, hung above the fireplace, whilst the heavy iron bed had been picked up bodily and flung across the room.

Pillows and bedclothes had been spewed about the floor.

There was one long, brightly coloured bolster lying against the wainscoting under the window. Tim looked at it twice before he realised that he had discovered Major MacMorris.

Forcing himself to hold the torch steady he made a quick examination. There was nothing that he could usefully do. The body presented that general appearance of a rag doll with all the stuffing out that high explosive produces where it lays its hands too intimately on a human being.

Lying beside MacMorris, on the floor, was an envelope. The flap was stuck down and the envelope itself was old, and crumpled, as if with much handling. Impossible to guess where it had come from. Off the table, out of the eviscerated cupboard or the ripped-up chest of drawers? Had it fluttered down from behind some picture? Or had it been by chance in MacMorris' hand at the moment of the explosion? He pushed it into his pocket for later inspection.

Tim had no real recollection of going back. The next thing he clearly remembered was sitting on the edge of the broken staircase. Sergeant Gattie was peering up at him.

'You found him, did you?' he said.

'He's in the bedroom,'said Tim. 'He's wearing pyjamas – I think.'

'Was he in bed, when it went off?'

Tim forced himself to think.

'He might have been sitting on the bed,' he said, at last. 'I don't think he was in it or he'd have been lying by the mattress and the bedclothes. They were the other side of the room. They might have protected him a bit.'

'And he's—'

'Yes,' said Tim. 'Yes. Very definitely. I've hardly ever in my life seen anyone more so.'

Sergeant Gattie peered up at him again. His face and head were white with plaster. It was so caked into his hair and smothered over his forehead that it was difficult to see where the handkerchief over his nose and mouth began. Only his black eyes were alive.

Tim felt an urgent desire to laugh at him, but he had a feeling that once he started he might not be able to stop.

'I should come down if I were you, sir,' said Sergeant Gattie. 'That sounds like the fire brigade arriving. We'd better give them a clear run.'

II

The following evening, after supper, Liz Artside put down her book and said, 'How much did I ever tell you about your father's death?'

'Never very much,' said Tim, looking up with a frown from a black covered exercise book in which he was working out something in pencil.

'I wasn't sure,' said Liz.

It looked for a moment as if that was the end of the conversation. Tim picked up his pencil again.

'I meant to explain about last night,' said Liz. 'I've been thinking about it. I expect it was the coincidence that set me off.'

'I knew that Dad got blown up,' said Tim slowly, 'and that it was an accident, and that it happened in Cologne, a little time before I was born. That's really all anyone's ever told me about it.'

Liz said slowly, 'It was an autumn evening, like yesterday, only rather darker and more overcast. I was sitting, looking out of the window. We had a flat in the Onkeldam suburb, overlooking the Rhine, just south of the city. From where I sat I could see Bill's headquarter building. It was a big house – an old school – further up, on the South Bank. He was working late that night. He didn't often work late. He usually got it all done in the day and he liked to sit at home in the evenings and plan what we were going to do when we got back to England.'

Tim looked up quickly. But there was no feeling there, suppressed or other. His mother's voice was as matter-of-fact as it always was.

That evening he had told me he would be late. There'd been some trouble. It was large scale looting by one of the Army contractors. He had all the papers with him to study. I think it was worrying him, a little. We had dinner together, and he left soon afterwards. I could see the window of his office. It was almost the only lighted one in the building. Then, suddenly, just like last night, when no one was expecting anything in particular, it happened.'

The same sort of explosion as last night?'

'Not really. They wouldn't have the same sort of explosives in those days, would they? It was a sort of white glare. Then the crash. Then lots and lots of smoke. I knew that something awful had happened and I ran down and out into the street. I'd forgotten about curfew. There wasn't a person or a car in sight. I ran all the way there, through the empty streets. It was nearly a mile, and I don't remember feeling tired at all, but it must have taken some time, because when I got there, there was a cordon round the building and they wouldn't let me in. They never let me see the body. I never saw Bill again.'

Liz was silent, looking back at her more than thirty years younger self, a serious, rather squat black-haired girl, scudding through the empty streets of Cologne. She had wondered afterwards why it hadn't killed the four-month old child she was carrying. Afterwards. Not at the time. At the time she hadn't given it a thought. It had started to drizzle, she remembered. She had been glad, because people were unable to tell if the moisture on her face had been tears or rain. It had seemed important then.

She was silent for so long that Tim said, 'I shouldn't go on if it worries you.'

'It doesn't worry me,' said Liz. 'I worried so much at the time that, in the end, I worried all the worry out of myself. I got calloused over. Nature's like that, she breeds her own anti-bodies. I haven't talked to you about it before, but it wasn't because it worried me – at least, not that part of it. It was the thoughts which came afterwards.'

Tim looked up sharply, but said nothing.

'There was a Court of Inquiry and I suppose there was an inquest as well, but I don't remember it. It came out that there had been a lot of explosive stored in the headquarters building. It seemed a bit odd. But I don't think people were quite so careful about things then. We'd just finished the biggest war anyone had ever heard of and I expect people were still a bit casual. It came out that the engineers had been dismantling the charges which the Germans had laid under the Rhine bridges. The charges had never been used, because the war was over before we got near the Rhine, but they had to be dug out eventually and disposed of. I gather they were quite primitive things – slabs of gun-cotton and detonators – and, of course, they'd taken out all the detonators, or thought they had.'

'But they hadn't?'

'So the Court of Inquiry decided. I didn't understand it all. There was talk about some gun-cotton which had been protected and some which should have been but hadn't.'

'Sheathed, I believe we call it now.'

'Something like that. It was just one of those ghastly mistakes that happens. The C.R.E. was the man I was sorry for. Brigadier Tom Havers. He was a nice little person, with a face just like a duck. It was the end of him, of course.'

'He got the sack?'

'Yes. I don't think he was cashiered. Severely reprimanded and lost seniority. He took the hint and handed in his papers. I never thought it was his fault at all, and I said so. We were very good friends after he left the Army.'

'Where is he now?'

'He's dead. He died a few years later – boredom, I fancy.'

'Was it an accident?' said Tim.

His mother did not reply directly. She got up and went across to the cupboard in the corner of the room and pulled out a heavy, old-fashioned, cash box. Originally, no doubt, impressive in green and gilt, it was worn with age and travel to a uniform drab. Tim could remember that box as long as he could remember anything. It was full of old Post Office Savings books, certificates, passports, licences, photographs; the hundred and one things that had once seemed valuable. From it she extracted a bundle of letters, fastened with a rubber band, and took out the top one.

It was evident that she knew just where it was and that she had taken it out lately.

She passed it across to Tim, who looked at it curiously.

It was on cheap grey paper, much folded, in the faded, chunky handwriting that he knew to be his father's. It was undated, and headed Trenches, near Ginchy'. It said:

'Darling Liz, a great day. I've got my "step". In fact, the chances are the next letter I write won't be headed "trenches", but Chateau – Something-or-other. In this part of the line even Brigade Commanders live in Chateaus (Chateaux?). If Roney gets the Corps – and no one deserves it more thoroughly – then it's not beyond the bounds of possibility – splotch – sorry, that was half a ton of flying pig landed near the dug-out door and blew out the candle. Don't worry about it, though. My privilege as Commanding Officer is to have the deepest and safest dug-out. As I was saying. It's not even beyond the bounds of possibility that they might leap-frog me straight up to Division! In which case, I shall be writing to you on embossed notepaper, and I shan't even post it. I shall get one of my gilded aide-de-camps to bring it to you personally. Seriously, though, I do sometimes wonder how all this is going to end. Most people at the top are doing jobs that are two, three and four grades higher than they could hope to hold down in peace time. To say nothing of the fact that we always treat the Armed Forces as Cinderella as soon as the war is over. I suppose the cynical answer is to make the most of it whilst it's there. You can hardly expect the government to maintain a war-sized army in peace time so as not to have to demote a lot of brass-hats. However, don't let's count chickens. Better to wait and see if we get up there, before complaining about being booted down again.'

'But he did get there, didn't he,' said Tim.

'He was an acting Lieutenant-General when he commanded at Cologne.'

'And how old? Thirty?'

'Thirty-one.'

'On top of the world.'

'So you might think,' said Liz. 'He'd just been offered a job in England, too. Commandant of the newly-opened School of Chemical Warfare.'

'Was it a good job?'

'It was a job. Even by 1920 any job was a good job. It carried the acting rank of Brigadier.'

'I see,' said Tim. 'But as he happened to die a Lieutenant-General, you got a very much higher pension.'

'That's right,' said Liz.

'Well, I don't believe it,' said Tim. He suddenly looked very red-faced, determined and young.

'Don't believe what?'

'What you're trying to tell me. That he might have killed himself because he saw the slump coming. No one would do that, at thirty-one, for himself, or anyone else.'

Liz looked calmly at her son for a moment and said, 'I don't really know that I believe it myself. But Bill wasn't a straightforward character. He was a terrific soldier. People who ought to know say that if he had lived he must have been at least an Army Commander in this war. He might even have run the whole show. Everyone who knew him trusted him, but at the heart of it all, he wasn't quite sure of himself. Bob understood him as well as anyone. You should ask him about it sometime. And another thing you've got to remember. After a long war a lot of people who have fought in it − really fought, I mean − are queer for a long time. Often it doesn't show, but it's there, and you've got to make allowances for it.'

'You may be right,' said Tim. 'I wouldn't know. I never did any real fighting. I was just a bag-snatching cut-throat. Ask the General.'

III

Rupert Cleeve sat on the piano stool in the small drawing-room and kicked his heels against the mahogany of that long-suffering piece of furniture.

Then he rotated solemnly, until the stool was as high as it could be made to go, reversed direction, and came down again to keyboard level. Then he looked at the clock on the mantelshelf, shut the lid of the piano with a bang, and walked across to the window.

The cook's cat, a large, dangerous animal, was squatting on the flat top of the ashlar wall that ran, knee high, round the sun garden. He was not easy to see, because he was so arranged that the dapple of evening light through the hedge blended confusingly with his tortoise-shell camouflage.

He was waiting for birds.

Rupert went up to his bedroom and pulled the bottom long drawer of his chest of drawers right out. Behind it, held in clips to the woodwork of the chest, and invisible whilst the drawer was in position, were a number of implements. One of them was a powerful looking catapult of thick rubber on a steel frame.

He took this out, and pocketed two marbles from a box beside his bed.

Then he shut everything up and went downstairs again. All his movements were neat and self-contained. He lived comfortably in the fifth dimension which a lonely child inhabits.

Back in the small drawing-room he went over to the window and eased it very carefully open.

It was a tricky shot. Rupert considered it with gravity. Safer to aim low, perhaps, and trust a ricochet off the coping.

He stretched the elastic, held his breath, and let go. There was a twang, a 'tock' of marble on stone, and a sharp oath from the cook's cat as it disappeared into the shrubbery.

When Rupert had retrieved the marble and put everything away neatly, he went to look for his father. He found him in the breakfast-room, struggling with a report on juvenile delinquency.

'Who got blown up last night?' he asked.

Cleeve looked up vaguely. Statistics. Trends. Home influence. Graphical reproduction of repeated offences.

'Who got what?'

'Blown up.'

'Major MacMorris.'

'Ah,' said Rupert.

'What do you mean?'

'It's pretty obvious who did it, I should think.'

'Oh.'

'It's that Bramshott Choir. They're trying to bitch up our Anthem.'

'Who taught you that disgusting expression?'

'It's not disgusting,' said Rupert. 'It simply means—'

'That'll do. And it's time you went to bed.'

It was time he went to boarding school, too. Time. Time. Time. The Chairman returned to his report.

Chapter Five

FIRST INTERVAL: TRIO (MA NON LEGATO)

BEROWNE:
'A lover's ear will hear the lowest sound
When the suspicious head of theft is stopped.'

'We'll give you all the help we can, of course,' said Tim. That's why we've come along. The only thing is, I've simply got to be in London by one o'clock.'

'I quite appreciate that, sir,' said Inspector Luck. He had hair that had once been auburn and plentiful but was now a sparse ginger, and a face like a tired fox. 'It's very good of you and Mrs. Artside to come along at all. Mind that step. That's right. I'd better go first and see if the door's open.'

He led the way out of the back door of Bramshott police station, and into a sort of large shed at the back. Battered furniture was piled round the walls. On trestle tables, under the long skylight, a jumble of smaller objects had been sorted out. An elderly police sergeant was making entries in a book.

'It's everything we could find,' said Luck. 'There's probably a good deal more, under the rubble, but we shan't get it until the demolition team has finished.'

'It doesn't look much for the contents of a fully-furnished house,' said Liz.

'As a matter of fact it wasn't all that fully furnished,' said Tim. 'On the ground floor I only went into the living-room, but I looked into the front room as I went by and it seemed pretty bare. Upstairs there was practically only one bedroom furnished at all, and one bed in another room.'

They inspected the sad miscellany of household goods laid out on the tables; disembowelled cushions, strips of curtains, pillows, bedclothes, a plaster dog, a selection of kitchenware, mostly intact, pictures, some of them almost unrecognisable, some undamaged. It took Tim back to Italy and Greece, and the collection of household goods which he had so often seen, heaped on to handcarts, dumped beside roads, torn, scattered, trampled on, soaked with their owner's blood.

He searched among the glass and woodwork of the pile of pictures and pulled out two framed photographs.

'I noticed these when MacMorris was talking to me on Wednesday night. They're Regimental groups. I don't know if you're interested in his background, but these might be a help.'

Liz and the Inspector came over and peered at them.

'That one's the Suffolks,' said Liz at last. 'It's a Minden Day photograph. You can see the roses. But it was taken a long time ago. Those pill-box hats went out before the South African War. I don't believe MacMorris was as old as all that.'

'This one looks as if it was taken in India,' said Tim.

'I don't suppose they belonged to him at all,' said Liz. 'It wasn't his house, was it? I mean, he hadn't bought it.'

'I understand,' said Luck cautiously, 'that it was rented furnished from a Miss Anglesea.'

'Oh, that's right then,' said Liz. 'Dolly Anglesea's father was in the Suffolk Regiment, and he went to India with them. Those photographs are nothing to do with MacMorris at all.'

'All the same,' said Tim. 'There was one that was him – or his twin. Quite unmistakeable. Dressed up as a one-pipper. And he had some sort of gong up, too. Not a campaign ribbon. Might have been the M.C.'

As he spoke, he was piecing together the fragments on the table. Seeing what he was doing the other two came and helped him. But nothing even remotely resembling a photograph of a Second Lieutenant appeared.

'Did you find the letter?' said Tim suddenly.

'Which letter, sir?'

'The anonymous letter.'

There was a pause. Then the Inspector said. 'Yes. Yes, we found that. The desk wasn't much damaged, you know. But just how did you happen—'

'Oh, don't be so mysterious,' said Tim. 'He showed it to me that night. In fact, he asked me what he ought to do about it. It wasn't the first he'd had.'

'And what did you advise him, sir?'

'I told him to show it to the police.'

'I see.'

'For some reason he wasn't too keen to do that himself. So he asked me to mention it to Sergeant Gattie. He knew I knew him.'

'And you did?'

'I work for my living during the week. There didn't seem all that urgency. I was going to cycle over on Saturday morning.'

'Pity,' said the Inspector non-committally.

Tim said angrily, 'I didn't know he was going to be blown up.'

'Of course not, sir.' The Inspector paused for a second and then said, 'You think the letter may have had some connection with—with the explosion?'

'Good Lord, but of course. I mean, that's rather more up your street than mine, but I should have thought it was obvious. Here's a man gets a letter threatening unpleasant consequences if he doesn't get out. Which he doesn't. So the consequences happen.'

'Yes,' said the Inspector. 'We've got all the papers back in my office. The letter's with them. There's not much more we can do here. Lock up when you've finished, Lawley. There was one thing we noticed straight away about that letter, and it did just make us wonder. It was stuck on to a quarto size sheet of paper. It's a common make, sold in all the shops round here. In fact – up these steps, Mrs. Artside – there was an opened packet of it in the bottom drawer of the desk. And another thing, all the letters and words which had been used to make it up came out of a local paper – the *Bramshott and Alderham Reporter* – it's an unusual type-case you see, so they were able to identify it for us at once. MacMorris was one of the people who took it – after you, Mrs. Artside – and so it did occur to us to wonder whether, for some reason – we shall never know just why – he might have rigged it up himself.'

'Lots of people take the *Reporter*,' said Tim. 'We do.'

The Inspector swivelled his faded eye on him.

'Why would anyone do a thing like that?' asked Liz.

'It's not unknown for a certain type of person to send themselves anonymous communications. I'm afraid we often have cases like that reported to us.'

'"Faire l'importance",' said Liz. 'Yes. It's possible. I shouldn't have thought he was quite the type. Is there any other reason to suppose that's what he did?'

'Well,' said the Inspector cautiously, 'there haven't been any other complaints round the neighbourhood lately. Once these anonymous writers get going they don't often confine themselves to one victim. Particularly if he doesn't seem to take any notice of them.'

'Something in that,' said Liz.

In spite of the Inspector's impeccable manner she was not at ease. She had never been very fond of Inspector Luck. His seedy bonhomie hid, she felt, an essentially vicious mind. She was fair enough to admit that he had given her absolutely no grounds for such feelings. Her two previous encounters had been when she had given away the prizes at a police Fete which Luck had been organising, and the occasion, some years since, when there had been some irregularity over Anna's status as an alien, which he had dealt with efficiently and courteously.

'Now, about Wednesday night,' said the Inspector, turning on Tim. 'Would you mind telling us about that?'

'Of course not,' said Tim.

When he had finished the Inspector said, 'About this noise you both heard—'

'He *said* he heard it. Me, I'm not sure.'

'Yes. Well, suppose for a moment there was a noise—'

From the way in which he said it, Tim felt some doubt as to whether he was being offensive or not. He decided to give him the benefit of the doubt. 'Suppose it wasn't the cat, or something like that. Did you happen to spot any way anyone could have got into the house without your knowing?'

Tim considered.

'It wouldn't have been impossible,' he said. 'Whilst we were talking in the living-room there's no real reason why someone, being a bit careful, shouldn't have got in at one of the ground floor windows and gone up the stairs. They don't creak much. I noticed that when I went up them myself, later. Or else, perhaps easier, he could have put a ladder up to a first storey window and got in that way.'

'Without being seen?'

'Oh, yes. I think so. It's the end house. And anyway, the next one's empty.'

'And you suggest he might have got out the same way *before* you went up to look for him. Which would account for your not finding anyone.'

'I'm not suggesting anything,' said Tim.

'Very properly,' said the Inspector smoothly. 'But you thought you heard a noise, and as a result of this you searched the house – quite thoroughly.'

'Yes.'

'And you didn't find anybody.'

'No.'

'Or anything suspicious.'

'I'm not sure that I know what you mean.'

The Inspector searched about, pulled a buff paper out of the litter on his desk, looked at it, and said,

'Well, you know, there was quite a lot of explosive in the house somewhere.'

'Is that the report?'

'Yes.'

'Can I look at it?'

58

The Inspector's hesitation was momentary, but both Tim and Liz noted it. Then he pushed the paper across.

Tim scanned it quickly.

'Yes,' he said, 'I see. Cordite. Probably in jelly form. Yes. It must have been quite bulky to produce an effect like that.'

'How bulky?' said Liz.

Tim demonstrated with his hands. 'A couple of ordinary sized suit-cases would do it.'

'Perhaps it *was* in two suit-cases,' said Liz. 'Did you look under his bed?'

'The explosion didn't occur in MacMorris' bedroom,' said the Inspector.

'How do you know?' said Liz. She was beginning to find these ex cathedra pronouncements irritating.

'The explosive experts have ways of deducing,' said the Inspector cautiously. He looked at Tim.

'You can tell by the electric light bulbs,' said Tim. 'That's one way. Explosion removes the glass, but the filaments are left behind. They get bent away from the source of the explosion—' He was reading the report again, 'I see it's suggested that the seat of the explosion was in the front section or frontside section of the house, and fairly high up.'

'That might be dining-room, spare bedroom, bathroom or attic,' said Luck. 'Can't put it closer than that.'

'Attic?' Tim looked up sharply. 'Box room, do you mean, or the smaller attic with the cistern in it.'

'It would be the small one, I think, sir.'

'Can you remember if cordite in jelly form gives off any smell?'

For the first time in the interview Inspector Luck managed to look genuinely surprised. 'I don't know,' he said. 'I can probably find out. Why?'

'I didn't look round the small attic much. It was pretty dark. And by that time I'd come to the conclusion that MacMorris had imagined the whole thing. But when I stood just inside that open door, I was conscious of an odd smell.'

'What sort of smell?'

'That's a hopeless question. It wasn't powerful. But sharp, and slightly acid. Like metal polish, but slightly less definite. And here's a funny thing – unless I'm just being wise after the event – but somehow my mind connected that smell with my service in Palestine.'

The Inspector considered this, his head on one side. Liz thought, uncharitably, 'He doesn't like it, because it doesn't fit in with some preconceived notion, so he's trying to pick holes in it.'

'But of course,' went on Tim, 'even if the explosive was in the tank room, it doesn't mean that the exploding device was there. That could have been anywhere.'

'Exploding device?' said the Inspector rather blankly.

There must have been something to set that little lot off. And I can't help thinking it was connected with the bedroom. So far as we know MacMorris was in his bedroom when the balloon went up.'

'Yes,' said Luck. 'But—'

More sales resistance, thought Liz. She said, sharply, 'Do *you* think the explosion was engineered by someone, or not?'

The Inspector, unexpectedly attacked in the flank, swung round with a grunt.

'I don't know that we've got as far as that, Mrs. Artside,' he said. 'This is only a first report.'

'You must be working on *some* theory. I'm just asking what your theory is. If you want us to help you ought to be frank with us.'

'Well,' said the Inspector unhappily, 'Since you put it like that – our idea at the moment is that there was a quantity of explosive somewhere in the house. It might have been in the tank room and it might not. And it went up by accident.'

'Sounds a bit far-fetched,' said Tim. 'Here's a man gets a threatening letter, and shortly afterwards he gets killed. I shouldn't have leapt to the conclusion that it was an accident. But then, I'm not a policeman.'

'We haven't reached a conclusion yet. And, as I have already indicated, we don't attach a great deal of importance to the letter.'

'Just why,' asked Liz, 'should an ordinary citizen keep two suit-cases full of high explosive in his attic?'

The Inspector had seen this coming. He was being pushed into a corner. Maybe he was tired of dodging.

'It's a matter of the highest security at this moment,' he said, 'but I think, in the circumstances, I should be justified in telling you.'

'Calculated indiscretion coming,' thought Liz.

'In our view, MacMorris may have been a professional burglar.'

'A country house burglar,' suggested Liz, gently.

The expression on the Inspector's face was delicious. He somehow contrived to look both sly and startled at the same time. Just as if a hen had changed into a duck right under the fox's nose.

Even Tim looked startled.

'It's all right,' said Liz. 'I'm not clairvoyant. It's just that Bob – Colonel Cleeve – was talking about country house burglars two nights ago.'

'And he told you about this one?' The Inspector's tone implied exactly what he thought about the security-mindedness of county councillors.

'No. He didn't. He happened to be talking about country house burglars generally. That's why, when you said burglar—'

'Now that the cat seems to be out of the bag,' suggested Tim pleasantly, 'why not tell us all about it?'

'There isn't a lot to tell,' said the Inspector. He was still looking worried. 'This one seems to have started to operate from here about the end of the war. 1946 was the first job that could be pinned down to him. There were hints that he lived in this part of the country. Nothing definite, you see. Cross-bearings. Then – it was in the spring of this year – a house near Henley – he was caught on the job.'

'You say "he",' said Tim. 'But did you know who it was? And were you sure all these jobs were being done by the same person?'

'We knew they were done by the same person. You know enough about police work yourself, sir, to know that that's one of the things you can be sure about.'

Tim nodded.

'You said they caught him?' said Liz.

'Not actually caught him. Not to recognise him. But he was disturbed on the job, and broke off without getting what he'd come for. Someone had the sense to telephone Scotland Yard at once. They warned us. The Chief Constable had road blocks put out. It was a system he had ready worked out for just such a case. They weren't to stop him. Just to report. He was checked through as far as the Bramshott cross roads. Then they lost him. There was a slip-up. Two parties went to the same road junction by mistake – and left the other unguarded. There was some fur flew about *that,* I can tell you.'

Liz could imagine it. Tom Pearce, the Chief Constable, was a man who lost his temper rarely but thoroughly.

'But surely,' said Tim, 'even if you lost him, someone would be able to identify his car.'

'He wasn't in a car, not that time,' said the Inspector, with a faint smile. 'He was on a motor-bicycle. Very neutral things, motor-bicycles. Easy to hide, too.'

'I believe MacMorris had a motor-bicycle,' said Tim.

'I believe he did,' said the Inspector. 'Three hundred others in this area alone.'

'It doesn't seem much to go on,' agreed Liz. 'I've got a motor-bicycle, but I don't rob country houses. Did anyone see what he looked like?'

'It was a dark, drizzling night. Most reports agreed he looked big – not tall, but thickish. Although that might have been because he was well padded up.'

'And how many of the three hundred motor-cycle owners matched up with that description?'

'Most of them. We didn't go a lot by description. We started checking up on people's past histories. We wanted someone who had come here in the last seven or eight years, and who had been busy during the war – and who might, perhaps, have lived in the Midlands in the late 'thirties. It's not certain. There were jobs done then that had the same sort of hall-mark.'

'And did MacMorris live in the Midlands before the war?'

'We don't know. As a matter of fact, we only just got going on MacMorris, but as far as we had been able to discover, he hadn't got any back history.' The Inspector chopped the desk lightly with the edge of his hand. 'He stops short, like that, the day he came here. There's nothing before that.'

'Did he never visit anyone?'

'Certainly he did.'

'Outside Brimberley, I mean. Up in London?'

'Very probably. We couldn't keep him in cotton wool. Anyway, as I say, we'd only really just started on him.'

'But you were having his house watched?' said Tim.

The Inspector allowed himself a brief smile.

'I understand you bumped into Constable Queen once or twice,' he said.

'He seemed to hang about a good deal under the trees in Melliker Lane. I never thought there was anything sinister in it.'

'Hanging about,' said the Inspector. 'That's what most police work is, hanging about. It's wonderful what you hear if you hang about long enough.'

'I expect it is,' said Tim shortly. 'Were you thinking of anything in particular?'

'Regular upper-and-downer you seemed to be having with Miss Palling on Tuesday night, Queen says.'

'Does he really,' said Tim. 'Well, I suppose it's all part of a policeman's job to crawl round eavesdropping. But if he happens, by mistake, to overhear a private conversation, does he have to repeat it?'

The Inspector did not seem in the least put out. He was looking at Tim, with his head cocked.

'Certainly he does,' he said. 'Everything that a policeman hears, sees and does goes down in the Occurrences Book. If it isn't to the point we can always forget about it. But it's surprising the little things that do come in useful.'

'I expect you know your own job,' said Tim coldly. 'It doesn't make it any pleasanter, for ordinary people, to know that they've been spied on.'

'For instance,' went on the Inspector, 'there was something Queen heard about people sticking knives into people's backs.'

It was impossible to say if Inspector Luck was smiling or not. Tim glared at him for a moment.

'I suppose, then, it's lucky for me no one thought of sticking a knife into MacMorris' back. Or I should obviously have been your number one suspect.'

'Oh, I shouldn't go as far as that, sir. No motive.'

'As a matter of fact I had a quarrel – a violent quarrel – with MacMorris about ten minutes before that conversation.'

'Had you, now?' said the Inspector. 'Yes, I believe I did hear something about that, too. These things get about, you know. Very frank of you to tell us about it, though.'

'I've nothing to conceal.'

'Of course not, sir. Well then – that's all for the moment. And thank you very much for coming.'

Mrs. Artside heaved herself out of her chair. She did not find herself liking Inspector Luck any better, but she was inclined to think that the honours of war were with him.

They stalked down the passage in dignified silence. In the charge room at the far end they found Sergeant Gattie, sitting at a desk, patiently filling in a yard and a half of pink form in triplicate.

He grinned at Tim and said, 'You been hauled over the coals?'

'Not really,' said Tim. 'Why?'

'Us going into the house before the fire brigade rolled up. Inspector didn't like it, I hear.'

'Didn't he now,' said Tim indifferently. 'What did he think we were doing? Destroying clues?'

The sergeant got off his stool and came round to the front of the desk. They were alone in the room. Mrs. Artside had gone on into the street.

'Did you ever know cordite jelly go off on its own?' he asked softly.

'No,' said Tim. 'I can't say I did. It usually needs a good detonating charge – and a detonator.'

Gattie nodded.

'You saw it happen,' he said. 'Which would you say? Detonation or explosion?'

'Detonation.'

'I thought so too. He was in his bedroom at the time. Any ideas?'

'If it had been the bad old days'—Tim found he had subconsciously lowered his own voice, too—'I should have plumped for the bedside lamp.'

'No go. The General had a view of the bedroom window. Says the light was on the whole time.'

'Well, there are plenty of other ways it could have been done. What about a contact switch in the bed. Would go off when he put his weight on it.'

'No sign of it. We got the bed almost intact.'

'I don't know,' said Tim irritably. 'I don't know. There are so many damn ways the thing could have been done. Contact, trembler, push-and-pull, photo-electric, time, temperature. There's no end to it—'

'Yes,' said Gattie. 'I agree. But here's what I can't make out. You know as well as I do, there's only one safe way of writing off the detonator – writing it off so that no one's ever going to find the least little bit of it, wire or screw or brass filing – and that's by putting it alongside the explosive. Then, when the thing goes off, it all gets blown up. Blown to smithereens, I mean, not just messed up.'

'Agreed.'

'Well, you see, it's pretty clear the explosive wasn't in the bedroom.'

'I haven't read the report properly, but I think that's right.'

'And there's no trace in the bedroom of anything like a detonating device.'

'If you've searched, and haven't found anything, I'll take that as gospel,' said Tim.

'Then how did MacMorris – who was in the bedroom – set off a lot of explosive – that was in another part of the house?'

'Perhaps he went out of the bedroom.'

'The General – who was doing his evening exercises in front of his window – saw MacMorris' shadow move across the window a few seconds before the balloon went up.'

'MacMorris' shadow?'

'Well – a shadow. He says it was MacMorris. No reason to suppose there was anyone else in the room.'

'I suppose not,' said Tim. He looked down at his watch and said, 'I'd no idea it was so late. I shall miss that train.'

'Which are you after?'

'The twelve-five.'

'You have cut it a bit fine. Better jump in the official wagon and I'll run you down.'

'It's very good of you,' said Tim. 'I've simply got to catch it.'

'You help us, we help you,' said Sergeant Gattie, flashing his grin again.

No more was said until they had sailed into the station. The sergeant was one of those competent drivers who make fast driving look safe and easy. The up-train was signalled but was not yet in sight.

'About what you were saying,' said Tim. 'If you're right about it – there are ways out of it, of course. Time devices and so on – but if you're right, what's your idea?'

'Well, sir. The stuff *could* have gone up by itself. Especially if it was in the tank room. The heat might have done it – or some sort of vibration.'

'That's the official theory,' said Tim.

'So what?' said Sergeant Gattie. 'Even the official theory's got to be right sometimes. Law of averages.'

Chapter Six

MARCHE MILITAIRE

HOLOFERNES: *'Most military sir, Salutation.'*

'Poor Liz,' said the General. 'I hear you've been subjected to the third degree. I hope your conscience is clear.'

'It's not a joke,' said Liz. 'That Inspector's a crook.'

'Really!'

'He's got a dishonest mind. He argues a priori. He commits catachresis. He suppresses his middles.'

'I wouldn't know about that. Personally I've always found him a decent enough fellow. You remember that time I lost Andy'—(Andy was an obscene bull-terrier for whom no one except the General had felt any affection at all)—'very worrying. I found him most helpful over that. How's he been upsetting you?'

There's nothing I can explain, but I don't like him. A pure case of Doctor Fell. I expect it will wear off. Have another cup of tea. What have you been doing with yourself today?'

'I've been spending a very trying afternoon,' said the General. 'Having a lady weeping on my shoulder.'

'Nonsense,' said Liz. 'You loved every minute of it. Look how you encourage me to weep on your shoulder.'

'Ah, but you're a dashed handsome woman,' said the General complacently. 'This was that silly old hen, Dolly Anglesea. She hasn't got a single brain to rattle in her skull. Her uncle was just the same. He lost us the Bullenpore Cup in 1895. As good as gave it away. We were in the middle of the last chukka but one, with a clear lead of two goals – look here, have I told you about this before?'

'What had Dolly got to say to you?' asked Liz hastily. She did, indeed, know the story of Tommy Anglesea's fatal blunder at Bullenpore in 1895. It had been no trivial blunder, and had not only cost his side the match but (according to Bill) had cost Tommy his Division in the 1914 war.

'About her house,' said the General.

'Yes. Very upsetting.' 'Can't see why. It's not as if she was living in it herself. And it's fully insured. She told me so. I believe she'll get more for it this way than she'd ever get by trying to sell it. And look at what she's saved herself. No legal fees, no bother.'

'All the same,' said Liz. 'It must be unsettling to have one's house blown to pieces. Not that it's anyone's fault but her own. Why ever did she let a man like MacMorris into it, in the first place?'

'I asked her that. Asked her what references he'd given. And, would you believe it – typical Anglesea – she'd never asked for any references.'

'Never asked for references?'

'That's right.'

'She must be cuckoo.'

'All the Angleseas are like that. I remember her father, once, at a mess meeting—'

'And yet,' said Liz, 'in another way, it does make sense.' She frowned and poured some more boiling water into the heavy silver teapot. 'The thing I could never understand was this. If MacMorris *wasn't* a soldier – and I'm beginning to believe that perhaps Tim's right about that, and he wasn't – why should he ever have pretended to be one?'

'People do that sort of thing.'

'Yes. But they don't come to live in this particular neck of the woods. You know that almost every male inhabitant here is Army or ex-Army. We're not *nosey* about it. We don't go round checking up on each other. If a man says, "Oh, I was on the administrative side" or "mostly on the staff", or something like that, we just gather he wasn't too proud of his Army record and we leave it alone.'

'Like when you ask a man where he was at school, and he says, "Oh, you won't have heard of it, a little place in the Midlands," so you don't poke any further.'

'Right. If he's been in the Guards or at Eton he'll tell you quick enough. So, admitted it was a small risk MacMorris ran. But why run it? That was the point. And the answer's just struck me. It was his only way of getting a house in this district. He couldn't produce any references. But he reckoned that with a woman like Dolly Anglesea all he had to do was click his heels and call himself Major and mention the old regiment a couple of times and she wouldn't worry about references.'

'Nor she did,' said the General. 'And if you're right, it means something else. It means that when MacMorris moved in here – from wherever he did come from – he had some particular reason for coming to this place. There must be lots of easier places to get a home – places where you needn't invent a phoney military past to get you in.'

'That's what I was thinking.'

The General swivelled in his chair, focused his frosty blue eyes on Liz and said, 'Yes. Yes. But why should it worry you?'

'Who says I'm worried?'

'I do,' said the General. 'What is it? Something that policeman said?'

'Not really. I told you, I don't like him much. But he wasn't offensive. It's just that you can see a mile away that he's got an *idée fixe* about this thing,'

'And you think it's the wrong one.'

'Yes. He's quite sure in his own mind – oh, damn. I can't tell you that bit, it was confidential. Anyway, he's quite sure that MacMorris had the explosive in the house for no good reason, and it blew him up accidentally.'

'Suppose he's quite wrong about all that,' said the General patiently. 'Why should it worry *you?*'

'It's going to take a lot of explaining,' said Liz. She poured a little of the hot water into the two Meissen china tea-cups, twirled each one slowly round in her strong fingers, and emptied it into the big silver slop basin. Then she looked up. The General was still watching her, his eyes snapping, but his face very friendly.

'When that first explosion happened – you know what I mean—'

'Yes.'

'When that happened, I shut my mind to it. I thought that was the best thing to do. Naturally, people were shy of talking to me about it. I didn't ask questions. I was sent a copy of the report of the Court of Inquiry. I tore it up. Then poor Tom Havers' Court Martial was in all the papers. I wouldn't read about it. So far as I was concerned, it was an accident. That was the official answer. That was the way it was going to stay. But you can't dragoon your thoughts forever. On and off, a long time after, I did find myself wondering.'

'I wondered sometimes, too,' said the General.

There was a moment of stillness. Then Liz said, 'I thought I was the only person with enough private information to piece that together. Do you mean to say it had occurred to you, too – that he might have done it himself?'

The General turned a shocked face on Liz.

'Bill take his own life? What—what damnable nonsense! Who put that into your head?'

'But I don't understand. Didn't you say that you sometimes wondered, yourself—'

'Suicide? The thought never entered my head. Bill couldn't have committed suicide. A moral impossibility. Men of thirty don't take their own lives – unless they're mad. And Bill wasn't mad, I can assure you.'

'Then what exactly,' said Liz slowly, '*did* you mean?'

'I was going to say that I sometimes wondered if perhaps people hadn't accepted the accident idea too quickly. Bill, you know, was working on a job that was going to blow a lot of other people sky high – higher than a tonne or two of high explosive. There was any amount of crooked work going on in Cologne at that time. I know, because I was there. You remember I was out there on that Observation Commission – it was the sort of job they were handing out to old has-beens at that time. It wasn't anything directly to do with me, but I couldn't help seeing what was going on. It was the first time since

Waterloo that we'd found ourselves as conquerors in a European country. And another thing. No one had worked out exactly how you put a war machine, in top gear, into reverse. I can tell you, from my own observation, that new trucks – war orders – went on being made *and delivered* up to 1921. Plenty of petrol. Plenty of tyres. Surplus steel. Red Cross supplies. Can you imagine the sort of opportunities a few unscrupulous men near the top could find in Germany – or in France – in 1920?'

'I knew a little about that,' said Liz. 'Bill told me something, but not much. He said there were some high-up civilian contractors involved. He was pretty worried about it. That's all I know.'

'If he was worried, you can bet the crooks were too,' said the General. 'However. That's dust and dead leaves now. We're never likely to know the exact truth. How does it tie up with this one?'

'It doesn't, of course,' agreed Liz, 'There's no logical connection of any sort. But, at the back of my silly old mind, what I feel is this. There have been two blow-ups in my life. I let the last one go. I don't want to funk this one.'

'Guilt complex. It's psychological. I remember the first time I went out after pig. Put up a monster. Overran him on purpose. I was afraid of him, you see. I had to shoot a tiger, on foot, to get it out of my system.'

Liz began to laugh, helplessly; and the General, after a moment, joined her.

'It's your metaphors,' said Liz, when she had recovered. 'So wildly inappropriate. I don't think there's a tiger in either of these explosions. Or a pig, for that matter. But I don't want to let it go by default.'

'What's in your mind?'

'I'd just like to find out who MacMorris was, and what he was up to.'

'Hmp!' said the General. 'Great respect for the police. If they haven't been able to do it, I don't suppose—'

'There are two things about that,' said Liz. 'The first is that the police had only just started looking into MacMorris. Luck said so. If they've got this idea in their heads that he's—I mean, about his having explosive in the house—'

'What was he? Burglar? Safe breaker?'

'All right. I didn't tell you. You guessed it. Yes. That's what they think. Well, mayn't they now never really look into him at all? There's not much percentage in a dead burglar. And suppose the sort of burglaries they were connecting him with should happen to stop now. Then they'll say, "We were right. Good riddance."'

'I don't think they're quite as easy to satisfy as that,' said the General. 'But go on—'

'The other thing is that I've got a sort of idea that they're inviting our help. I think that's why Luck was allowed to be so indiscreet. It was obvious to me he was doing it on orders from above. I think they calculate that if you want to find out about a person it's not a bad idea to start by enlisting the interest of his neighbours. We're so well brought up round here that we never appear to ask any questions but somehow we manage to keep our ears flapping.'

'My dear Liz! What an expression! However, I do see what you mean.'

'Particularly in a place like Brimberley.'

'So you suggest we start an investigation of our own. Not a criminal investigation. A sort of inquiry into MacMorris' past.'

'You'll help?'

'Of course,' said the General. 'I've never done this sort of thing before, but I've a feeling I shall be rather good at it. I took up golf at seventy-five.'

'Bless you,' said Liz.

'I shall begin on the War Office.' The General's eyes positively shone at the idea of beginning on the War Office. 'Have you got any particular ideas yourself?'

'Not an idea, but a photograph.'

'A photograph? Can I see it?'

'I wish you could. But it's gone. That's one of the things that makes it so interesting.'

She explained about the photograph.

'And you're sure it wasn't one of Dolly's that went with the house

– like the groups?'

'Tim says not. It was definitely MacMorris. About fifteen years younger. In service dress. Wasn't service dress for officers abolished in the first year of the war?'

'Officially it went out in 1940. All ranks were supposed to wear battledress. A lot of people went on wearing it, though.'

'Tim says he had a feeling it was pre-war. And then that medal ribbon—'

'Yes. That is odd. Doesn't sound like a campaign ribbon. Those usually went in batches. And it looked like an M.C.?'

'Tim says so.'

'He ought to know. It's not impossible. Young officers were getting M.C.'s in the thirties. Palestine, and so on. But still, MacMorris—?'

'It sheds rather a surprising light on his character, if it's true,' said Liz.

'How are you going to work this photograph – if you haven't got it.'

'Tim noticed the name and address of the photographer.'

'I see. Seems a slender lead. Mayn't be significant at all.'

'I don't think,' said Liz slowly, 'that the photograph itself is significant. But there's one point about it you can't argue away. Someone did take the trouble to remove it. It can't have been blown to pieces, because it wasn't anywhere near the heart of the explosion. And I don't believe the police can have overlooked it. They don't overlook things like that.'

Then what's your idea?'

'I've got three ideas,' said Liz, 'and you shall have them in order of unlikeliness. The police may be suppressing it themselves for some reason. Someone may have got in after Tim left and removed it. Or MacMorris himself may have spotted Tim taking notice of it – he was quite a sharp person – and may have removed it from the wall and hidden or destroyed it,'

'If that's right, he must have calculated it could lead people back to him.'

'Just exactly what I was thinking,' said Liz.

II

When the General reached his own house he looked at his watch and saw that it was nearly six o'clock. There were certain duties connected with this hour in his daily routine: the wireless to turn on so that clocks might be adjusted to the time signal; Sandy (Andy's successor) to be fed; hens to be dealt with.

He coped with all this, and poured himself out a drink, the first of the day. Then he sat down with it in the fat leather armchair in the room which was still called his study, and allowed himself the luxury of some reflection at large.

He thought about the War Office.

To-morrow was Saturday. Saturday morning was a good moment for an attack on the War Office. Nowadays he had noticed that most officers liked to put in a token appearance on Saturday morning, but they were more than usually free for gossip.

There were quite a number who might be useful to him, men whose fathers or grandfathers he had known. One or two whose active careers had just overlapped his. Ceremonial duties with the Gentlemen at Arms had kept him in touch with them.

The front door clicked.

That would be Sue. Friday evening. She would have been out helping Mrs. Macintyre with library night at the Institute. Now she was going to cook the supper which Mrs. Bannister, the daily, had put ready.

He wondered, and not for the first time, whether she didn't do too much of that sort of thing. Social work, housework. All work and no play. She was only just eighteen. At eighteen, a girl ought to be out and about nearly every evening. Dances, balls, dinner parties. Simla in the nineties. Early morning rides round Jakko. His wife-to-be coming into a dance at Vice Regal Lodge on her father's arm. Low fronts; tight sleeves; ostrich feather, bracelets winking with such tiny diamonds as an impecunious subaltern could afford. A young lady named Vivienne who, he had once fondly imagined—he coughed severely and switched his thoughts back towards the present.

Sue was attractive to men. The General, who had watched the process, would have been hard put to it to say just when it had happened: at what moment she had stopped walking and talking and thinking like a schoolgirl; at what moment she had become conscious of her body as an asset and her clothes as a weapon. He himself had been dimly aware, for some time, that the change had taken place, but it had only been brought home to him at the Staff College Ball. Indeed, some of the remarks he had overheard had seemed to him to verge on indecorum. He had had to be very stiff with old General Manktelow.

But was there anyone definite in view? A succession of eligible hussars, lancers, riflemen, guardsmen and horse gunners had danced with her and, subsequently, asked her out to parties, mostly refused.

At one time he had imagined that Tim was the one. The thought had troubled him a little. At first analysis Tim was all right. No money, agreed. But in Army circles one tended to be suspicious of a young man with money. On the other hand, his stock was undeniably excellent. They didn't come any finer than Liz and Bill Artside. Liz herself was the daughter of Sally Hope who, come to think of it, had been a Coutts. And the Artsides had been solid stuff for generations. If Tim had been a horse, thought the General, I'd have backed him both ways for speed and stamina. But he wasn't a horse. He was a man. And the General had a slight feeling of unease about him. Was it the fact of his having grown up without father or brothers? Or was it something to do with the war? Difficult to say. But once you got to know Tim you realised that he had a lot of the qualities of an iceberg. He was solid; he was dangerous if you crossed his path; and there was a good deal more of him below the surface than showed above it.

However, said the General, as he drained his glass, that didn't answer the main question. Did Sue go for him? And if so, how far and how deeply? He had heard about the quarrel they had had on Tuesday evening. That was a bad sign – or a good, according as you viewed the prospect.

If he really thought the matter important enough he could, he supposed, ask Sue about it.

Or could he?

The truth was that the General was more than a little afraid of his granddaughter.

III

'My dear Hubert,' said Major-General Rockingham-Hawse, 'how splendid to see you. They told me you were on the war-path and I hoped you'd come and look me up. We usually get such dreary visitors in establishments. You're looking very fit.'

'Of course I'm looking fit,' said the General. 'I *am* fit.'

How fat Rockinghorse was getting! It must be the effect of sitting in an office all day. He would have to find an opportunity of warning him tactfully of the dangers he was running.

'How's Tiddler? I hear he's settled in your part of the world.'

'I ran into him the other day,' said the General.

'He's looking very old. I'm afraid another winter will break him up.'

'Will do if it's anything like last winter,' agreed Rockingham-Hawse, glancing complacently round his own steam-heated office. 'Terrible climate. I wonder we don't all pull out and go to live in Kenya. Have you seen anything of Bunji lately?'

But Bunji was somewhat summarily disposed of. The General felt it was time to get down to business.

He had given considerable thought to his tactics, in the train, on the way up, and had decided that a modified form of the truth would serve best.

'I'll tell you how you can help me,' he said. 'You may have read in the newspapers about a man at Brimberley who got his house blown up.'

'I not only read about it, General, but remembered that you lived at Brimberley, and wondered what the poor chap might have done to offend you.'

'Well,' said the General, 'I might have blown him up if I'd thought of it, but actually it wasn't me, this time. The theory is it was an accident.'

'Rum sort of accident.'

'Well – yes. As a matter of fact that part of it's rather confidential.'

'Top secret, eh?'

'That's it. Political.'

The General was well aware of the paralysing power of the word 'political' when spoken inside the War Office. Rockingham-Hawse immediately pursed his lips, said, 'Ah, yes. I see. Yes,' and looked inscrutable; a feat which was not difficult, as his well-baked, finely glazed face offered little foothold for changes of expression.

'The fellow had been going round posing as a Major.'

'Before he got blown up?'

'Oh – yes – definitely. Had been calling himself Major MacMorris, getting a lot of credit on tick, and that sort of thing.'

'A phoney?'

'I think so. That's what I want to find out – quietly – if I can. I think he was a phoney all right. But if by any chance he wasn't, well, you see, it might be awkward.'

'It certainly might. You said his name was MacMorris "Mac", by the way, or "Mc"?'

'Mac, I think.'

'What sort of age?'

'Forty-ish. We had the idea that if he did any soldiering it was before the last war. There was a photograph—'

The General explained about the photograph and Rockingham-Hawse brightened considerably.

'Have you got it?'

'I'm afraid it seems to have got blown up, too.'

'I see. Do you know his Christian names?'

'I haven't been able to find anyone in Brimberley who was on Christian name terms with him, but it's thought to have been James.'

'I expect he registered somewhere. Coal or chicken food or something. The police—'

'I expect he did,' said the General smoothly. 'And I expect the police could find out, but at the moment I'm not particularly anxious to trouble them.'

'Political?'

'Political.'

'Well, we'll probably be able to find something for you. We've got pretty good officers' records here. And it's surprising how people keep in touch with us, even after they've left the Army. A lot of them are on reserves of one sort and another. I expect we shall be able to eliminate nine candidates out of ten straight away.'

'It's very good of you,' said the General, and meant it.

'Not at all. It may take a little time but we should be able to get on to it. Always supposing—'

'Always supposing,' agreed the General, 'that MacMorris *was* his name. That's a possibility, I agree. But if he was using a false name and rank that proves something too.'

'Wouldn't go round changing his name unless he'd got something to hide,' agreed Rockingham-Hawse. 'Well, that's that. I'll give you a ring when I find out something.'

'Afraid you're not getting rid of me as easily as that,' said the General genially. 'There's something else. Although I don't suppose it's in your department. I want to look at some old Court Martial proceedings.'

'That'll be the J.A.G. Let's walk along and see if Porky's in.'

Major Hogg was in, and was pleased to see the General. He was too young to have had much contact with him professionally but his father had been adjutant when the General had been Second-in-Command of the regiment in South Africa.

The General wasted no finesse on him, but simply told him what he wanted.

Major Hogg said: 'As far as the Court Martial goes there shouldn't be any difficulty about that. We keep Court Martial papers almost indefinitely. In fact, I was looking at some Peninsular War ones the other day. Courts of Inquiry are a different kettle of fish. If the Inquiry produced results which led directly to disciplinary action, then you might find copies with the court papers – or, on the other hand, if the whole thing was obviously going to be done again almost immediately at a Court Martial, I expect we shouldn't bother to keep the earlier record.'

'Where do Court of Inquiry papers go?'

Major Hogg said hesitantly, 'Now you're asking me something. They belong to the unit that holds the court. I expect they'd keep them, for a time, at Regimental headquarters – with the war diary and the G.1098 and junk like that. Always supposing they do keep them. An active regiment hasn't got much room for bumf.'

'But this wouldn't have been a regiment. It was a headquarters. A Corps headquarters, I think.'

'Well, that's a bit more hopeful. Which Corps?'

'Whichever Corps,' said the General slowly, 'was running Cologne in 1921.'

Major Hogg's face fell.

'It's a long time ago, isn't it?' he said.

'Certainly not,' said the General. 'Do you realise that by 1921, I had practically finished my military career?'

'It all depends how you look at it,' agreed Major Hogg.

'It was the year I went to my prep school. Now, let's think about this. We'd better look up "Pronto" Phipps. He knows all there is to be known about moribund formations. They hate killing anything off in his department. Put everything into "suspended animation". Makes you think of a live codfish in ice, doesn't it? All his records go into cold storage.'

Colonel Phipps, who was a tall, thin scholarly man wearing the faded ribbons of the D.S.O. and Croix de Guerre, welcomed the General with serious enthusiasm, but looked doubtful when he heard what he wanted.

'I could find what Corps was in charge of Cologne in 1921,' he said. 'There would be no difficulty about that. I only hope it *was* a pukka Corps, and not some improvised arrangement. There's always complete chaos when we win a war. God knows what would happen if we lost one. *If* it was a proper set-up, and *if* someone thought it worth while preserving the records – we did with some of the last war Divisions, I know – prestige reasons – then it's just possible the papers will be at Staines.'

'Staines?'

'Yes. There's no place for storing records here. The Department took over an old car factory at Staines in 1930 and we've been keeping papers there ever since. There's a character called Sergeant-Major Bottler in charge of it. He's about the oldest non-commissioned officer still serving. If anyone knows where to put his hands on it Bottler will. I've got to go to Staines on Monday, anyway—'

'It's very good of you.'

'Not a bit. Glad to help.'

The General walked out into Whitehall. As he was passing the Cenotaph a thought occurred to him. It was, he considered, absolutely typical of the whole organisation that no one had ever bothered to inquire why he wanted the papers. Absolutely typical.

He hailed a taxi and made for his club.

Chapter Seven

SOLO: WITH UNEXPECTED TENOR SUPPORT

MOTH:

*'No, my complete master, but to jig off a tune at the tongue's end,
canary to it with your feet, humour it with turning up your eyelids, sigh
a note and sing a note, sometime through the throat, as if you swallow'd
love with singing love; sometime through the nose, as if you snuff'd up
love by smelling love; with your hat pent-house-like o'er the shop of
your eyes; with your arms crossed on your thin-belly doublet, like a
rabbit on a spit, or your hands in your pocket, like a man after the old
Painting, and keep not too long in one tune, but a snip and away: these
are complements, these are humours, these betray nice wenches—'*

The day had started well for Liz.

She had never before had occasion to walk up the Charing Cross
Road, being aware of it only as part of the taxi route between the
shopping territory of Oxford Street and the railway terminals of
Victoria and Waterloo. Now that she was able to devote herself to it in
detail it seemed to have a certain fascination.

She had walked up, past the facade of St. Martin- in-the-Fields, to
what she imagined must be the beginning of the road itself. It was not
at all easy to be sure, since it was composed chiefly of theatres, which
of course had no numbers, and then a good deal of underground
station; but just as the station stopped she had found a bookshop,
numbered 34, and a milk bar, 36, and then she knew she was on her

way.

There seemed to be quite a lot of bookshops and milk bars (as well as the more ordinary bars). There were also shops which sold contraceptives. Liz was enchanted. She knew all about contraceptives in theory, and almost nothing in practice. They were things which one got, if one needed them, from one's family doctor. It had never occurred to her as possible that there could be shops which dealt in nothing else; shops which were prepared to display such things, even to advertise their peculiar attractions, in their windows.

The general public seemed to hurry past them in a sated way, but Liz remained anchored for a full five minutes, until, through the glass window, she observed the assistant, who had been sitting behind the counter reading a newspaper, to be eyeing her curiously. Whereupon she moved on.

Apart from the bookshops and the milk bars and the contraceptive shops there were doorways.

The doorways were, on the whole, helpful, because they had numbers over them. In some the doors were shut, in others, open. A few had no doors at all. Liz peered into one such hinterland. It seemed to be a communal hall serving a dozen one-roomed businesses. As Liz was looking curiously about her, a bulky woman with frizzled hair came slowly down the steep interior stair. She came so slowly, and so entirely filled the narrow staircase, that she looked more like a lift coming down a shaft than an ordinary person coming downstairs.

She started at Liz who stared back.

The woman said something abrupt in a foreign language. Liz shrugged her shoulders. The woman shrugged hers, turned ponderously, and disappeared into the back parts.

Liz went on down the street.

She could not help reflecting that it made a nice change from Brimberley.

Her troubles really started when she found that not only did No. 233 not exist, but that it could never have existed. Charing Cross Road came to a stop somewhere just over the 200's. Careful research disclosed a shop on the right-hand side, near the Tottenham Court

Road Tube Station, numbered 208. The other side seemed to tail off at somewhere about 197.

This brought her up all standing.

Could the numbers have been changed? She put the question to a policeman, who admitted that he did not know and referred her to a postman. The postman, an old cheerful man, said that he had been up and down the Charing Cross Road for forty years and hadn't noticed any change to speak of. Was she certain that the number really was 233? People's writing on envelopes, he had found, was quite unreliable. He had himself once gone all the way, in the snow, with a letter to 76 Bradford Mansions only to find that the address was intended to be 16 Beaufort Mews. Perhaps this one was meant to be 133. He rather thought that 133 Charing Cross Road was a public house.

Liz thanked him and took herself into one of the milk bars, where she ordered a cup of coffee. She felt deflated. Before starting out she had ascertained that the firm of 'Ardee' did not feature in any telephone or trade directory. Now, if she had got the address wrong, it looked as if she had wasted her trip to town.

She thought about the postman's suggestion, but it hardly seemed helpful. This address had not been in handwriting. It had been printed. How could Tim have mistaken '1' for '2'? There was not the slightest similarity.

She took out an envelope and printed 233 squarely on it. She turned the envelope round and looked at it upside down. It looked no better this way, so she righted it again. At that moment the glimmer of an idea lit in her mind.

She took a bus right back to the place she had started from. She trudged once more, slowly up the pavement on the East side where the odd numbers ran. This time she found No. 15, which was a tobacconist's. No. 21 had sunk without trace. Then came a large corner block which looked big enough to have swallowed up two or three numbers.

Pursuing her idea, she turned right at the corner. Sure enough, a little way down the side street, there *was* a door, on the right-hand side. And on the fanlight was painted the number, 23B. Taken all in all it was a triumph of deductive reasoning.

She peered into the doorway.

Judging by the nameplates and cards, screwed, tacked and pinned to the inside of the doorpost, the occupants of 23B were a versatile crowd. Reading from the bottom upwards there appeared, on the left, Mr. Skouros, who reconditioned furs, The Registered Office of Bancos Ltd. (philatelic dealers), Miss Chartrelle (hair therapist) and Miss Yvette Colouris (occupation unstated). On the right were Messrs. Crake and Crake, accountants, the U-Know Press Cutting Agency. Angus Romanes (consultant) and—wait for it—yes! Ronald Dowbell, photographic artist.

'Ronald Dowbell,' said Liz. 'R.D. – Ardee – Bob's your uncle.'

She advanced up the stairs.

The premises of Ronald Dowbell occupied the whole of the top storey and looked as if they had been there for some time. A door at the head of the staircase invited her to knock and enter and Liz knocked and entered. After this the proceedings slowed down. There seemed to be no one at home. It was a small, almost bare waiting-room, furnished with a table, three chairs to match and an enormous old-fashioned screw-operated letter-press.

Liz sat down patiently and tried to read the magazines. None of them was less than six months old.

After about ten minutes of this, she got up and walked round the room. There were three doors leading from it. She knocked at them in turn. Nothing happened. She then opened them. The first revealed a large cupboard full of shelves, and a single, old, wrinkled umbrella hanging, like a strip of dried seaweed, from a nail. The second door was locked. The third opened on to a corridor.

The corridor seemed to go on quite a long way. Evidently the premises of Ardee were somewhat larger than they seemed from the outside.

She stopped to listen. At the far end she seemed to catch a murmur of voices. She walked towards it. The voices came from behind a door at the very end. One was gruff and peremptory and male. The other was indeterminate.

'Sheep as a lamb,' thought Liz, and gently opened the door.

A dwarf with a hunched back and an alarming scowl was doing something with an enormous camera on a truck. A young man, with a little, monkey face and waved hair was sitting under several bright lights, in front of the camera. Both seemed startled to see Liz.

'I'm very sorry,' said Liz. 'I wanted to find out if anyone was about.'

'Whadyer want?' said the dwarf.

'I wanted some attention.'

'We only deal with the trade.'

'Oh,' said Liz. 'And just how do you know that I'm *not* the trade.'

The young man giggled. The dwarf continued to stare at Liz as if he hardly believed she existed.

'Whadyer want?' he said at last. He didn't seem able to think up anything better.

'What we'd better have,' suggested Liz, 'is a word in private.'

'Don't mind me,' said the young man. 'I'm quite comfy.'

The dwarf gave him a dirty look, then pushed past Liz, out of the door, and down the corridor. It wasn't exactly a gesture of courtly invitation, but Liz grasped her umbrella a little more firmly and followed. He led the way into an office. It was a small room, and rendered smaller by the clutter which filled it. The walls on three sides were lined with shelves and the shelves were jam-packed with papers. They covered the table. They encroached on to the floor. They continued, in piles, on top of shelves, reaching up to the ceiling like tropical undergrowth blindly seeking the light.

'Now wassit about?' said the dwarf brusquely.

He did not sit down, although there was a chair behind the desk, and Liz was unable to, since the other chairs were both deep in unfiled correspondence.

'When you send out photographs,' she said abruptly, 'do you put Ardee – A-R-D-E-E – on them?'

'We useter,' said the dwarf cautiously.

'So a photograph with Ardee on it must be one of yours?'

'Could be.'

'If I described a photograph to you, do you think you could trace it?'

'What do *you* think?' The dwarf's eye flickered up and down the shelves. Liz saw his point. She tried another tack.

'Do you do private sittings?'

'Private,' said the dwarf more thoughtfully. He managed to invest the single word with a deep edge of grimy disreputability.

'I mean,' said Liz hastily, 'if someone just walked in and asked you to take his photograph, would that be the sort of business you'd do?'

'Certainly not. We work for the trade.'

Liz nearly said 'What trade?' but funked it.

'You work for agencies?'

'That's right.'

'Which ones?'

'All the big ones.'

From the depths of her memory Liz fished up a name.

'Bart's.'

'That's right. Bart send you?' For the first time Liz seemed to be making sense to him,

'Not exactly,' she said. Thank you all the same. I may be back.'

'Any time,' said the dwarf impassively.

Liz trudged back up the Charing Cross Road. The attendant was standing in the doorway of the contraceptive shop. He recognised Liz and winked at her. Liz winked back.

Bart's office was at the top of the building behind the Collodeon Theatre. It, too, was up three flights of stairs, with no lift, but at that point any resemblance to the Ardee Photographic Studios ceased.

To begin with, it was full of people; not the helpless, costive crowd traditionally associated with such places, but a fluid one. People came in and held short and serious conversations, with a young man who was perched on a sofa reading a shiny periodical, with a young lady who came in from time to time from the back premises, with each other. When they had finished their conversations they went, and others came. Everyone talked rapidly but confidently. Everyone oozed personality. Everyone seemed to be roughly two and a half times their normal selves.

Liz, sitting squarely in a corner, decided that it was, in principle, not unlike a French eighteenth-century salon.

Eventually, by doing absolutely nothing, she attracted a certain amount of attention, and during a lull in the proceedings the young man came over and sat down beside her and asked, was there anything he could do for her?

'Just a word with Bart,' said Liz.

'A word with Bart?' said the young man. 'Oh, I don't—what exactly was it about?'

'Nothing important,' said Liz shortly.

This seemed to disconcert the young man. He looked covertly at Liz again, trying to rationalise her old but nicely-cut tweeds, her expensive shoes, her impossible hat.

'Was it personal?'

'In a way,' said Liz.

'Financial?'

'I suppose you could describe it as that.'

The young man got to his feet rather thoughtfully and said something to the girl. The girl cut short a conversation with a grey-haired old bouncer in full morning dress and went out of the room.

Five minutes later she reappeared and asked Liz for her name. Liz gave it, spelling it patiently. The girl disappeared, reappeared, and said that if Mrs. Arsite would come along Mr. Bart was free for a few minutes.

As she followed the girl Liz realized that everyone in the room had stopped talking and was trying to calculate, on insufficient data, who she might be. She felt a little surprised at herself.

Bart was as she remembered him, a round brown indestructible ball of a man with the thick lips and high cheeks of his Russian parents, and the manners of a man who had been doing immense favours to other people since before he can remember and is getting a bit tired of it. It was clear that he did not recognise Liz.

'I see you don't know me,' she said, as cheerfully as she could. 'Why should you? It was fifteen years ago. I was running the Bramshott and

District Pageant – the last big one we had before the war. I borrowed two professional players from you – one for Charles the Second and Sidney Herbert and the other for Nell Gwynne and Florence Nightingale.'

'But I remember perfectly,' said Bart, untruthfully. 'I have no doubt we can help you. Again a pageant? Yes?' He looked approvingly at Liz. 'I have exactly the man. Last Tuesday he is Canute at Canvey Island. This weekend, Guy Fawkes, at Staines. Versatile.'

'Well, no,' said Liz.

'Not a pageant?'

'Not a pageant. Something quite different. It was really your help I wanted.'

'Oh.'

'It's not—I mean, I'm not collecting for anything,' said Liz hastily. 'It's your professional help that I want. It's a curious story.'

'Curious stories. I hear them a hundred a week,' said Bart.

'But this is quite uncommonly curious,' said Liz. She told the story quickly. She was aware that she was there under false pretences, but she did not intend to abandon the ground until she was actually thrown out.

It was difficult to tell if Bart was interested or not. He said, 'Yes, of course I know Ronald Dowbell. They do a lot of work for us. Theatrical work. We are their biggest customers. But why should an Army officer go to them from us? I do not understand that.'

'He wouldn't,' said Liz. 'I expect he just walked in – like I did – and they took his photograph. The thing is, I can't make them search for the original, but you could. I'm sure they'd do it to oblige you—'

'Perhaps—' said Bart. He was too much of a gentleman to add what was plainly uppermost in both their minds.

At that moment a small door behind Bart's desk swung open and a big, black-haired man came in. There was no need to speak his name. His face said it for him. He was without doubt the greatest tenor in the world.

Bart jumped to his feet, bounced forward with outstretched hand and said, 'A pleasure. My dear Florimond.'

'Florrie!' said Liz.

The black-haired man shook Bart by the hand, came forward with calculated deliberation, and kissed Liz, first on one cheek, then on the other.

It was as if someone had turned on a large electric fire and pink lighting had sprung up all round the cornices.

'My dearest Liz,' said the famous voice. 'What gifts the Gods do drop into our undeserving laps. I come in, expecting to do no more than a little business with ugly old Bart, and who do I find—?'

He waved a hand. It was a gesture to the leader of the orchestra. It was a signal to the electrician. More sympathetic spotlights. A soft preliminary note of music.

'My dear Florimond. You know Mrs. Artside—?'

'The name,' said Florimond, 'is Liz. Do I know her? The answer is "Yes". I have been in love with her for thirty years. Even since she was six,' he added gallantly.

Now how was it, thought Liz, that some people could say things which they didn't mean and which they didn't even mean you to think they meant, and yet you liked them none the less? Italians, especially.

'What chance brings you here? Do not tell me. I shall guess. Bart has at last found a composer talented enough to write an opera around your personality.'

'I had no idea,' said Bart. 'Does Mrs. Artside—?'

'She has a perfectly natural basso. Rounded. Unique. Hamlet as a woman you have seen. Now Falstaff. Conceive the possibilities.'

'Now really,' said Liz. 'Behave. It's no use, Florimond, I'm not for sale. Sit down.'

Florimond seated himself obediently, yet with a swirling gesture that turned Bart's office chair into the imperial throne of the Romanoffs.

'I did not come here for an audition,' she went on. 'I came here to get Mr. Bart's help.'

'Which I am certain he will give to you.'

Bart was certain, too. So was Liz. Rarely had anyone's status altered quite so rapidly. If Mrs. Artside was a friend of Florimond, if she knew him well enough to tell him to sit down and stop talking, then Bart was prepared to spend the whole day humouring her.

'Mrs. Artside was just explaining it to me when you came in,' he said. 'A photograph—'

'Ha,' said Florimond. 'An indiscreet photograph, taken in your youth. Some cad who has it refuses to give it up. A horsewhip—'

'No, no. Nothing like that. I'll explain it again.'

When she had done so Bart said: 'That should not present any insuperable difficulty. I have a certain influence with the firm of Ronald Dowbell. In fact, a controlling influence. His records will certainly be available. The question will be, can anything at all be found? You say fifteen years. His filing system, I know, lacks method.'

Liz could not but agree.

'However, I have in this office a young man who worked there for some years. He shall go across and see what he can find. No thanks, please. If you would perhaps come back here after lunch—'

Liz had arranged to lunch with a friend who lived in Putney and having little idea of comparative distances between different parts of London had made up her mind to go by bus. (If she had been told that Putney was nearly three times as far from Oxford Street as Bramshott was from Brimberley she would not have believed it. Everything in London was naturally next to everything else.) It was therefore nearly four o'clock before she got back to Bart's.

Bart had gone but the young man was waiting patiently for her. He had with him a number of photographs of men in military uniforms. They were a curious collection, ranging from a Colonel of Ruritanian Hussars to a gentleman in that easily recognisable Eastern European uniform which is made up of jackboots, baggy trousers, a blouse and a flat hat. Among them Liz had little difficulty in identifying Lieutenant MacMorris.

'So that's the chap, is he?' said the young man. He peered at the photograph. 'Don't fancy I know him. He's not a regular – not now, anyway. Here's all the dope we've got about him.'

He handed Liz a sheet of paper, half covered with typescript, which she read with a growing sense of fantasy.

'Is this—are you sure this is right?'

'Oh, that's gospel,' said the young man. 'Some of the dates may be a little out but the gist of it's all right. We're very careful about that sort of thing here. Have to be.'

'Well, thank you very much,' said Liz.

'Not at all,' said the young man. 'Only too pleased to be of any help.'

II

Whist as played at village whist drives, as Tim had discovered, bore little resemblance to any other card game. The rules were comparatively simple. Suits were led out in turn, starting with the highest card in that suit that you happened to possess. Trumps were played last. (So much so that if, in error, you led a trump early on in the game it was etiquette for your opponents to indicate your mistake by some such observation as 'Hearts are trumps this time,' whereupon the lead could be withdrawn without penalty.) Scoring was at the flat rate of one point per trick, but an additional prestige point could be gained by leading your first card so quickly that no one else had had time to sort out their hand.

Once he had mastered these rules Tim found the Brimberley whist drive quite good fun. They were cheap. One and sixpence, including refreshments.

There was plenty of time to talk to one's friends between games. And in the ordered coming and going that constituted the mobile element of the whist drive one could hardly help running into people one knew.

As, for instance, Sue.

Sue was two tables away, circulating anticlockwise. He was in the opposite planetary system. If they both won this hand they would find themselves momentarily in conjunction, though as opponents, at the same table,

Tim looked at his hand and calculated his chances.

Sue was now playing against Mrs. Ransome, who cheated and, therefore, won more often than not. He, on the other hand, was playing opposite Lucy Mallory, who was quite hopeless, against the Vicar and his wife, rather a hot partnership. On the other hand, the organiser had just announced that clubs would be trumps, and he saw that he had no fewer than six of them.

It was a close call, but he did it. He was almost thwarted at the last moment by Lucy, who first trumped his last (and winning) diamond and then failed to trump the Vicar's winning spade; but he bludgeoned his way to seven tricks with his run of clubs and rose to his feet to see Mrs. Ransome looking slightly pink about her prominent ears, and Sue coming towards him.

Sue also appeared to be put out.

'Really,' she said, 'that woman ought to be warned off. I don't mind her revoking, but when it comes to putting her handbag down on two of our tricks and trying to claim them for her side – what are trumps?'

'Hearts,' said Jim Hedges, 'and I hope you got plenty of 'em. Miss Susan, because I haven't got but two.'

'That's all right, Jim,' said Sue. 'I've got some nice hearts. It's clubs I'm right out of. Oh, I didn't really mean that as a hint, but I suppose I might as well trump it, since you've led it – well played again – eight – nine – ten – that's eleven tricks to us. Thank you so much, partner.'

She moved on.

Mr. Sunley, the Bramshott solicitor, who had been partnering Tim, got up and moved into the opposition seat and observed, 'I am not sure that cards bring out the best in the opposite sex.'

By ten o'clock the prizes had been distributed and the party was breaking up. Tim caught up with Sue as she was leaving.

'May I walk home with you?' he asked.

'Yes,' said Sue shortly. 'If you behave yourself.'

They walked in silence for some time. Tim said, 'I've wanted a chance to apologise for the other night.'

'There's absolutely no need.'

'Well, I think there is. Particularly now that—'

'Now that the little man can no longer stand up for himself.'

'All right,' said Tim doggedly. 'I told him I was sorry – and now I've said it to you.'

'Short of an announcement in the press, that would seem to wrap it up,' agreed Sue.

After a further hundred yards Tim chanced his arm again. 'I only wish,' he said, 'that you wouldn't be quite so beastly to me all the time.'

Sue stopped, and there was enough light for him to see the danger signals. However, when she spoke it was in a deceptively moderate voice.

'Just exactly why should it matter to you how I behave?'

This was not a question to which there seemed to be any easy answer.

'I—' said Tim. 'I can only say—well, it does matter to me. I'm—' Under her young eyes he funked it. 'I'm fond of you,' he said at last.

'I see.' Sue looked him up and down carefully. 'That's rather one-sided, isn't it? I mean, why should the fact that you are fond of me be supposed to affect *my* outlook? Or perhaps I've missed the point.'

'I did think, at one time—' said Tim, and stopped. He was being manoeuvred into an impossible position.

'You thought at one time that I rather went for you,' said Sue. 'Right. So I did. When I was six I loved the gardener. He was a Scotsman, and he had the softest brownest sidewhiskers. Later on it was the geography mistress. Then it was you. I can't explain it, but I expect it was something to do with your uniform and the medals and all the jolly hush-hush business of being behind enemy lines and killing people and spying.'

Tim remembered reading about a Red Indian who had been skinned alive. They started with his feet. He appreciated just how it had felt.

'I see,' he said at last.

'You were only a phase,' went on Sue, plying the knife kindly. 'It didn't last long. There are too many soldiers round these parts for the actual idea of a soldier to stay glamorous. And, when you look round you, there doesn't seem to be all that future in being a soldier's wife.'

'But I'm not a soldier.'

'No,' admitted Sue. 'I suppose not. But you're not exactly a civilian either. What *do* you do for a living? Not,' she added as Tim remained uncomfortably silent, 'that I'm at all interested. Particularly if it's security.'

'Well, yes,' said Tim. 'In a way, it is.'

'Then you *are* doing a Secret Service job?'

'I—look here'—said Tim—'you know damned well that if I was I couldn't say.'

'Of course not,' said Sue. 'And, as I said, I'm not really interested. But whatever it is, it doesn't sound like work to me.'

They moved on in silence. By the time they reached your thigh, Tim seemed to remember, the pain was so agonising that you became numbed by it.

'Tell me,' he said at last. 'Is it that you don't like me, or is it that you don't like the idea that I'm not doing a proper job of work – living on my mother? Go on – say it if you think it.'

'But I never said I didn't like you,' said Sue. 'I'm afraid this is where we part – I'm calling on Mrs. Hitchcock. And what a warning *she* is against marrying a soldier. Good night.'

III

'He was *what?*'

'An actor.'

'Not a soldier?'

'Only on the stage.'

'Good God,' said the General, adding, automatically, 'Sorry, Liz.'

'He wasn't even really an actor. He did walking-on parts. His steadiest employment was in the Gilbert & Sullivan Chorus. Iolanthe.'

'And which was he? A peer or a peri?'

'Don't be catty,' said Liz, and added, 'Te turn te tiddy turn. "A Lordly vengeance will pursue all kinds of common people who oppose our views or boldly choose to offer us offence."'

'Then what was the photograph? That wasn't anything from Iolanthe.'

'That was his big part. Lieutenant Harkness in the Ace of Clubs. Did you see it? Just before the war.'

'Certainly not. Did you?'

'Once – after a good dinner.'

'Then you remember MacMorris?'

'Not exactly. He hadn't a very long part. He comes in at the end of the Court Martial scene and hands Major Rutland a revolver and says, "The Regiment is a bigger thing than you are, Major."'

'My God,' said the General.

'He was on the stage, in a sort of way, till the end of 1944. That's about a year before he came here.'

'Then he never fought in the war at all?'

'No real reason he should,' said Liz fairly. 'According to this he was forty when it started.'

'Impossible. That would make him well over fifty.'

'Actors have their secrets—' began Liz, and was interrupted by a bellow of laughter from the General. He rarely laughed, but when he did the effort was unstinted. He was unable to speak for a long time.

'The Regiment,' he gasped at last, 'is a bigger thing than you. Oh dear, oh dear, oh dear.'

'It does explain quite a lot. In fact, I should say it answers all the questions except the important ones. Such as, why did he come *here?*'

'Sense of humour. Ha ha ha. Second Lieutenant Harkness. Ho ho ho.'

'Improbable,' said Liz calmly. 'A joke's a joke but it would wear thin after five years or so. But suppose you're right. Suppose he retired here and called himself Major MacMorris from a misguided sense of humour. Or for no particular reason at all. People don't *have* to have a reason for everything they do. Then tell me this. What did he live on?'

'Live on?'

'No one,' said Liz, 'could stand the life of an ageing third-class actor, a hanger-on of the West End stage, unless he had absolutely no other means or way of living. The only reason for persevering would be the hope of a lucky break – which would give you enough to retire on. Well, he didn't get it.' She looked again at the crumpled sheet of paper in her hand. 'His parts got smaller and smaller. So small, they almost became invisible. Yet suddenly, he managed to retire. And to live down here. Not luxuriously, but well enough.'

'Perhaps he did get that break. Not on the stage. Something else.'

'That,' said Liz, 'is just what I was thinking.'

Chapter Eight

LIZ MARCATO: TIM RADDOLCENDO

COSTARD: *'Thou pigeon-egg of discretion.'*

"So you see,' said Liz, 'MacMorris wasn't a Major. He wasn't in the Army at all.'

'Yes.'

'What do you mean, "Yes"?'

'I meant,' said Inspector Luck patiently, 'that we had already ascertained that fact.' He added, with a smile that could have meant anything, 'We, too, have our avenues of information, though not perhaps at the same level as General Palling.'

'If you've found that out, then I expect you know who he *really* was.'

'Well—'

'Play the game. I'm not going to tell it all to you for the fun of hearing you say, "As a matter of fact we knew it all the time." Either you have found out who MacMorris was or you haven't.'

'As a matter of fact,' said the Inspector crossly, 'no.'

'All right, then. He was an out-of-work actor called Don Trefusis. At least, that was the name he used with the agencies and on the stage. I can't believe it's the name he received at the font.'

'Don Trefusis.' The Inspector made an inconspicuous note.

'If you should experience any difficulty in tracing his antecedents, Bart's Theatrical Agency in the Charing Cross Road will tell you all you want to know about him. Unless,' she added with an ill-bred grin, 'your union insists on you using your own avenues of information.'

'Well,' said the Inspector, 'I'm very obliged to you, I'm sure.'

'Chalk it up to me next time you catch me driving without a tail-lamp,' said Liz. 'The real point is, where do we go from here?'

'I don't quite—'

'Lord love us. That's only the beginning. It's nothing at all by itself. Don't you see the possibilities it opens up.'

'Well – ' said the Inspector. He seemed to be choosing his words with more than usual care. 'Since we know, now, that MacMorris wasn't really a soldier, he had to have been something else. The fact that he was formerly an actor doesn't seem, by itself, to prove anything very much.'

'Mills of God,' said Liz. 'Of course it doesn't. But ask yourself two questions. If he was going to play at soldiers, why come here? If you were going to pretend to be a policeman you wouldn't go and live at Scotland Yard. Or, come to think of it, might you? Double bluff? No, I don't think so. Too subtle, and out of character.'

She looked inquiringly at the Inspector who opened his mouth and closed it again slowly, exactly like a fish at feeding time.

'The second point is even simpler. What did he live on?'

'As to that,' began Inspector Luck judgmatically, 'I take it—'

'I suppose you're going to suggest that he came into money.'

The words thus neatly whisked out of his very mouth, the Inspector was forced to fall back on looking cross and inscrutable.

'The poor old actor,' said Liz, 'who hasn't had a part in six months. Last pair of shoes worn out staggering through the snow, from agency to agency, now staying in bed to keep warm and preserve his only suit. Enter the family lawyer. "Mr. Trefingle? Your aunt, Lady Trefingle, has died and left you a hundred thousand pounds. Here's five hundred on account. Apply to me as soon as you want some more." Corn. If you can believe that you can believe anything.'

'I didn't say—'

'And suppose he had come into money – some real steady settled income – dividends, that sort of thing. Then tell me this. Why didn't he have a bank account?'

'How on earth,' said the Inspector, 'can you know that he didn't?'

'Well, I don't know it. I haven't been inquiring round the banks. Not that they'd have told me anything if I had. But I do happen to know that he paid all his local bills in cash. Even quite large ones. And don't ask me how I know *that*. I do know it. I've got friends.'

It was then that the Inspector decided to come off whatever high horse he had been riding. He said, and without too much stuffiness in his voice: 'So what do you make of it?'

'There, now,' said Liz. 'That's a fair question. I've had longer to think about it than you so I'll give you my idea first. I think he must have found a gimmick. That would account for the money, and it would explain why he came down here to keep an eye on it. You've got to nurse a gimmick, or, like the Snark, it fades away.'

'A—?'

'American expression. It doesn't translate into one word in English. It means—it means some secret source which produces a steady income which you don't have to work for. Sometimes it's just a trick – like knowing how to make three lemons come up together on the fruit machine. But it can be even easier than that. You know something, and someone is prepared to pay you not to say it. Then it really is money for nothing. Like famous film stars, who get paid large sums for *not* acting.'

'Then the supposition would be—that someone in this area – yes, I see. It's a bit vague, isn't it?'

These things are always vague to start with. What you have to do is get busy and trace MacMorris' friends. Who came to see him? Who did he call on, openly? Who did he visit secretly? Who knew him *but pretended not to?*'

'Yes,' said the Inspector. He did not sound very happy about it.

'Isn't that right?'

'I suppose so. Yes. He's been here six or seven years, you see.'

'He wasn't very social man,' said Liz. 'He was in the choir – and just what we're going to do for a tenor for our Harvest Festival Anthem I don't like to think. He played a little tennis – Lucy Mallory used to partner him. He knew General Palling, and the Vicar. He sometimes rode Bob Cleeve's horses and he once tried to buy a car off Jim Hedges. He knew me – I wouldn't have described him as a friend.'

'Yes,' said the Inspector again. 'Well, it's been very good of you. Thank you very much.'

'That sounds like a brush-off,' said Liz. 'Give me a straight answer to a straight question. Are you going to follow up what I've told you?'

'I don't think,' said the Inspector in an exceedingly reasonable tone of voice, 'that I'd be at liberty to discuss actual police plans with you.'

'Fair enough. But I warn you. When I was a girl my headmistress wrote on my report "Has little brain, but when she does get an idea she sticks to it." And just so that you won't think I'm doing anything behind your back, I'm warning you. My next call this morning is on Tom Pearce.'

When she had gone the Inspector went across to the shelf and got down his well-thumbed dictionary. First he tried the 'G's'; then the 'J's'. He didn't have any luck in either.

Pearce (whose Christian name was Cecil, but a fellow Devonian at Peel House had called him Tom, and the name had followed him round ever since) looked like a successful banker. He was, in cold fact, a successful Chief Constable; which is a role in which real success is a good deal harder to come by than in any bank.

He attended to all that Liz had to say, without interrupting, coiling it all away in the orderly recesses of his mind.

At the conclusion of it he turned his candid, grey eyes full on to her and said, 'Tell me, Mrs. Artside, are you dissatisfied with the Inspector's handling of this matter?'

This was such a sharp jab below the belt that it took Liz a little time to get her breath back.

'No,' she said. 'I don't—I mean to say, I think he's made the right moves so far. I expect he would have found out about MacMorris' past soon enough. I wouldn't have got it myself without outrageous luck.'

'Then—'

'All the same, it's not quite fair to ask me if I'm happy about his handling of the case. He hasn't really started to handle it yet. And I've got a feeling – no more – that he's going to backpedal on it.'

'Luck doesn't give one the impression that he's over-flowing with mental alertness or bursting with vigour,' agreed the Chief Constable. 'All the same, in my view, he's a good policeman of a rather old-fashioned sort. And I don't think it's fair to prejudge him.'

'All right,' said Liz. 'Just so long as he hasn't prejudged the case. MacMorris was a cracksman. MacMorris had cordite. MacMorris blew himself up. End of cracksman. End of case.'

The Chief Constable opened his eyes slightly.

'Did Luck tell you that? About MacMorris being a cracksman?'

Liz hesitated.

'Yes,' she said. 'Wasn't he supposed to?'

'So long as he had every confidence in your discretion,' said the Chief Constable with a smile that travelled almost all the way up to his eyes. 'I don't suppose any great harm was done.'

II

'It's like trying to swim through a treacle pudding,' said Liz.

'Never tried it,' said Cleeve. 'Sounds a bit dispiriting.'

'It is dispiriting. But there's a broad distinction between being dispirited and being choked off. I refuse to be choked off.'

'That's the stuff.'

'And don't you dare blow your silly moustache at me and give me your "poor little woman" routine. Because I warn you, I'm serious.'

'You're not only serious,' said Cleeve, blinking at her. 'You're terrifying.'

'Then instead of trying to gammon me, just explain what it's all about?'

'Don't want to appear obstructive. But what's all *what* about?'

'You know as well as I do. Why is it that everyone has made up their mind to sit heavily on this case? Why is it being played down? Even the papers are calling it an accident now. Not that anyone has troubled to explain just why a retired Major (alleged) should have enough cordite in his attic to blow his house into two bits. Maybe a public brought up on Giles and Low thinks that *all* retired Majors keep explosives round the house. And there's nothing about the anonymous letter, I observe.'

'The anonymous letter,' said Cleeve. 'Yes, it's a real puzzler, that. I honestly think, if the truth were known, MacMorris wrote it himself.'

'Why?'

'That's one of the things that's giving Tom Pearce and his boys a headache.'

'All right. I accept that the police may want to keep quiet about the letter, particularly if they think it was a fake. But why are they conditioning themselves into thinking that the whole thing was an accident? And don't tell me they aren't. I had an hour of Luck this morning and I could hear the needle going round in the grooves. MacMorris was a burglar. MacMorris blew himself up. Good riddance.'

'Hmph.'

'Do you think it was an accident?'

The Chairman turned the light of his countenance fully upon Liz. His washed blue eyes were the colour of the clear evening sky after a blatter of rain; and just about as communicative.

'I don't know,' he said at last. 'I honestly don't know. Twenty-four hours ago I should have said, "Yes." Now I'm not sure.'

'Because of what I unearthed in London?'

'Partly because of that.'

'Was it you who told Luck he could tell me about MacMorris' past?'

'Yes,' said Cleeve, without even blinking.

'Because you guessed I'd scuttle round and find something out for you quick.'

'Yes.'

'I did, too,' said Liz.

'And now I'm going to say something to you, in return,' said Cleeve. 'Something you'll have to keep quite quiet about. *If* we can succeed in persuading everyone that the MacMorris case is closed, *if* people can be induced to stop thinking about it, and think, instead, about the Harvest Festival Anthem, and Guy Fawkes and their Christmas shopping, then, and only then, we may be able to do something useful.'

'I don't quite see—'

'My dear Liz,' said Cleeve gently, 'You know this part of the world. They're quite level-headed folk. But just what sort of crisis do you think we should provoke if they realised that there was someone living among them who was capable of blowing up any one of them, in their beds, to-night? Particularly as the police can't offer much protection until they discover just *who* is gunning for *whom* and *why*.'

III

When Tim got home that night he cracked his shins on the dining-room table, which had been moved out into the hall, and, when he had edged past it and into the dining-room he found the chairs arranged in two rows and the portable harmonium blocking the sideboard, and it came to his mind that Monday was treble practice night.

This reminded him of something else, and he went to look for his mother, who was in the kitchen, with Anna, icing cakes.

'Have we found another tenor yet?' he asked.

'As a matter of fact,' said Liz. 'I think we may have. Thanks to Luck.'

'Luck?'

'Not luck, Luck. When I saw him this morning he happened to mention that Sergeant Gattie was the absolute mainstay of their police choral society. Gattie was very modest about it when I saw him, but I really think he might do it for us.'

'Well, thank goodness for that,' said Tim. 'Singing that tenor solo was not one of the things I was looking forward to most. Come to think of it, this will be the second time Gattie has saved my bacon.' When Liz looked inquiring, he added, 'In Jerusalem, in 1947, he shot a gentleman in a bowler hat who was on the point of tossing a hand grenade into the back of a car I was driving. What are we doing about supper?'

I'll think about that when I've got rid of the trebles. Why don't you go down to the church and give a hand with the flowers?'

'Because I don't know the first thing about flowers.'

'I don't imagine Sue is all that expert, either. Couldn't you hump round the heavy lectern vases whilst she does the actual arranging?'

'Why, yes. I could do that,' said Tim. 'Yes. I could certainly do that.'

'I thought you might be able to,' said his mother.

There were lights in the church, and voices. As Tim opened the door it was plain that he interrupted an argument.

Lucy Mallory stood by the lectern, clasping an armful of early-autumn foliage. Sue was in the pulpit. She had a bunch of white asters in one hand, some straggly gypsophila in the other and a flush on her cheek.

'Why, hullo, Mr. Artside,' said Lucy.

'Hullo, Tim,' said Sue. 'If you dare do it, I shall probably never speak to you again.'

Tim looked slightly taken aback but discovered that this broadside was aimed at Lucy.

'What nonsense,' said Lucy. 'Anyway I'm sure Mr. Artside hasn't come here to listen to us girls quarrelling.'

'I'm not quarrelling,' said Sue, giving the asters an angry shake. 'And as he's involved he's got a perfect right to know about it.'

'How's he involved?'

'He's in the choir, isn't he? Until we find out who did it we're all involved.' She shook the asters again, and Tim, who had been conscious that it reminded him of something, realised that it was exactly the way old Canon Bessemer used to shake his finger when he spoke of sin.

Tell me all,' he said.

'Hand me those two vases then,' said Sue. 'I suppose you came here to help, not just to gossip. It's about Maurice.'

'Maurice Hedges?'

'Who else?'

'What's he been up to now?'

Maurice was the eldest of the Hedges children, a boy with a long, serious, Hanoverian face and the gravity that went with the headship of a large family.

'That's just what we don't know,' said Sue, 'but Lucy caught him in Mrs. Simpson's shop trying to change a ten shilling note.'

'It doesn't sound a desperate crime,' said Tim.

'That's not all of it,' said Sue. 'You'd better tell him, Lucy. If you're determined to split to the Vicar it'll have to come out, anyway.'

'When Maurice saw me come into the shop,' said Lucy, 'he bolted. It looked so fishy I asked Mrs. Simpson what it was all about. She was a bit surprised too. Apparently he came in, put down this ten shilling note, and asked for some sweets. None of those kids ever have any money of their own. If his mother had sent him down with a big order of groceries she might have given him a ten shilling note, you see. But if it was just sweet money it would have been a bob, or half-a-crown at the most.'

'Still doesn't seem enough to hang him on,' said Tim. 'Did Maurice actually succeed in changing the note? I didn't quite get that bit.'

'No. As soon as he saw me he picked the note up and bolted. But I saw, and I asked Mrs. Simpson and she'd noticed too – it wasn't a new ten shilling note. It was one of those purpley ones – they stopped making them before the war, when they brought in the brown sort. You remember them?" I remember them all right,' said Tim. 'You don't see many of them about now, but as far as I know they're still legal tender.'

'Ah,' said Sue. 'That's just it.'

'Just what?'

'One of the notes the Vicar put in the offertory box from his American girl friend was a purple.'

'How do you know that?'

'He told Gattie, Gattie told Queen, and Queenie told me.'

'It all seems a bit second-hand,' said Tim.

'Well,' said Sue. 'I'm not sure. If it was just a question of the type of note I'd be inclined to agree. As you say, there are still plenty of them about. But why should Maurice have a note at all?'

'They're not paupers,' said Tim. 'His father runs a taxi – to say nothing of a garage.'

'Then why did he bolt?'

Lucy said, 'Now you're arguing against Maurice. When I first told you about it you said you thought he hadn't taken it.'

'I didn't say he hadn't taken it. I said you wouldn't be able to prove it. If you go and tell the Vicar he's bound to do the wrong thing. He's such a silly man. Then you'll have started something you can't finish.'

'That's up to him,' said Lucy. 'I think he ought to know about it. Don't you?'

'I'm not sure,' said Tim. 'I think Sue's right, in a way. If Hallibone possibly can put his foot in it he will. And if he rubs Jim Hedges up the wrong way we shall lose five-sixths of our trebles.'

'Yes, but,' said Lucy unhappily, 'don't you see? People are being suspected. If it really was Maurice—'

'It was a beastly thing to do,' agreed Tim. 'And if he did it he ought to be belted. But we ought to hear both sides of it. Why don't you have a word with my mother? She's got all the trebles for practice to-night and she could have a chat with Maurice. If he's got an explanation we might as well know about it.'

'All right. I'll do that,' said Lucy.

'If you nip along now,' suggested Tim, 'you could catch her before the practice starts.'

When Lucy had taken herself off they worked for some time in silence.

'It doesn't sound good, all the same,' said Sue, at last.

'I've just remembered something else. That practice night, Maurice was late. He came in a few minutes after we'd all started.'

'Did he, though.'

'Yes. I noticed it at the time, because the Hedges children usually come in a gang.'

Tim was balanced on the pew-back, trying to edge a heavy vase on to the cill of the lancet window beside the porch. He waited until he was back on the pew-seat before he replied.

'As to whether Maurice did it,' he said, 'I wouldn't know. As to whether the Reverend Halitosis will make a mess of the situation if you tell him, there can be no two opinions. He will. He has got as much tact and sense as a child of seven. Indeed, I know plenty of children of seven who have more savvy than he has.'

'Who cares about the Vicar's feelings? We demand justice.'

'All right,' said Tim. He was standing on the seat and in the dimness, he looked, thought Sue, perfectly enormous. 'All right. Let justice be done though the sky fall. I must confess that I've never thought stealing a bad crime. It is a crime, of course. But for me it comes way down the list, a long way after cruelty and ingratitude and cowardice and self-indulgence. If there are degrees of theft, I suppose that stealing from a church is one of the least attractive, because you are probably stealing from the poor.'

'Come off it, Robin Hood,' said Sue. 'I want to lock up.'

They walked down the path together. Tim was glad of the dusk. It was difficult to pin it down, but he felt that the evening had started rather well.

'Are you going home?'

'I can't. Grandpa's up in London at what he calls a Gentleman's Dinner. Lucky him. On those evenings I make do with a snack.'

'Where?'

'Where else than at that well-known combination of the Ritz and the Savoy, Gwen's Tea Parlour.'

Tim knew Gwen's Tea Parlour. It was a Brimberley institution. He had himself sampled, in times of necessity, the glaucous egg on a partially warmed pile of beans that constituted Gwen's staple supper dish.

'I know what,' he said, 'why don't we walk out to the Swan? What with the treble practice at home and one thing and another I shan't get anything to eat myself till God knows when.'

'The Swan,' said Sue. She looked at Tim speculatively for an instant. 'Do you know, that's not a bad idea at all.'

The Swan had started life as a simple country pub. It stands on the corner where the Brimberley side road runs out into the London-

Bramshott bypass. The big world, speeding past in its big cars, has liked the look of it and has gradually turned it, as the big world often does, into something larger, louder and nastier than nature had originally intended. However, it offers lights, drinks, and reasonable food at stiffish prices.

It was all of two miles from Brimberley, so they stepped out. They were both inclined to silence. When they got there they had a glass of sherry in the Tudor Bar, followed by a meal in the Jacobean dining-room. Sue behaved well. She did not cast an anxious eye down the price list, nor did she ask if Tim could afford certain of the dishes. She assumed that as he had asked her out he had enough money to pay for it all. She disposed of a chop and a mug of cider and they had their coffee in the Queen Anne lounge.

'Lucky, lucky some people,' said Sue. She had made a pile of the glossy weeklies, and was looking at the latest copy of *Country Life*, which depicted the glories of Belton Park, in Essex.

'It's a dump, really,' said Tim. He looked over her shoulder at the double page of photographs. 'The chap who took those did a smart job. You wouldn't guess from them that the gardens are overgrown, the roof lets in the rain, and only the East Wing is really habitable at all.'

'Don't be such a realist,' said Sue. She lay back in the chair, relaxed. Like a kitten she was expanded with warmth and food and drink.

'What about a liqueur?'

Sue considered.

'Are you planning to seduce me in that haystack on the way home?'

'It's an idea,' said Tim.

'Then no liqueur. I shall have to be able to see to bite straight.'

Soon after that they started back. It was a perfect night. The day which had started in mist and ended in drizzle had cleared with the coming of darkness and now every star looked like a hole fresh punched in the sky.

They walked side by side, and every now and then the back of Tim's hand brushed against the back of hers. If it meant anything to Sue she gave no sign.

He had never felt more conscious of her. Not her face. That was a forgotten blur. It was her body that was real to him. The girl's body that was now a woman's body. The exciting length of her from hip to ankle.

As they approached the haystack, he very slightly slackened his pace. Sue very slightly increased hers.

They passed the haystack.

In fact, there was nothing Tim would have liked more than to have seduced her. Only his complete, his fatal lack of experience stood in the way.

At the top of the hill the lights of Brimberley came into view.

Then Sue started singing, very softly, 'She'll be coming round the mountain when she comes.' After a minute Tim joined in, and they walked down into Brimberley together, Tenor and Alto in approximate harmony.

As he reached his own front door Tim realised that he had not told his mother that he would be missing supper. Unlike most women, this was not one of the things that worried Liz. If people were late, meals could be put into ovens. If they missed them altogether, there were always the hens that would benefit. She did not, as most women, feel the thing as a personal insult. Nevertheless, Tim would have telephoned if he had remembered and he felt a twinge of conscience as he opened the front door and realised that his mother was in a flaming temper.

She was speaking into the telephone.

'No, I do not,' she was saying. 'I don't agree. I can't make it any plainer. I—do—not—agree.'

The telephone squeaked back faint defiance.

'You can have it in writing,' said Liz. 'Set it to music, or publish it in the *Times*.'

A lot more squeaks.

'It's no good,' said Liz. 'We can stand here talking from now till eternity. I'm afraid it won't change my mind. Good night.'

She slammed down the receiver and said, 'Oh, it's you, is it, Tim?'

'I'm sorry I didn't let you—'

'That was the Vicar.'

'I guessed it might be.'

'He's got about as much sense as a baby that kicks its nappy off and then cries because it's sleeping in a puddle.'

'Did you say that to him?'

'Did I? I forget. No, I don't think I actually said it. What I did tell him was that he had to choose between his miserable ten shilling note and his Harvest Festival Anthem.'

'What did he say to that?'

'Something about his principles. I didn't hear it all. I was too angry.'

'Who told him – about Maurice?'

'I did.'

Tim looked baffled.

'Lucy told me, and I tackled Maurice about it after practice. He's an absolutely truthful child. He looked me straight in the eye and said, "I didn't take any money from the box in church." I believed him.'

'Sounds straight enough,' said Tim.

That's what I thought. So I rang up the Vicar and told him – in case he heard it by some roundabout way. He said he thought we ought to report the matter to the police. I told him that if he did he would have to resign himself to non-choral services for the rest of his stay here.'

That ought to hold him,' said Tim. He spoke so absently that his mother looked up and said, 'What's wrong?'

'Nothing's wrong,' said Tim. 'I've had an idea. That's all. Nothing to do with anything you've been saying. Just an idea.'

When he reached his own room he stood thinking for a moment, then walked across to the cupboard where he kept his suits. Which coat had he been wearing on the night of the explosion? It was either the old blue or the slightly less old grey. He felt through the pockets, and it was in the side pocket of the grey that he found it. A crumpled, faded, envelope, sealed up, with nothing written on it.

Tim hesitated before opening it. It had belonged to a man who was now horribly dead. Had fallen with him, almost on top of him, twirling and fluttering above the blast that had ripped him apart.

It contained a single sheet of paper, as crumpled and as faded as the envelope. On it, in a shaky, uneducated hand, was written 'Brasseys. Ask for the Captain. Talk about whisky.'

Chapter Nine

SPIRITOSO

COSTARD: *'Well, sir, I hope, when I do it, I shall do it on a full stomach.'*

The idea remained, lodged somewhere at the base of Tim's skull, throughout that week; through Tuesday night's very successful choir practice – Sergeant Gattie was voted to be an acquisition; through two unsuccessful attempts to get Sue to himself again; through a lot of ordinary hard work by day and some gritty sleep by night.

On Friday evening he called on a Mr. Smith.

Mr. Smith had an office in Holborn. The firm for which he worked was called (if the discreet notice board was to be believed) Metal Parts & Sundries, and the office in which he sat had a name plate outside it which suggested that Mr. Smith was an assistant consultant.

Mr. Smith greeted Tim cheerfully. He was a sandy-haired little man, with thick glasses and a Herbie Morrison quiff. He said, 'That was a very nice job you did for me, Artside. I'm very happy about that.'

Thank you very much,' said Tim. 'We strive to satisfy. Can you give me ten minutes of your time?'

'Technical?'

'Highly so. Look here. I want to blow you up.'

Mr. Smith did not seem upset by the idea. He drew a scribbling pad towards him and started a slow doodle.

'I've got a lot of cordite packed away in an upstairs room in your house. In the loft, say. You're the householder. I can't say exactly what you're going to do, but sooner or later you'll go to bed, I don't know when. You don't always go at the same time. Maybe you'll have a bath, maybe you'll just wash your hands and teeth. Then you'll go to your bedroom—'

'Bedside lamp or overhead?'

'Both. And both in use. You may even listen to the wireless. There's a portable set beside your bed.'

'Do I put my suit away on its hanger, in the cupboard? Or do I throw it over the back of a chair?'

'I'm afraid I don't know.'

Mr. Smith reflected.

'I take it you'll want the actual detonating device destroyed.'

'Certainly. It's absolutely essential that no sign shall be left. The official theory has got to be that the stuff in the loft went off by accident.'

'Time or remote control, or something like that.'

That's the sort of thing. When I was in Palestine I knew something about it but I'm rusty now. I want to find out what the up-to-date ideas are.'

'Is there enough explosive to kill your man if he happens to be still on the ground floor when it goes up?'

'It might. But it'd be chancy. Quite a solid little house. If he'd been two floors down, he might have got away with it. He'd have had a hell of a headache, but it mightn't have killed him.'

'If you've really got no idea when he goes to bed – he might sit up till three in the morning if he got interested in a book. It almost rules out time, doesn't it?'

'I was never very happy about time. The thing went off too pat; when he was in his bedroom, but not actually in bed.'

'Brimberley,' said Mr. Smith indifferently.

Tim nodded.

Mr. Smith returned to his doodling.

'It sounds,' he said eventually, 'as if it might be a push-and-pull job.'

'Come again.'

'It's a new gadget. Or, strictly, an old gadget with modifications. It's rather neat. Say you set it on a door. You open the door. That winds up the device. As soon as you shut the door again it goes off. Either immediately, or after an interval. That's the two-way. Then you can have a variation on that; the three-way type. When you open the door that winds it up. When you shut it that arms it. When you open it *again* you set it off. Very useful, that one, if the man you're after is suspicious of you.' Mr. Smith almost blinked in his enthusiasm. 'You take him into the room with you, you see. You open the door yourself, and show him in. Then you say, just wait a minute, and go out and shut the door behind you – and take yourself off. If he's suspicious, he'll keep pretty quiet. He won't go round turning on switches and touching things. But the one thing he won't mind doing is opening the door. He's seen you do it twice. He knows it's harmless. Only this time is the *third* time and it's no longer harmless.'

'I see,' said Tim. 'Applying it to my man—?'

'Easy. Ordinary landing light with a two-way switch, one switch by the stairs, one at the other end of the passage by your bedroom. You turn the landing light on at the stairs when you come up to bed. That's movement number one. Last thing at night, when you've finished washing, and so on, you turn the light off, at the bedroom end. A five second delay fuse. Enough to let him get into the bedroom and shut the door, but not long enough for him to get into bed.'

'Yes,' said Tim. 'Yes. That fits well enough with what was observed. How long would it take to rig up?'

Mr. Smith looked doubtful.

'I could do it in ten minutes,' he said.

'And leave no signs?'

'They wouldn't be very easy to spot. There'd be nothing at all in the bedroom. One extra wire from each switch on the landing. The actual timing and setting devices would be screwed into the explosive. They'd disintegrate.'

'Thank you,' said Tim. 'Yes. Thank you very much. I need hardly say—'

'Oh, discretion itself,' said Mr. Smith with a blink.

Tim stepped out into High Holborn, into a slant of cold rain.

Darkness had fallen and the lamps were lit. The tide, which sets eastward here as Londoners scurry home to their firesides, was already slackening.

Brasseys lies behind Sloane Square. It is a name which Londoners have associated for sixty years with good food. Three generations of diners-out have passed through the swing door, between the twin bow windows, one with its ten different sizes of champagne bottle, the other with the giant scarlet lobster in plaster-of-Paris.

You go straight into a cramped ante-room and bar, with stairs leading off it on both sides. At the back is a long partition of screens. Behind the screens the dining-room. You can still see, if you look carefully, that it was once a gymnasium. There is the big double skylight in the roof, with the long, brass rods and the cog wheels by which it was opened, and there are hooks in the high roof from which ropes once hung. The inner room is now a comfortable mixture of Regency sporting prints, red plush, brass rails and balloon glass. If it is not quite as full as it used to be in its hey-day, it is still popular.

The scene was just warming up when Tim arrived. The family parties, who had been eating early to get to a theatre, were finishing, yielding place to more leisured and serious diners. In one corner three naval sub-lieutenants were examining the wine list with suspicion. A clergyman and his wife were saying that on the whole they thought they would just start with clear soup. A very fat man was superintending the addition of hot garlic sauce to a plate of scampi.

Three people came in at the same time as Tim. One was an untidy but intellectual-looking young man who was walking with the extreme care of one who is drunk, but unhappily not quite drunk enough to have reached unawareness; with him a blonde. Behind them a moon-faced man, the back of whose neck recalled to Tim someone he was certain he knew. Irritating. Couldn't place it. School? Army? Palestine? Tim dismissed the problem. There was work to do. He picked up the long, hand-written menu and studied it carefully for clues.

A frail old waiter who looked like a windblown leaf, if it is possible

115

to imagine a windblown leaf in a tail coat, drifted up behind his elbow and awaited his pleasure.

'Is there anything you can particularly recommend?' said Tim.

'The whitebait's nice,' said the waiter.

'Whitebait, then. And steak,'

'The steak's not so good tonight.'

He looked like an honest man.

'Duck?'

'Very good, indeed, sir. Orange salad, spinach, straw potatoes.'

Tim said he thought that would do. The waiter produced a black shagreen-covered wine list which was a little smaller than a family bible.

'A pint of beer,' said Tim.

'A pint of beer,' said the waiter and drifted off.

It took the usual unconscionable time to serve, but it wasn't a bad dinner. When he had eaten it all up, and had rekindled a spark of hope in the waiter's breast by ordering a small kummel, Tim felt fortified for the next move.

The dining-room was quite full now, full of the aroma of garlic, of methylated spirits, of newly ground coffee, faintly hazed with the incense of cigar smoke and good humour. It was a moment for the laying down of lines and the drawing up of blueprints for the future. It was the moment when your ankle would touch someone else's under the table and out of that light contact unimaginable things would be born.

The untidy young man had progressed several stages beyond self-consciousness and was trying to balance one soda water syphon on top of another. The moon-faced man caught Tim's eye and looked away. Now *where* had he met him?

Tim shook his head angrily, and beckoned to a superior waiter who was propping up a pillar beside the service door. The superior waiter ignored him as long as he could, and then advanced at a speed which implied that he was not used to being beckoned to by men who drank pints of beer.

Tim waited patiently until the man had come to anchor behind his left elbow.

'I wonder if I could have a word with the Captain,' he said.

'The Captain, sir.'

It was difficult to detect whether or not there was a question mark at the end of it.

'I'm told he can get me a special line in whisky. Is that right?'

'Oh, whisky,' said the superior waiter, as if that made sense of it all.

He sailed off. Tim thought that he was moving a little faster. The wind was behind him this time.

A short interval ensued in which he heard a stout party say to the innocent girl who shared his table, 'always save your chemist's bills, my dear. You're an actress. You can put them in for expenses against your surtax. Save two hundred pounds a year by that. Two hundred pounds. That's not to be sneezed at, you know.'

The girl confirmed that she would not sneeze if anyone offered her two hundred pounds, and the superior waiter reappeared.

'Would you come with me, sir?' he said.

Tim followed the man out into the ante-room. The jostling crowd was no longer there. It was either eating its dinner or had gone on. The room was quiet and deserted. They turned left, up the shallow stairs, through a door and along a short passage.

The waiter knocked, bent his head to listen, opened the door and stood aside for Tim to go in. The gesture was as clear as words. His part of the job was done. Tim was now on his own.

The man who was sitting behind the big, cluttered, desk was vaguely familiar. It was a picture in the fashionable weeklies. Sporting event? The turf? Greyhound racing, perhaps. He had sandy hair, dropping into old-fashioned sideboards in front of his ears; a yellowish leathery face, the lower folds of which rested on a high Edwardian collar.

He did not get up but looked vaguely towards an empty chair. Tim sat down.

'I understand you wanted to see me.'

'You're the Captain?'

'My friends call me that.'

Hardly a snub. Just a remark.

'Pleased to make your acquaintance,' said Tim, getting as much geniality into it as he could. It was not easy. There was something formidable about the old man and something chilling.

'I'm sorry to bother you. I didn't really intend to burst in on you like this. But a friend of mine told me that you could put me on to something quite special in the way of whisky.'

'A friend of yours? He knows me?'

'Toby Carshalton,' said Tim readily. '16th Hussars.'

'Carshalton?' said the Captain impassively. 'I don't remember the name. But I have many friends in the Army. Tell me, Mr——?'

'Artside.'

'Mr. Artside. When he recommended my whisky, did he particularly mention Scotch or Irish?'

It was as clear to Tim as anything could be that this was some sort of pay-off line. If he got the answer to this one he was in for a dividend. The trouble was that he lacked any sort of inspiration. Silently he cursed MacMorris for giving him only half the story.

Before the silence could become awkward he said, 'I don't know that he mentioned that especially. If you know Toby you'll know what a vague sort of chap he is at times—'

At this moment he happened to look up and his blood chilled.

He was looking into the eyes of a wolf.

Just a flash. Then it was the dear old Captain again. But he could no more mistake it than the Styrian peasant could have mistaken it when, at dusk, in the lonely depths of the forest, he looked more closely at the friendly old man who was guiding him and saw the sprouting hair, the lengthening white teeth, the yellow fire in the shallow eyes.

Tim had no more to say and his mouth was dry. The Captain continued to look at him, thoughtfully now. It was an awkward silence to break.

At that moment the door opened and a man came in without knocking.

Tim found it difficult, afterwards, to remember what he looked like.

He was a youngish man, with a suggestion of the Latin in his hard brown face and black hair. He was well dressed, and carried himself with the confidence of a man who expects to be deferred to wherever he goes. Tim got the impression that he, and not the Captain, was the real owner of the room.

He glanced at Tim for a moment, and then walked over to the fireplace and helped himself to a cigarette out of the box on the mantelshelf.

'I did think,' said the Captain, in a voice which conveyed a warning, 'that we might have a customer here. I was led to think it.'

'Oh, yes.'

'A customer for our whisky.'

'Yes?'

'But it didn't work out that way.'

'A pity,' said the newcomer, with an insincere smile. 'In that case—'

Tim accepted his dismissal. He rose to his feet and said, 'Well, if there's nothing doing I'll be getting along. Sorry to have bothered you.'

Neither man said anything to that. He was conscious of two pairs of eyes watching him as he closed the door.

When he reached his table he was surprised to find that his coffee was still hot. He felt that he had been away a lot longer.

He drank it slowly, in time with his slow thoughts. When you are clearing out the sty, he thought, there is no mistaking the moment when the prongs of your pitchfork, driving through the piled trash and straw and rubbish, touch on the concrete of the floor itself. He had run up against the hard competence of professional crime and his arms were still tingling with the shock.

Yet it seemed to have nothing, less than nothing, to do with the amateur goings-on at Brimberley. They were different equations, without a common factor.

He signalled for his bill and two men began to move. Both were big men and neither of them had been serving him before.

He realised that he had made a mistake.

He should have paid his bill and got out whilst the going was good.

It was all done very smoothly.

One of the men stationed himself in the alleyway in the line between Tim's table and the door. The other came straight for him. He had the bill on a salver in his big right hand. He looked like an army gym instructor, one of those menacing men who used to tie you in knots and bounce you genially on the mat.

Only this time he was going to be bounced on the pavement, face downwards, and not genially. To teach him to keep his silly little nose out of things that did not concern him.

As the man approached, Tim got to his feet and got clear of the table. The man came on, until he was right up to him, leaned forward courteously, and stamped on Tim's toe.

As Tim's head jerked forward, he raised the salver so that the edge of it caught Tim on the bridge of the nose.

A scene, thought Tim, through the sharp pain. A scene. That's all they want. They'll say I started it. Then they're covered.

'our bill, sir,' said the gymnast. 'And I hope you won't forget to add a nice big tip.'

Tim kicked him, as hard as he could in the small space available, on the shin. He might have been kicking a wall.

The man put down the salver without hurry and his big hands came up and felt for the lapels of Tim's coat.

It was at this moment that the untidy young man, two tables away, knocked over one of the lighted methylated spirit stoves. It rolled on to the floor and burst with a little pop.

The blonde screamed.

The untidy young man looked unspeakably horrified at what he had done. He then picked up an open bottle of brandy, and poured it helpfully over the wavering nest of fire on the carpet.

A sheet of flame rose from the floor and for an instant everything stood still.

Then, as Tim tore himself out of the hands of his startled opponent, pandemonium broke loose.

There was one chance. The front door was blocked by the second man. He dived for the service door.

The gymnast came after him, fast. The service door was a swing door, but even so Tim doubted if he could negotiate it in time. Then, out of the corner of his eye, he saw the gymnast go into an involuntary dive. He had become entangled with the untidy young man, who was behaving like a demented fire brigade.

With the crash of that fall still ringing in his ears, Tim burst through the service door.

That a waiter should have been coming through it in the other direction carrying a tray of madras curry was bad luck, on the waiter. The incident hardly checked Tim who, as opponents on the rugger field had discovered, was slow off the mark but devilish difficult to stop once he got fairly under way.

Tim hurdled the body of the waiter, skidded through the first wave of curry, took the short passage in five steps and erupted, through a second swing door, into the kitchen. Three men in white caps and aprons jerked their heads up together, as if they had been strung on the same wire.

'Fire!' shouted Tim. 'Police. Fire.'

The men continued to stare. Through the doors they could hear a growing hubbub.

'Way out?' shouted Tim.

One of the men gestured feebly.

Tim wrenched the door open and found himself in an alley. At the end of it was an archway, with an iron gate across it. The gate solidly and completely filled the archway, and it was padlocked.

There was a row of dustbins against the wall.

Tim got up on to one, felt for the top of the wall, and scrabbled up.

The top was dirty, and slippery with rain. Tim balanced for a moment. Ahead of him was a pit of darkness.

At that moment angry voices broke out from the room he had just left.

He turned on to his stomach, lowered himself to the full length of his arms, and hung for a moment. He hoped there was nothing spiky below. Then he dropped.

His landing place proved soft and yielding. As he got to his feet he decided that it was a bale of partly scraped sheepskins. The smell was powerful and unmistakeable. There was a heap of these bales. He slithered off them and felt his way forward.

He had time to notice that it was still raining.

It was an open yard, at the back of some sort of factory or workshop. The building was barred and inaccessible, but he could see a wooden gate, and the street lamps beyond.

The gate was high, but there might be room to squeeze over the top. He went back to the wall and fetched, one after the other, a dozen bales of skins, which he piled, two deep, into a sloping ramp behind the gate.

From the top he saw that he could manage it. Apart from the steady drip of the rain all seemed quiet.

He hoisted himself over the door with a squeeze. There was one hitch, followed by a sharp tearing sound, and then he was dropping down into the street.

Before he had time even to get to his feet, two unwinking lights had him captive.

A long car slid up and a voice said, 'Can we be of any assistance?'

There was no choice. The rear door opened and Tim climbed in. Someone flicked on an interior light and he saw that it was the moon-faced man he had noticed in the restaurant. There was another man with him in the back and another in the front beside the driver. They were none of them in uniform, but Tim had no difficulty in guessing who they were.

'Been killing someone?' asked the moon-faced man. His voice was unexpectedly authoritative.

Tim glanced at his hands. What with the soot and the sheepskins they were quite something.

'It's Artside, isn't it?'

Tim looked at him. 'Wait a minute,' he said. 'It's been on the tip of my tongue all the evening.'

'Has it not! I was afraid, once or twice, that you were going to shout it across the room.'

'Beasley?'

'Getting warm.'

'Bazeley. Jaffa. 1947. Right?'

'That's right,' said Detective Inspector Bazeley. 'But I'm damned if I'm going to shake hands until you've had a wash.'

An hour later Tim was feeling a lot better. He had had a bath, and his clothes had been dried and brushed.

'Now perhaps you wouldn't mind telling me what it's all about,' he said.

'You take the words out of our mouths,' said Inspector Bazeley, with a glance at his assistant, Detective Pontifex.

Tim considered.

'I'll strike a bargain,' he said. 'If I tell you what I was doing there, will you tell me what you were up to?'

Bazeley considered.

'You can check up my references, if you like,' said Tim. 'I'm quite respectable. Tom Pearce, our Chief Constable, will give me a chit—'

'I'll take you at your face value,' said Bazeley. 'You used to be quite reliable in Palestine. You shoot first.'

'From my end,' said Tim, 'there isn't a great deal to tell. I got a tip through a man – a Major MacMorris—'

It was evident that the name meant nothing to them.

'It led to the idea that if I sought out a character at Brasseys, called the Captain, and started to talk to him about whisky, then things would happen. I did. They did.'

'They certainly did.'

'All right,' said Tim. 'Now your turn.'

Inspector Bazeley said, 'This really is absolutely not for publication. I'd get the sack if anyone knew – however. It's fencing. Big time fencing.'

'I see. Any particular line?'

'There's no tie-up with any one crowd. They'll take anything provided they can handle it. And provided the profit margin's big enough.'

'I've never known a receiver who didn't feel cheated unless he made eight hundred per cent on every deal,' agreed Tim.

'It's diamonds mostly. Country house stuff. If you'd said "Old Scotch" that would have been diamonds in an old-fashioned setting. Vat 17 – that you wanted £1,700 for them.'

'I see,' said Tim. 'I see. I never got further than the opening gambit. I wonder what they thought I was up to?'

'I know what I *hope* they thought,' said Bazeley. 'I hope they thought you were some amateur who didn't quite know the ropes. If they *did* think that, then they may carry on. We don't want them to close down. Such a useful little honey-pot.'

'And I suppose you've had them under observation for some time.'

'Just over a year,' said Bazeley calmly.

'And you've got a list of everyone who went in and out?'

'Not everyone. It's a pretty busy place. Anyone who turned up at all regularly, or seemed to be too pally with the Captain.'

'I suppose I couldn't look—'

'Well,' said Bazeley. 'No. I'd need higher authority before I did that.'

'All right,' said Tim. 'Let me put it this way. If I gave you a name, would you be prepared to tell me if that name was or wasn't on your list.'

'I expect I could do that. I'd have to find out.'

'Splendid.'

Quite suddenly he felt desperately tired. He looked at his watch. It was just past midnight.

'We can give you a shakedown, here,' said Bazeley.

'I'll tell them to get your bed ready,' said Detective Pontifex. 'We'll put you in the D. T. Cell. I'm told it's very comfortable.'

'I'd better do some telephoning first,' said Tim.

If his mother had gone to bed, which he doubted, the telephone would have been switched through to her bedroom.

He got the number and heard the bell ringing. It went on for a long time.

Worried, he tried the General's house. The result was the same.

This was inconceivable. On occasions of emergency, when he had had to get hold of him, the General, who was the lightest of sleepers, had answered in a matter of seconds.

He tried both numbers again, feeling the sweat prickling cold on his body with a premonition of disaster.

In the end he gave it up, and after a little thought and research he asked for Bob Cleeve's number.

The receiver came off the hook so quickly at the other end that someone must have been waiting with a hand outstretched.

'Tim,' said his mother's voice. 'Am I glad to hear you! No, it's all right. We're all of us all right. Yes, *all* of us. We're out at Bob's place. There's nothing you can do. No, nothing. But come down as quickly as you can in the morning. Something not very nice.'

Chapter Ten

MARCHE MILITAIRE

(CONTINUED AND CONCLUDED)

ARMADO: *'We will put it, as they say, to "fortuna de la guerra".'*

On the morning of that Friday, as the General and Sue were finishing breakfast, Bob Cleeve's large, maroon-coloured Bentley poked its nose into their front drive.

Sue opened the front door, ducked a fatherly kiss from Bob, and showed him into the breakfast room, where the General was unfolding the *Times* which it was his habit to read, pretty carefully, from cover to cover each day.

'I've got a Chairman's conference at Westminster,' Bob explained. 'Juvenile delinquency again. Thank you very much, Sue. I wouldn't say no to a cup of your coffee. You're looking particularly ravishing this morning. Must be because you've got such a clear conscience. The Press are going to be admitted and I don't mind betting that it'll be a regular jamboree. There's something about juvenile delinquency that stirs the heart and soul of our newspaper-reading public.'

'Well, it's uncommonly kind of you,' said the General. 'If you really are going up I'd be pleased to come with you. I take it you'll be going through Staines.'

'Can't avoid it.'

'Splendid. And how very kind of you to look in on the off chance.'

'I didn't come to see you,' said Bob. 'I came to look at Sue. And, by

126

Jove, she's getting more worth looking at every day.'

Sue snorted and went on with her breakfast.

As the big car scudded along the pleasant stretch between Bramshott and Wentworth the General, feeling that silence would have been a sort of discourtesy, explained to Cleeve, in outline, what he was doing.

'It's worth a try,' said Cleeve. 'But I think you'll be lucky if you find anything. You know what Courts of Inquiry were like. By the time the talking was over you felt so fed up that you shoved down the shortest account you could, consistent with not getting a rocket from the convening authority. "Court of Inquiry assembled this blank day of blank to inquire into the loss of Gunner Bloggins' boots. Gunner Bloggins in evidence said, I am Gunner 99999 Bloggins—".'

'Yes, yes,' said the General. 'I've done plenty of them. All the same, this wasn't Gunner Bloggins' boots. Someone had blown up the Commanding General. That may have made them a little more long-winded.'

'I hope you're right,' said Bob.

The car swooped down Egham hill, by-passed Egham on the left, and entered the mile of gasometers and cafes that leads to Staines bridge.

'We shall have to pack our conference up at four o'clock,' said Bob, 'whether we've finished or not, but I can't guarantee to be here before five. Will that do?'

'It's extremely kind of you,' said the General. 'I think the place is somewhere behind here, on the right. Put me down at the bridge and I'll find it.'

It had once been, and still looked like, a motor-car factory. The wire-mesh entrance gates were shut and the commissionaire's hutch stood empty.

The General found a bell and rang it.

After a pause a door in the building opened and a man came out and crossed the yard. He was in neat battle dress, with shoes instead of boots and gaiters, and he wore the crown of a warrant officer on his forearm.

From the name and the rank the General had inferred someone with a red face, a lot of body and a hearty manner. Sergeant-Major Bottler was, therefore, a surprise. He was small and grey-haired and he wore steel-rimmed glasses. Only a certain self-sufficient neatness in his carriage and movement suggested the old soldier.

He said, 'General Palling?' and saluted.

The General raised his bowler hat punctiliously, and the Sergeant-Major unlocked the gate.

'I gathered from the War Office something of what you wanted, sir. It's going to be a bit of a job to find it. Mind your head.'

They ducked under the open porte-cochère, cut in a large steel door which had evidently not been fully opened since the day when the last car had rolled off the production line. They were in a roomy building, something between a barn and a hangar. A little light filtered through overhead windows. It was quite warm.

'We have to keep the heating going,' explained the Sergeant-Major. 'Otherwise the damp would get at the papers. It comes up off the river. Damp and rats. They're the two things we have to worry about most. You wouldn't think rats could live on paper. But I believe they do – the little beggars. Only last week I found a nest of them, right in the middle of a bunch of A.B.104's. Hold hard, sir. We'll have some light on the scene.'

He clicked down two switches and a battery of big, overhead lamps opened up.

The whole floor space, as the General now saw, was honeycombed with wooden shelves. Not proper book-shelves, but slats resting on upright boards. On the lower shelves were different sizes of black tin boxes with drop-fronts. On the upper the papers stood piled in folders. The shelves ran up to a height of about eight feet. Above them, grey over the swinging electric globes, loomed the vast obscurity of the factory roof.

'There's bats up there,' said the Sergeant-Major. 'If you shine a torch up you can see them. Would you care to step into my office, and I'll just show you how we're arranged.'

The Sergeant-Major's office was a cheerful little room; a kettle humming on the stove, a cat sleeping in the corner; a snug cabin in a grey wilderness. The Sergeant-Major unrolled a plan which showed the layout and opened filing cabinet after filing cabinet as he demonstrated the arrangement of his huge charge. It was difficult to imagine anyone having an affection for a thousand tonnes of paper, but when a man is in love with his job it shines in his eyes and speaks through his speech.

The General found himself warming to the Sergeant-Major.

'It'll be in the north east block, that's certain, sir. All the disciplinary proceedings are there, except sex. We keep sex in separate boxes against the north wall.'

'How satisfactory,' said the General. 'I mean – I don't think sex comes into this one.'

'The next point is, when were the papers lodged? We can't file them according to the year they relate to, you see, because that would mean opening every blessed paper and reading it, and that I can't do. So we file them in years of lodgement.'

'I can't tell you that,' said the General. 'Not exactly. It can't be before 1920 – probably later. But not likely to be much after 1924. They broke up those war-time formations pretty quickly.'

'Then we're cross indexed under countries. India, Egypt, Far East, and so on. This would be Germany, I take it.' The Sergeant-Major rattled his thumbnail through a dozen cards. 'Occupation Forces, we called it then. It's all B.A.O.R. now. Anyway, that'll be enough to get us into the right section.'

'I think it's extremely helpful,' said the General. 'I'd no idea it was all arranged in such a businesslike way.'

'We try to be businesslike,' said the Sergeant-Major, much gratified. 'Would you come this way? That's right. We'd better bring dusters. I get round the whole lot once a month, but it soon settles again.'

'Now see here,' said the General. 'Don't you bother to do the actual searching. I'm sure you've plenty to do. And I've got all the time in the world. I'll soon get the hang of it.'

All in all, the General could not remember when he had passed such a satisfactory morning.

Almost at first dip he picked out the papers of that extraordinary business in which Tricky Pellow had almost lost his commission. Indeed, *would* have lost his commission had not justice been tempered with a good deal of imagination; a piece of long-sighted clemency which paid off when Pellow did so well in the South African War.

Thinking of Pellow, somehow put him in mind of Masters, and a disastrous piece of horse-coping, a matter in which he had been called on himself to give evidence. It gave him quite a shock to find his own name. 'Colonel Palling stated that, in his opinion, the fact that the horse had thrown General Pargeter during a ceremonial parade did not, in itself, prove that the horse was vicious—'

How important it had all seemed at the time. How little it all mattered now. General Pargeter must have been dead half a century. Masters? Masters had died on the Somme, like a lot of other good fellows.

At this point the General was diverted from a train of melancholy by the happy discovery of the papers relating to the Covent Garden Ball rumpus.

When he had finished with these he looked guiltily at his watch and found that it was nearly two o'clock. So he went out to see if he could find some lunch, which he did, eventually, at a café which had been designed to deal with the summer boating trade but was now some weeks past its normal time for hibernation and inclined to be resentful about it.

During the afternoon he addressed himself more seriously and methodically to his task and by four o'clock he was getting warm. At one moment he thought he had it. He had untied a bursting buff folder labelled (promisingly enough) 'Occupation Forces, Cologne. Headquarters Records'. They were in no sort of order, but that he was on the right track was proved by the fact that Lieutenant-General Artside's name appeared with increasing frequency.

He was hampered by the fact that he could not remember the exact date on which the explosion had occurred. He seemed to remember that it was some time in October of 1920. He searched again through the file and discovered an odd thing. There were papers connected with every other month of the year, but nothing at all for October.

He went through it once again, to make certain. Then he looked at the backs of the other folders in that box. None of them seemed even remotely promising.

The General put the Cologne folder away, in the front of the box, and went to find Bottler.

'I suppose you get a lot of visitors,' he said.

'One or two a day, most days,' agreed the Sergeant- Major. 'Mostly from War Office and Records. They come down to borrow papers.'

'Borrow?' said the General sharply. 'But you'd keep a record of any papers they took away.'

'Certainly sir. Any particular file you had in mind?'

'It's box M.B. – I've jotted the number down somewhere—here it is – 56.'

'M.B.56.' The Sergeant-Major consulted his filing system. 'No there's nothing out from that—except that—wait a moment. Well, now, that's an odd coincidence. It really is.'

The General waited patiently.

'There's nothing booked out from that file but I do remember it was looked at. Normally, I wouldn't remember a thing like that, but—M.B.56—you see, sir. That's my wife's initials, Madge Bottler, and it was her exact age. The day it was looked at was her birthday.'

The General thought hard.

'How old is Mrs. Bottler now?'

'Fifty-seven last April. April 10th.'

'I see. Then it was on April 10th of the year before that someone went to that file. I expect you keep a visitors' book.'

'Certainly.' The Sergeant-Major opened a ledger. The General noticed that his own name and rank had already been neatly entered.

Against April 10th of the previous year there was only one name. Major Robinson.

'I'm afraid I don't really remember anything about him,' said the Sergeant-Major apologetically. 'It was just the coincidence, you see, of the file and the number, and on that particular day.'

'Hmp. The rank's not very helpful either. There were a lot of very old Majors left over from the first war, and a lot of very young ones out of the second. Never mind. As you say, it was an outside chance that you remembered it at all.'

A rich-sounding motor horn spoke from the street.

'I'll have to knock off now,' said the General. 'That sounds like my lift home.'

The Sergeant-Major followed him out. It was Cleeve all right. He was hunched up over the wheel and what little could be seen of him looked depressed. The juveniles must have been more than normally troublesome.

The Sergeant-Major walked round and held the door open for the General. He shut it after him, and saluted. The General turned down the window, put his arm and shoulder out, and shook hands warmly.

'You've been most helpful and considerate,' he said, 'and it's been a real pleasure meeting you.'

The Sergeant-Major looked startled but pleased. He stood for some time staring after the long car as it gathered speed up the road.

'I don't know about you,' said Cleeve at last, 'but I haven't yet found time for any tea. There's rather a nice little place in Egham – that's it – with the bottle glass windows. They make good toast, and plenty of it.'

He still seemed worried. Evidently there was more than juvenile delinquency on his mind. When he said, as soon as they were alone with their tea, 'I saw Tom Pearce last night. He's not at all happy about things,' the General had no need to ask him what business he was talking about.

'He's not the only one,' he said. 'I can't remember seeing Liz in quite such a state before.'

'Liz is a damned level-headed woman,' agreed Cleeve. 'But in this particular instance I think she and the police are worrying about different things. She's worried that they aren't taking her discoveries seriously. That's where she's wrong. They are. It's what happens next that worries them.'

'Yes,' said the General. He was cutting the crusts carefully off a round of toast.

'MacMorris was blackmailing someone. We might as well say it. We've all been thinking it. So someone decided to get rid of him. Very understandable reaction. It's just the way he carried it out makes it so frightening. It's not the sort of way I'd choose myself – too complicated and chancy. But you can't deny that it was damnably effective. It not only destroyed MacMorris, it destroyed all the clues, too. You saw the house—'

'Yes,' said the General. 'All the same, there was the suggestion of an unbalanced mind in it.'

Cleeve looked up sharply.

'A madman,' he said.

'Yes. Or a madwoman. You haven't really got much line on the sex of the murderer, have you? Single blonde hairs on the sofa, and so on. If there were any, they went sky high with the fingerprints and everything else.' He added, 'Don't mean a raving lunatic. Someone with an element of unbalance in their make-up. The idea of wiping out a single threat with a great big explosion. There's something elemental about that.'

The two men sat on in silence for a few minutes. The toast was, really, very good. It was buttery and soft enough not to worry the General's teeth.

In the end he broke the silence himself.

'It's a point of difference,' he said, 'between dangerous animals and dangerous people. Animals just go on quietly being killers. They don't let circumstances worry them. Humans are different. However sound their nerve may be, if they feel themselves pressed, they do stupid things. That makes them more dangerous in a way. But it makes them easier to catch.'

'I hope you're right,' said Cleeve soberly. 'It's getting dark already. We're in for some rain.'

In fact, rain was falling as they went out to the car.

II

Earlier that afternoon Liz walked up to the far end of Brimberley to call on Jim Hedges.

The garage and motor repair shop lay beyond the bridge over Brimber brook which circled the churchyard at that point.

Liz had never before penetrated beyond the penthouse in front where she paid for the oil and petrol and bought an occasional spare part for her motor-cycle. She had not realised the full depth of the interior building.

A car, stripped to its chassis, and tilted at an uncomfortable angle on props and jacks, waited patiently for the hand of the surgeon. Jim was beyond the car, busy at a bench. He was using a bright pair of long-nosed pliers to tiddle a copper wire along a steel channel. His huge, oil-blacked hands worked with curious delicacy and precision.

It has taken three generations to do it, thought Liz, but we've bred him at last, the natural mechanical countryman. Spanners now, not scythes; horse-power instead of horses. But just as patient and just as instinctively clever with the new toys as he had been with the old.

'Sorry to disturb you, Jim,' she said.

The noise of the charging-plant must have killed the noise of her approach, but when she spoke the big hand did not jump a fraction of an inch.

'Well now, Mrs. Artside,' said Jim. 'Motor-cycle trouble or choir trouble?'

'Choir trouble,' said Liz. 'Treble trouble.'

'That makes it five to one it's something to do with my lot.'

'That's it. It's one of yours. Has anyone said anything to you?'

Jim put down the pliers and wiped his hand on a piece of rag. He looked worried.

'I heard something,' he said. 'You know how it is in a village.'

'I know how it is in a village,' agreed Liz. 'And that's why I came round. What's the strength of it, Jim?'

'I haven't spoke to Morry yet,' said Jim. 'He's at school, see. I was going to talk to him this evening. What do you think, Mrs. Artside?'

'I don't think he took it.'

'It didn't sound like our Morry,' agreed Jim. 'Nor I couldn't quite see how he was supposed to have done it. He's not what you'd call a pick-lock. Not like his old man.'

'Can you pick locks, Jim?'

'Most of 'em,' said Jim, suddenly grinning. 'But it's not a thing I've taught the kids yet. You never know with a parlour trick like that. What I did wonder'—Jim looked serious again—'if it's right he had a ten shilling note, he can't have come by it honest. Sixpence a week and their lunch money. That's all they get, unless it's a birthday or Christmas. But I did wonder if he might have got hold of it here. Those kids are all in and out, and I don't lock the money up, which I ought to, I know—'

'It sounds a much more likely explanation,' said Liz. 'I always found Maurice truthful myself. When I asked him straight out, had he taken it, he said, "I never took any money from the box in the church." Straight out. Just like that. It did occur to me to wonder, afterwards, if he wasn't being a little *too* truthful – if you see. Just telling the literal truth and hiding behind that.'

'I'll talk to him this evening when he gets home,' said Jim. 'I'd rather it turned out to be my money he took. Keeps it in the family. Not that it'll save him from a walloping he'll remember, if so he did do it.'

When Liz got outside she stood for a moment wondering what she wanted to do next.

The afternoon had been growing steadily darker. There was rain, and plenty of it, piled up in the dirty, over-blown clouds to windward.

On Fridays she usually spent the evening with the General. And if Tim had anything to keep him in London he would arrange it for that evening. Today, however, the General had gone up to Staines, to look at some papers. To rustle about, amongst matters long dead.

Long dying, but now dead.

The rising wind was whipping the trees, stripping off their last leaves, baring their branches for the stark severity of winter.

'Stop brooding,' said Liz to herself. 'Life isn't really like that at all. It's the weather, and the uncertainty. You want a cup of tea, and a good gossip.'

She set out briskly, back over the bridge, across the churchyard, down the small strip of High Street, keeping along it until she was past the speed limit signs, and saw the poplars that marked the turning into Melliker Lane.

Sue was at home. Liz heard her start downstairs as soon as she rang. Then, rather to her surprise, the click of the key being turned back. The Pallings' front door usually stood on the latch.

'Am I glad to see you,' said Sue. 'I've been sitting here having the willies.'

'Me too,' said Liz. 'It's something to do with the weather. Can I help you get tea? I pine for tea. Tea and toast.'

'For goodness sake, yes,' said Sue.

They went along to the kitchen. Liz put the kettle on and Sue cut some bread.

'If I'd known what it was going to be like this afternoon,' she said, 'I'd never have allowed grandfather to go. It started getting dim soon after lunch. If I'd had any sense I'd have cleared right out, and taken a bus over to Bramshott and gone to the cinema or something. But instead I sat in my room and tried to catch up with jobs. I thought I would sustain myself with virtue.'

'Fatal,' said Liz. 'When you feel the blues coming on you've got to go out and do something violent and silly.'

'It wasn't too bad until I heard the ticking.'

'You heard what?'

'Ticking. When I sat quite still I could hear it distinctly.'

'But—'

'It's all right. I ran it to earth. It was the gas meter under the stairs. After that I started hearing little men. Sometimes they were upstairs, sometimes down.'

'They get about,' agreed Liz. 'Was that when you locked the front door?'

'That's right. Let's take it upstairs. I've got a good fire.'

They went to Sue's room. She had, for her own, the big front room, on the first floor, with the bow windows. It was a nice room, with just that shade of uncertainty in the decorative arrangements that reminded Liz of her own youth.

Over a cup of tea Sue looked levelly at Liz and said, 'And just what's wrong with Tim these days?'

Liz tried to consider the matter dispassionately, whilst half of her mind was weighing up the form of the question, to see if she ought to read something into the fact that it had been asked at all.

'He was always a difficult boy,' she said. 'Nice, but difficult. I don't think it was only because he never had a father. Something to do with it, but not much. Then, the 'thirties were a bad time for a boy to grow up in: I don't imagine, when we're far enough away to look back at them, that we're going to be awfully proud of the 'thirties. Then again, he was too good at games. And that made everything a bit too easy for him at school. He didn't have to work his way to the top. He got there by divine right, because of some knack of co-ordinating wrist and eye, which meant that he could score runs at cricket or points at racquets, or whatever it was the school needed at that moment to make them happy. He must have got all that from his father. I never had any eye for that sort of thing. I was a promising boxer, though, at the age of ten.'

'Have some more tea,' said Sue. 'I suppose the war didn't help.'

'Yes and no. He got straight into Special Service – almost as soon as they invented it. Games again. He'd played football with someone who was starting a special unit—'

'I know,' said Sue. 'Awfully good chap, Artside. Played scrum half for the 'Quins. We *must* have him.'

Both women suddenly giggled.

'Anyway,' said Liz, 'it saved him from life in a wartime officers' mess. And I think it democratised him. I don't believe that what he did was any more dangerous or uncomfortable than a front line soldier's job, but the point of it was that it was mostly solo stuff – at the most he might have a sergeant or a couple of men with him. One of the men he worked with most was a private in the Middlesex Regiment.'

'Does he still keep in touch?'

'I'm afraid he's too grand,' said Liz sadly. 'He owns a whole chain of second-hand car shops. He still sends Tim a box of cigars at Christmas.'

There was silence for a bit. The rain was thickening now, coming down in a solid, heavy curtain.

'He's bit wrapped up in himself,' said Sue at last, as if she was answering some thought of her own.

'Before the war,' said Liz, 'I thought I understood him as well as any woman of my age could understand a boy. Now I hardly know a thing about him. He might do anything in the wide world.'

'Just what does he do?' said Sue. 'I suppose I oughtn't to ask really.'

'There's no harm in asking,' said Liz, 'because all I can tell you won't make you much wiser. After he came back from Palestine—and was I glad to see him get clear of that!—worse than the war – and so unnecessary – as I say when he got back he had a shot at a lot of things. Forestry estate management. I'm not sure he didn't even try bee-keeping. But they all seemed to want capital or experience which were the two things he was short of. Then, quite suddenly, one day, he announced that he'd got a job. That was that. Every day he puts on a dark suit and a clean collar and trots off with all the other commuters to this job, whatever it may be. It brings in money every week. Not much, I think, but enough. He doesn't seem to have to be at the office terribly early, and he usually gets home in good time. I don't suppose he stays away for the night more than two or three times in a year. And that's really all I know about it!'

'Does his job take him into Essex, by any chance?'

'Not that I know of. Why?'

'Oh, I don't know. Something he said. Listen, isn't that Bob's car?'

Both women went over to the window. Sue's hearing must have been extraordinarily acute. The car had only just turned into Melliker Lane. Its headlights cut out a path through the dancing rain.

As they watched the car swung out to make the turn into the drive.

Liz felt Sue gripping her arm.

Then she saw it, too.

She wrenched at the window and started to shout abruptly.

Out of the very corner of his eye, Bob Cleeve noticed the window swing open and, with the reflex of a good driver who sees something he cannot at once account for, he braked lightly. The noise of the engine drowned any shout.

Too late, he saw it too and stood on everything.

There was a twang like a bowstring as the taut rope across the gate hit the car. A crack as the windscreen buckled. A sharper crack as one of the gate-posts heeled and snapped, and the car, skidding wildly, thrashed the gravel and turned broadside on across the width of the drive.

Then, for a long moment, no sound but the drumming of the rain.

Chapter Eleven

SECOND INTERVAL: CLAMBOYS

ARMADO : *'Why tough signior? Why tough signior?*
MOTH; *Why tender juvenal? Why tender juvenal.'*

'Easy does it now,' said Cleeve. He was bleeding freely from the face, but seemed otherwise intact. 'Easy again. I'll shift the seat.'

There was a bruise, already puffy, on the General's forehead, a bruise from which blood was beginning to ooze dark and slow. His eyes were shut.

Sue's face was as white as her grandfather's.

'Ring the doctor,' said Liz. 'Bob and I can manage now. And stop looking like a frightened duck. He's survived worse bumps than that.'

Cleeve got one arm under the General and, Liz helping, they lifted him, curiously light, she thought, as though under the outer husk of his clothes, age had been stealthily eating up her friend.

During the slow passage from the car to the front door the fresh air and rain must have achieved something, for the General opened his eyes, shook his head, winced and shut them again.

They propped him on a chair in the hall.

'The fire's upstairs, in my room,' said Sue over her shoulder. 'Oh, is that you, doctor? Sue Palling here. Yes. Could you come across right away. Only be careful when you get to the gate. It's blocked. A sort of car smash. Yes, it's the General. Right away, if you would.'

'We'd better carry him up,' said Liz. 'Warmth's the thing.'

'If you say so,' said Cleeve. 'Disturb as little as possible would be my diagnosis.'

'Walk,' said the General, faintly but firmly.

And walk he did, helped on either side.

They put him on the sofa, in front of the fire, with a rug over him.

'Hot sweet tea,' suggested Liz.

'Nonsense,' said the General. 'That's the treatment for shock. This is concussion.'

They were still arguing when the doctor arrived. He was young and brisk and confident.

'Slight concussion,' he announced, when he had finished cleaning up. 'You'd be better in bed. I'll put you up a sedative.'

'I've had concussion more times than you've had birthdays,' said the General. 'Never been to bed for it yet. Always found a glass of red wine useful.'

'The great thing is not to worry,' said the doctor. The General eyed him malevolently out of his bloodshot right eye. His left one was so puffed as to be temporarily useless. 'And you'd all be better for dry clothes. We don't want three more patients.'

He clattered off down the stairs. Sue went down to let him out, and came back again.

'He's absolutely right,' said Liz. 'I'm soaking. That was real rain. Is your car still functioning?'

'What? Yes, I think so,' said Cleeve absently. 'Just the windscreen. It'll be a bit draughty.'

'If you could run me back to my house, I'll get changed and arrange for someone—'

'I don't like it,' said Cleeve suddenly and sharply.

'Sue'll be all right for a bit. We can arrange for a nurse later.'

'Of course I shall be all right.'

'Nurse,' said the General. 'Who for?'

'Curiously enough,' said Cleeve, 'it's not you or Sue that I'm worrying about at all.'

This achieved its object. There was a moment of silence.

'What do you mean?' said Liz.

'Look here. You're all assuming that rope was put there by the

141

same—the same madman who destroyed MacMorris. Aren't you?'

The General started to nod but thought better of it. Liz and Sue said 'Yes'.

'All right. But doesn't it strike you as a chancy and inefficient way of knocking us off?'

Liz said, the puzzled look still on her face, 'Do you mean that he wasn't to know you'd both gone up to town. Because if so, it's only fair to say that I mentioned it to half a dozen people, in Brimberley alone.'

'That's one aspect of it,' said Bob. 'But it wasn't exactly what I had in mind. Granted that anyone *might* know that we were due back after dark, why set about it that way?'

'It seems to have worked reasonably well,' said Sue. She sounded cross.

'Slight concussion,' said the General defiantly.

'By a series of flukes, he got some results,' agreed Bob. 'But tell me this, General. If it hadn't been pelting with rain, would you have allowed me to bring you to your front door?'

'Certainly not,' said the General. 'If anyone's kind enough to give me a lift I invariably jump off at the end of the lane.'

'Right,' said Cleeve. 'And if it hadn't been for the same rain, I don't believe I'd ever have hit the rope at all. I'd have seen it in plenty of time and stopped. Or been going so slowly it wouldn't have mattered. And why a rope? It couldn't be strong enough to wreck the car. A steel hawser, now—'

'For goodness sake,' said Sue. 'Perhaps he hadn't *got* a steel hawser.'

'What are you getting at, Bob?' said Liz.

'I'm getting at this,' said Bob. 'Every Friday, after dark, throughout the winter, Liz comes to this house on that motor-bicycle of hers, which she rides to the public danger. Just imagine her pelting round that corner and getting the rope under her chin.'

'Good God,' said the General, sitting up.

'And that's why I don't particularly want Liz out of our sight. At least, not until Tim's back, and can keep an eye on her.'

'Where *is* Tim?'

Liz said, 'I can usually get hold of him when he stays up on a Friday.

142

There's a number I can ring. It's a friend's flat.'

'All right,' said Cleeve. 'Give it a try. But if you can't get hold of him, I'm going to take you all home with me. I've got plenty of beds – and hot baths,' he added as Sue sneezed. 'I'm going out now to extract the car.'

The friend was in his flat when Liz rang, but knew nothing of Tim's movements. Which was not surprising, as Tim was, at that moment, conversing with Mr. Smith of Holborn.

'All aboard, then,' said Cleeve. 'Bring your toothbrushes and pyjamas. The house can supply the rest. We'll prop the General up in the back seats with cushions and a rug, and Liz to hold his hand. You sit in front with me, Sue. Mind the upholstery. There's glass everywhere. All set? Then tally ho!'

Three hours later a warm, well-fed, reasonably easy-minded and very sleepy trio were sitting in front of the big open hearth in the drawing-room at Clamboys Hall.

The leaping firelight threw the rest of the big room into shadows. Sue was half sitting, half lying in a box-like brocaded sofa so wide and deep that she seemed to be trapped in its folds. Liz squarely filled a chair on one side of the fire, opposite her host on the other. The General was in bed and was thought to be asleep.

'And the deuce of a job I had getting him there,' said Sue. 'He won't remember that he's no longer a child of sixty.'

'As soon as people remember their age they curl up and die,' said Liz.

'He's a tough nut,' said Cleeve. 'Very bad luck, actually. He hit his head on the window stop. If it hadn't been for that he'd have got off quite lightly.'

'Have the police made anything out of it?'

'I shouldn't think so. They've shone their torches on the ground and stamped around a bit. They won't be able to do anything useful until it's light.'

The door at the far end of the room opened and Rupert came in. He was wearing a dressing-gown and his hair was tousled from his bath. He said good night composedly to everybody in turn and withdrew as quietly as he had come.

'Chickens and hens,' thought Liz. 'How little the young thing looks like the finished product. In five years' time he'll be long and pimply and will have forgotten how to come into a room.'

'You'll have to look after him,' she said out loud.

'Do all I can,' said Cleeve, startled. 'Why?'

'His voice, I mean. He's the only real treble we've got. Without him the Hedges quintet are as sheep without a shepherd. Where's he get it from?'

'Must be on his mother's side. His father never had any voice to speak of. He's a good-looking boy, isn't he?'

'He's a banger,' said Liz. 'Pity he's got to grow up really. You ought to be able to preserve him in his status quo. Under a glass case. Like Lenin.'

Cleeve affected to consider the matter. 'I don't think he'd fancy that,' he said. 'Very active boy. He's got a war on with cook's cat. I saw the cat go up a tree after a bird the other day, and Rupert going after the cat. I don't know which of 'em climbed better. The bird got away but the cat didn't.'

There was such a warmth of affection in Cleeve's usually impersonal voice that Liz and Sue caught each other's eyes and smiled.

'I sometimes wonder if he isn't lonely here. It's a big house, you know, and only servants to talk to. I'm not here a lot, and even when I am I can't give him all the time I'd like. He had a governess up to this summer. Strong-minded woman. But no real stamina. She had a nervous breakdown in July. He's been running his own trail since then.'

'I don't think he minds being on his own,' said Liz. 'He's the most terrifyingly self-sufficient boy I've ever had anything to do with. How old is he now?'

'Ten and a bit. I'm afraid it's got to be boarding school. Got a lot of prospectuses here. I'd like you to look at 'em, Liz. They're all the same, though. Staffs of graduates. Young, energetic headmasters assisted by wife and mistresses. Twenty acres of playing fields and own dairy herd. Boys not driven but brought forward by kindness. It all sounds remarkably unlike any preparatory school I can remember but perhaps things have changed since I was a boy.'

'I think they have changed a bit,' said Liz.

'Rupert doesn't need kindness. He needs competition,' said Sue sleepily from the depths of the sofa.

'What nonsense,' said Liz. 'All children want kindness. That's right, isn't it, Bob?'

'I'm not sure,' said Bob. 'I'm kind to him. But that isn't policy, it's weakmindedness. Anyway, what children want and what they need are different kettles of fish. Too much pampering, bring 'em forward quickly, no fruit worth speaking of. Cut 'em back now, good crop later.'

'Children aren't Ribston Pippins,' said Liz. 'And what's more, I don't believe you believe a word of it.'

'I *believe* it,' said Cleeve. 'I don't practice it. Fact is, I always let personalities creep in too much. Whenever I get a problem – and I've had a few – say it's juvenile delinquency. My mind's eye doesn't see the average juvenile delinquent. It sees Rupert. If you see what I mean,' he added, for Liz seemed suddenly to have lost herself.

'Yes, I do,' she said at last. 'It's a national failing.'

'Some really frightful case is being discussed. A boy of thirteen, say, who has been living for the last three years by systematic robbery and violence. And all the time I'm trying to be horrified about it something inside me insists on saying, "Well, he must have a lot of guts, anyway. Better robbery than charity."'

'That's purely Elizabethan,' said Liz.

'Do you know, I think I might have been quite happy in the reign of Good Queen Bess,' said Cleeve sadly. 'I know they hadn't got drains and dentists, but think of the compensations. A man could cut out his own path for himself. If he hurt other people, that was just too bad for them. If he got hurt himself, no squealing. *And every single penny that he made he kept.*'

'No television either,' said Sue from the sofa. She was almost asleep.

'It wasn't all fresh air and freedom,' said Liz. 'What about religious persecution? What price the Star Chamber?'

'Don't pour cold water.'

'I'm not pouring cold water. I think you'd have looked splendid in a ruff. And I'm sure you'd have given the Spaniards hell. As it is, you've got the next best thing. A lot of this house is Elizabethan, isn't it?'

'All the middle bit. And talk of religious persecution, we've even got a Priest's Hole. Rupert spends hours looking for it. I had to put my foot down, though, when I found him boring holes in the panelling with a brace and bit. Who says bed?'

Liz and Sue said bed.

At that moment the telephone buzzer sounded. The extension was on the table beside Liz's chair. She lifted the receiver.

And as she had guessed, it was Tim, at last.

That night, in her comfortable bed, with her feet on a stone hot-water bottle, Liz found herself curiously wakeful. Clamboys lay about her, five centuries of it, shifting slightly in its sleep, as an old house will.

Thought ran into dream, and dream woke again into thought.

At one moment they were all in the stern-cabin of a high-pooped ship-of-war. Bob, florid and magnificent in silks, with a leg to rival King Hal. The General, dressed in black, slight, upright and severe. Tim, bulky and happy with the sword on his hip. Sue showing all that a girl of eighteen was allowed to show in the reign of the first Queen Elizabeth and looking shockingly attractive and desirable. Even Rupert was there, improbably demure, serving the party on bended knee.

Four bells sounded. Or would it have been the stable clock? Liz had a feeling that one important person was missing, and frowned with disappointment when she realised who it was. Look as she would she could not see herself anywhere.

The frown was still on her face when the maid woke her at nine o'clock the next morning. She got up and looked out of the window. The gale had blown the rain clear out of the sky.

She was, had she known it, the last in the house to get up.

At seven o'clock Sue had roused herself, put on an old pair of flannel trousers and crept quietly downstairs. Clamboys was one of the last houses that still retained an adequate staff, and people were moving in the kitchen quarters.

The front door was unlatched.

She went out into a lovely cold morning that hit her like a friendly slap on the face. When she reached the stables someone was clanking a bucket and whistling.

She lifted down the light saddle from the peg, picked up the bridle and saddled Rosie, the bouncy grey. As she led the mare, clowning gently, towards the open door, Bob Cleeve appeared. Despite the cold of the morning he was in his shirt sleeves.

'Morning, Sue,' he said. 'If you'll hold your horse for a minute I'll be with you. I want to knock some of the stuffing out of that brute Bolo.'

'All right,' said Sue. 'But not too far or too fast. I've only got thin flannel trousers on me.'

'And remarkably shapely you look in 'em,' said Cleeve with a grin. He disappeared into the end stall and an outburst of clattering and snorting recorded the protests of the terrible Bolo against early morning exercise.

At about the same time the General's bedroom door opened and the General emerged. He looked cautiously about him and then tiptoed towards the nearest bathroom. He had been threatened with breakfast in bed and was determined to take no chances of such humiliation. Once let women get the upper hand of you and you might as well hem your own shroud.

Although it took him the best part of an hour to do everything that had to be done, when he finally got himself downstairs, he found that he was first at the breakfast table, and he had almost finished his meal by the time his host and his granddaughter appeared.

'What are you doing down here?' said Sue.

'Finishing breakfast,' said the General complacently. 'You two been out riding? I very nearly came with you myself.'

'You—'

'Remarkably good kedgeree, this. You ought to try a plateful with your ham.'

'All right' said Sue. 'All right. But just wait till Liz sees you, that's all.'

'I'm not afraid of Liz,' said the General. But nevertheless he finished up his breakfast and pottered out into the garden. Dangerous woman. It didn't do to take chances.

But when Liz came down she had other matters on her mind. Her first inquiry was, had anyone telephoned?

As soon as she had finished her breakfast she rang up her house. It was Anna who answered. No, apparently Tim was not back. No sign of him. And no message. Was anything wrong?

'There's nothing wrong,' said Liz. 'Why?'

'Everything feels wrong,' said Anna. 'I been hearing things. It's not nice in this house alone. The boards get creaking. And last night, when I was going to bed, a man came to the door. I didn't know whether to open it.'

'Did you?'

'Yes. I opened it when he'd rung the bell a bit. It was the Vicar. Something about the choir treat.'

'Well, goodness,' said Liz. 'What's wrong with that?'

'Nothing's wrong with it,' said Anna. 'But I don't like it.'

'All right. There's no reason for you to hang about. Tim's got his own key. You go and spend the rest of the weekend with Mrs. What's-her-name? The one you spend your afternoons off with. She'd be only too pleased to have you.'

'Mrs. Antonovich,' said Anna, sounding brighter at once. 'Yes, I could stay with her. Would that be all right?'

'See you on Monday morning,' said Liz, and rang off thoughtfully.

Anna was a stolid person, not easily upset. She had never before raised the slightest objection to being left alone in the house. If Anna was beginning to panic, then something had better be done.

With sudden resolve she helped herself to a stick from the rack and set out for a walk. Clamboys stands on the southern edge of the heathland which runs, almost unbroken, from Brimberley to Woking. It is good country for walking, being sandy and open and traversed by a maze of tiny footpaths, most of them decorated with War Office notice boards which warn unauthorised persons of a variety of fates which will overtake them if they wander at large (unexploded gas shells). From long experience Liz ignored these and trudged in a haphazard circle which brought her back to Clamboys at lunch-time with a big appetite and a mind at rest.

In the course of her morning's walk she had come to certain conclusions. They were not attractive conclusions, but it was a comfort to have reached some measure of finality.

After lunch, when they were finishing their coffee, they heard a car drive up and shortly afterwards a maid came in and said something to Cleeve. Cleeve looked startled, muttered, 'I wonder what the devil he can want,' and shot out of the room.

The Chief Constable was waiting in the library. He was looking as serious as he ever allowed himself to look.

'I thought you ought to know,' he said, 'that our friend has been at it again.'

For a moment Cleeve looked blank.

'A Major and Mrs. Lucas. Their country house in Essex, at Belton Park. Made a clean sweep of the family jewels. Diamonds and emeralds. All very nice stuff.'

'Kept in an unlocked, downstairs drawer, I suppose,' said Cleeve.

'As a matter of fact, no. They usually keep it all at the bank. They just happened to have it out for a big dinner party and dance to-night.'

'Our friend showing his usual, accurate sense of timing. Was there anything concrete to connect it with him?'

'Quite a bit,' said Pearce. 'In fact, I should say myself, that there isn't room for any doubt at all. Major Lucas had put the stuff in his own wall-safe in the study. Quite a nice little job with one of the new precision-combination locks. Well, as you know, that's just our man's cup of tea. In fact, I don't think there's another man in England who can open them by kindness alone. A dozen in America. One in Australia. Two or three in Palestine.'

'Yes. Anything else?'

'He got in at a first storey window without leaving much trace. So that probably means a folding steel ladder. And he used a motor-cycle for transport. That's him too.'

'Are they sure about that?'

'They've found where he parked it in some long grass outside the walls. And he was seen, at least, it's fairly likely it was him – shortly after he got away. The local bobby was sitting in a hedge waiting quietly for a chicken-steal to come off and he saw him go by.'

'What time?'

'Three o'clock, or near it.'

'Any sort of description?'

Thick-set chap. Well wrapped up. Difficult to say whether he was young or old. In fact, just what we got the only other time he was seen.'

The two men looked at each other. In the sudden silence Sue's voice could be heard, two rooms away, and the rumble of a reply from Liz or the General.

'If you're right,' said Cleeve, 'and God knows it's got all the trimmings, then one idea goes clean overboard. MacMorris never had anything to do with the country house jobs.'

'I'm not sure that I ever really thought he had,' said Pearce slowly. 'He fitted, in theory. He was a solitary man, with very little background to him. But – I don't know. Somehow or other I could hardly see him belting across country on a motor-cycle, jumping walls, climbing up home-made ladders. It all seemed to me to add up to someone a good deal younger. Or at least,' he added carefully, 'someone very active for his age,'

'He can't be all that young,' said Cleeve. 'You told me yourself, he's been going for nearly thirty years. I don't suppose he started when he was at school.'

'Do you remember Lockspeiser?'

'Lockspeiser? No. Yes. Wait a minute. Wasn't he a bank-note forger. Way back before the first World War. I think I do remember him.'

'It wasn't a him. It was them.'

'Them?'

'Three of them. The founder of the firm – he must have started up the business well back in Victoria's reign. No one really knows when he *did* start. In fact, no one knows much about him. The second Lockspeiser – no family connection, just an accomplice – carried on where the old man left off. Same plates, same methods, same distributors. He even helped himself to the old man's name. We know more about him. He's still alive – in Ontario, Canada. A most blameless old party. We've got nothing definite on him. Before he left this country with his pile he handed over the outfit, goodwill, name and all, to Lockspeiser III. That was the one we caught.'

'But,' said Cleeve, and then stopped and said, 'Hmp.'

'Once you think of it,' said Pearce, 'this has got all the elements of a Lockspeiser. If you think of the three things a country house operator wants. The general technique. It's not taught in night schools. You've got to learn it somewhere. A skill with certain types of lock. Windows, small drawers, small safes. Then, last but not least, he wants to have his finger on a good receiver. When he decides that he's too old to play the active part himself, what's to prevent him taking in a young partner? It could become a family business. Father to son.'

'What a horrible idea.' Cleeve sounded genuinely upset.

'It's not as uncommon as you'd think,' said Pearce, 'And look at the dates here. The first series starts some time after the Kaiser's war and goes on until 1939, when it stops. The second lot starts a year or two after Hitler's war.'

'Your explanation,' said Cleeve painfully, 'being, I take it, that the younger man was otherwise engaged during the recent war. And needed a year or two to train up afterwards.'

'I think so,' said Pearce. As he got up he added, inconsequently, 'I'm sorry, too, you know. I'll keep you in the picture. I think something's bound to break soon. Don't bother to show me out.'

On his way down the hall the Chief Constable paused for a moment. The door of the little gunroom, on the left of the front door, was ajar and someone was watching him through it.

The door swung open and Liz appeared.

'Come in here a minute,' she said. 'I'm sorry to lurk, but there was something I had to say, and this was the only way of catching you alone.' She pulled the Chief Constable inside and slammed the door.

'An unexpected pleasure,' said Tom Pearce breathlessly. 'I'd no idea you were in the neighbourhood.'

'I won't take a minute,' said Liz, 'but I badly need a piece of information and you're the only person I can think of who can get it for me quickly. I could ask Tony, but he's abroad.'

The Chief Constable was not absolutely certain, but he had an idea that Tony was the Home Secretary. He bowed cautiously and asked what it was she wanted to know.

'Have you heard of a man called Feder?'

'Otherwise Barry?'

'That's the chap. Bob was talking about him to the General and me the other night. He was one of the first expert country house burglars, wasn't he?'

'I rather fancy he's dead.'

'Oh, that's all right,' said Liz. 'I didn't want to be introduced to him. I wanted to know something about him. I wanted to know *exactly how he was caught.*'

'Well, yes. I should think I could find that out for you. Is it urgent?'

'If I'm right,' said Liz in her deep voice, 'it's just about the most urgent thing you've ever done in your life.'

On Sunday morning, after breakfast, the General was so far recovered that he insisted on walking to Morning Service. He had a black eye, turning yellow at the edges, and a square of sticking plaster over his forehead, and he created quite a sensation among the congregation in the tiny church in the Park. It was plain to Sue that he would shortly be demanding to go home.

Just before lunch Tim telephoned. He was speaking from his house.

'How long have you been back?' said Liz, in some surprise.

'As a matter of fact,' said Tim, 'I got back yesterday evening.' He sounded quite unrepentant and Liz knew, from the tone in which he spoke, that it was not the least use asking him any questions.

'I hope you had a comfortable night,' she said.

'Not a single gremlin,' said Tim. 'I cooked my own breakfast, too. We seem to be a bit short of butter. When are you all coming back?'

'Well,' said Liz, and stopped. It had been generally accepted that they were to stay at Clamboys until Monday morning at least. She took a sudden decision. 'After lunch today,' she said.

She was alone, at that moment, with the General, who nodded his vigorous approval.

'I'm too old to be quite happy in other people's houses,' he said, 'however comfortable. You'll have to break it to Sue, though. She likes the riding.'

However, when the point was put to Sue she proved unexpectedly agreeable. She seemed to have something on her mind, too.

As the Clamboys car was approaching Brimberley she leaned forward and slid the glass partition across, thus excluding the ancient Clamboys chauffeur from their confidences.

'On Friday night,' she said, 'when you asked Bob where Rupert got his voice from – he said – or rather he didn't say quite what I expected—'

'You spotted that, did you?' said Liz. 'I thought you were asleep. You're quite right, though I don't think people know it in these parts. Rupert isn't his son. His father and mother were very old friends of Bob's. They were killed in one of the London raids. Bob's treated Rupert as his own son ever since. In fact, I doubt if Rupert knows the difference. He was less than a year old when it all happened.'

'Funny,' said Sue. 'I'd always thought of Bob as a widower.'

'Crusted old bachelor,' said the General. 'Why? Are you after him for yourself? Very warm man.'

'Try not to be vulgar,' said Sue coldly. 'Here we are. We'd better drop you first, Liz.'

When the car reached Melliker Lane the General and Sue got out. The right-hand gate-post still stood at an odd angle, but otherwise all signs of the accident seemed to have been cleaned up.

The General waited until the big car had rolled away, then he drew a deep breath.

'I feel,' he said, 'just as I used to when I got back to the fighting after a bit of leave. A nice holiday, but I'm glad it's over.'

He stumped up the two shallow brick steps and unlocked the door of his house. His granddaughter followed, a good deal more slowly.

Chapter Twelve

FALSE POINT: COUNTER-POINT

ARMADO:
'For mine own part, I breathe free breath.
I have seen the day of wrong through the little hole of discretion, and, I
will right myself like a soldier.'

Early next morning the General came to a stop in the middle of his
loosening-up exercises and frowned. Facing him was the open window.
Something, or someone, was moving in the fields behind the house.
Pulling on a jacket, for it was barely eight o'clock, and there was a bite
in the morning air, he strode across to his dressing table and reached
for his field-glasses. They were a good pair, which he kept for bird
watching.

When he got back to the window the figure had disappeared. The
General drew up a chair, rested the heavy Zeiss glasses on the window
ledge and waited.

Presently he caught a glimpse of brown and white, whipped up the
glasses and focused them at speed.

It was Tim. No doubt about it. He was not taking any particular
pains to conceal himself. He seemed to be loafing along the hedgerow
which divided the big back field, his hands in his pockets, his eyes on
the ground.

The General grunted, returned the glasses to their case, took off his
jacket and continued his careful routine. Up, down. Steady. Up, down
(crack) steady.

When he felt a light perspiration breaking out all over him, it would be time for his bath.

Tim was not really loafing. He was walking slowly, certainly, but he was walking carefully.

He had arrived at the end of Melliker Lane that morning with no very set purpose. His excuse was that he wanted to see for himself the damage to the gate-posts; (and if Sue had happened to look out of the window and wave to him, well, he would have been happy to wave back). Also he wished to test out an idea that had come to him.

You thought of Melliker Lane as a cul-de-sac. So far as motor-traffic went, this was no doubt correct. The made-up surface stopped opposite the shell of the MacMorris house. It was obvious however that when the road had been laid its planners were prepared, at need, to carry it further. The end had been sealed off temporarily with a line of hurdles and a small quickset hedge which had grown, through neglect and the passage of time, into a formidable obstacle.

If you squeezed round the end of the fence – there was a sort of established opening used first by cats, then by small boys, and later, apparently, by heavier traffic – you found that the continuation of the metalled road was a cart track, now almost indistinguishable from the field in which it lay,

'Must have led somewhere once,' observed Tim to a fat thrush who was cracking a snail on a stone. He moved slowly along, his eyes on the ground. The cart track wandered, slow and laborious as the carts that had made it, up the hill at an easy slant, along the crest, and down the reverse slope. Ahead showed a square of alders and brambles. In the middle, an affair of tumbled bricks and rotted timbers, stood the remains of a barn. The track ran up to it and stopped. Beyond the barn was something more ambitious. It was a service road, between high banks, badly made, but practicable in dry weather for most makes of car.

The intervening crest hid the spot from the Melliker Lane houses. In fact, it was out of sight of any house. A sad, lonely spot. Tim, who had lived in the district, off and on, for most of his life, had never suspected that it existed.

He squatted. There were tracks of some sort on the rough surface. Tyre tracks, he thought. Impossible to say what type, or how recent. Then, in the dust, something more interesting. A dribble of black oil. A car had stood there, and not too long ago.

Tim started down the lane. It curved always to the right. Soon it must come out – oh, here it was – as he had thought, on the side road that joined Brimberley to Bramshott.

The end of the lane was marked by a heavy, padlocked gate. Tim frowned at the padlock. It was unexpected. Then he looked more closely at the gate, and laughed. The cross bar had broken away, and the chain, padlock and all, could be lifted off in one piece.

'That's the way he came, all right,' he said softly. 'Old man dynamite. Knows the district. Runs his car up to the barn. Chance in a million if anyone saw it. Pussyfoots along the cart track and through the hedge into Melliker Lane. Back the same way. Safe as houses.'

He became aware that a car was approaching. Brakes squealed. It was Sergeant Gattie who looked out, teeth flashing white under the black bar of his moustache.

'There you are,' he said. 'Save me a lot of trouble. You're wanted.'

'Who by?'

'The Inspector wants you. Step in. Mustn't keep the great man waiting.'

Tim looked up and down the deserted road. Then he got into the car, fitting his square bulk neatly into the seat.

'What's it all about?' he said.

'Nobody ever tells me anything,' said Gattie. 'I'm just the boy round that office. Fetch this, carry that. Drop everything and pick up Mr. Artside.'

Now that he had got Tim in the car he seemed in less hurry to start.

'You ought to take steps to improve your own prospects,' said Tim. 'Catch this blower-up-of-other-people's-houses and they'll make *you* an Inspector.'

'Or the country house joker,' said Gattie, looking slyly sideways at his passenger.

'Oh, yes. He'd do. Maybe they're the same person,' he added helpfully.

'That's an interesting thought,' said Gattie. He let in the clutch and they moved slowly off down the road towards Bramshott. The young morning sun was clear of the trees, now. It was going to be a lovely day. They had gone some little way before the sergeant added, 'Any particular reason?'

'Nothing special,' said Tim. 'Economy of effort really. You want a chap for dog-stealing. And another chap for cat-stealing. So artistically satisfactory if they turn out to be the same man. Two birds, one stone.'

'I see,' said the sergeant.

'I'm full of ideas like that. At one time it did occur to me to wonder if this mightn't be a Kilmartin case.'

The car barely slowed.

'What horrible ideas you do get,' said Gattie at last. 'Where did this one come from? Your artistic conscience again?'

'No. There was something a little more substantial this time,' said Tim. 'Or I thought there was.' He had slewed round sideways in his seat and was looking at the sergeant. 'Very possibly I was wrong about it. I don't know.'

'I surely hope so,' said Gattie. 'It's not a thing we want in this country, is it? Here we are. I'll just run her into the yard. By the way, I should have asked you. Have you had your breakfast?'

'As a matter of fact, I have,' said Tim. 'Why? Is this going to take a long time? I'm a working man.'

'So's the Inspector,' said Gattie. 'A real hard worker the Inspector.' They were inside the building now. The charge room was empty. 'Bit of an awkward mood this morning. I'd mind my step, if I were you. You know the way. Straight along the passage.'

Tim had been a sort of policeman himself. As soon as he got into the Inspector's room he realised one thing clearly. The Inspector was on the move. There comes a time in every case when the policeman in charge feels it shift under his hand. It is beginning to crack. All he has to do is to keep hitting, and it will break up into pieces. Pieces small enough to be classified and docketed and tied around with pink tape and served up to the Office of the Director of Public Prosecutions. Conquering a very slightly cold feeling in the bottom of his stomach Tim seated himself in the chair in front of the desk and said, 'Good morning, Inspector. How can I help you?'

'You can help me most by answering one or two questions.'

'Is this the sort of interview at which I ought to insist on my legal adviser being with me?'

'That's up to you, sir.'

'I see. Well. On the whole I think I'll take a chance on that. Unless you start to savage me.'

'This is just an unofficial inquiry,' said the Inspector. 'I want to satisfy myself on one or two points. I shan't even have a note taken of it.'

'And if you *don't* satisfy yourself you can get official later. I know the form, thank you.'

'Of course. Yes. You were in the Palestine police after the war?'

'Not the police. The Gendarmerie.'

'That was an unofficial police force, I believe?'

'Highly unofficial.'

'And before that – during the war – you were a parachutist?'

'I don't see that it's relevant, but if we're going to relive my military past, let's do it properly. I was never in Airborne Forces. I was a member of a private thuggery called the Special Air Service. I served in it in North Africa, in Greece and, a little, in Italy. I was a temporary acting Major, which means that you have the responsibilities of a Major and the pay of a Captain – and can be sacked as a Lieutenant. If you want a second opinion on my performance as a soldier I can only refer you to General Palling.'

'Yes,' said the Inspector. 'Many of your missions in Greece were sabotage missions.'

'Don't let's beat about the bush,' said Tim. 'I had a great deal to do with explosives in the Army. Exceptionally so. During the active part of the war I learned to use them, and in Palestine I learned to dodge them. I'm a little rusty now of course – fashions in explosives change almost as quickly as fashions in dress. But I have ways and means of keeping up to date. For instance, I know Tobias, the top M.I.5 explosives man. I called on him the other day, and he gave me a quick refresher course.'

'The other day?'

'Friday evening, to be exact.'

'I see,' said the Inspector. 'It's good of you to be so frank.'

'Never keep anything from the police,' said Tim.

'A very sound rule,' said the Inspector. 'What do you do for a living now, Mr. Artside?'

'For a living?'

'Your job, I mean.'

'Well now,' said Tim. 'I'm not sure that I'm prepared to tell you that. My job has nothing to do with the matter you are investigating. It's irrelevant. I didn't undertake to answer irrelevant questions.'

'Then you refuse to say?'

'I just don't think it has anything to do with the matter in hand,' said Tim steadily.

'Very well,' said the Inspector. He sounded ominously pleased with himself. 'I expect it will come to light sooner or later. Would I be right in saying that it is a job that takes you out into the country a good deal?'

'Well, I expect that's right,' said Tim.

'And that you have a car – a small 1940 Austin, that you keep in a garage near King's Cross, and use for your——er—your trips into the country.'

Tim's eyes flickered for a moment.

'I wouldn't be surprised,' he said.

'The garage, I believe, knows you as Hodges.'

'I don't think,' said Tim, 'that the garage actually knows me as anything. It's "Hodges' car" as far as they are concerned. And they know that I have authority to use it.'

'That doesn't quite tally with my information,' said the Inspector. 'Do you mean that the garage man doesn't call you Mr. Hodges?'

'Certainly not. I call him Ron and he calls me Tim. Very democratic part of London, King's Cross.'

'All right,' said the Inspector. 'Does your job take you into Essex at all?'

'It has done.'

'Belton Park?'

For the first time Tim really did look surprised. 'Don't tell me,' he said, 'that you've had a little man in a bowler hat hidden in the dickey. Extraordinary. Yes, I was at Belton about three weeks ago.'

'Not since then?'

'Not to my knowledge. It would be a long way to walk in your sleep.'

'You weren't there by any chance on Friday night – or early on Saturday morning?'

Tim began to say something. Then stopped. 'What's all this about?' he said abruptly.

'Just answer the questions.'

'Not on your life. As you yourself pointed out, this isn't an official inquiry. Unless you tell me why you're asking these questions I shan't say another word.'

'I'm sorry you've adopted this attitude,' said the Inspector smoothly. He reached out his hand to the bell under his desk.

'Good Lord above,' said Tim. 'I remember now. It was in the papers yesterday. Major Lucas. Big robbery. The country house gang suspected.'

'You read about it in the papers?' said the Inspector in his ominously toneless voice.

Tim took no notice of him. He was struggling with suppressed emotion.

'Look here,' he said. 'Just at what time – or between what times – the widest margin possible – was this job done at Belton Park? There can be no harm in telling me that, surely.'

The Inspector reflected.

'The period we are inquiring about,' he said cautiously, 'is between midnight on Friday night and about four o'clock on Saturday morning.'

'All right,' said Tim. 'Then if you'll take the trouble to ring up West

End Central Police Station – you might ask for Detective Inspector Bazeley – you'll find that I spent Friday evening from about eleven o'clock onwards in their hospitable company. Shortly after midnight, I was given a bed in the cell ordinarily reserved for extreme cases of Delirium Tremens. I was not actually locked in, I agree. But at approximately two o'clock in the morning a gentleman was brought in who had celebrated his seventieth birthday by drinking half a pint of methylated spirits and I had to vacate my couch. I spent the rest of the night in the sergeant's room with three sergeants. Is there anything more I can do for you?'

'If—' said the Inspector heavily. 'I mean, I don't suppose—'

'I'm not making it up, if that's what you're hoping,' said Tim. 'Why should I? You'll telephone them as soon as I'm gone. Incidentally, I suppose I can go?'

'Why, yes,' said the Inspector. 'Yes, of course. I'm sorry to have detained you.'

'Don't mention it,' said Tim. He got up and was walking towards the door when a thought occurred to him.

'If you're looking for someone in our circle,' he said carefully, 'who *hasn't* got a very good alibi at about that time, then perhaps I can help you there, too.'

Luck looked up. The light was behind him and Tim could make nothing of his expression.

'I telephoned my mother that night,' went on Tim. 'After two bad shots I found her with Bob Cleeve out at Clamboys. Sue and the General were with her. She told me about the joker tying the rope across the gate. I was a bit worried. I wondered, you see, if they were taking the thing quite seriously enough, or if they ought to have some sort of protection. So I rang up Queen, at his cottage. His wife said he was out – had been for some time – didn't know when he'd be back. So I tried Gattie. No answer at all. Then I tried you, Inspector. The station didn't know where you were. Curious.'

Luck had half turned in his chair and Tim could see his face now. It was not pretty.

'I've heard some unwarranted attacks on the police in my time,' he said at last. 'But for sheer impertinence I think that beats the band.'

He was so angry he sounded almost human.

'Possibly I've got a warped mind,' agreed Tim. 'But then, you must remember, I spent some time in Palestine. I remember one case particularly – an Inspector Kilmartin – the old racket. Pretended to be protecting the Arabs from the Jews, but actually robbed them indiscriminately. He made quite a pile before he got found out. Both parties hated him. The Jews got him first. Threw him over the Gehazai bridge with a live hand grenade in both pockets. You ought to ask Gattie about him. He knows the details.'

II

'I'm glad you could all get here,' said Liz. 'I had to bring the practice forward to Monday, because they're starting on the heating tomorrow, and you know what a row that makes.'

'Couldn't be worse than us,' murmured Tim to Sue. He had quietly transferred himself to MacMorris' place leaving Lucy Mallory to Sergeant Gattie.

Sue frowned and opened her anthem sheet ostentatiously.

'There's one new hymn for Sunday. At least, not a new hymn but a new tune. It's Bax. Modern, but good.' She sketched it through on the harmonium. 'I particularly want it to go well, because all the old diehards will be saying "*That's* not the right tune". Let's try it through. Take the last verse. Mezzo forte.'

The choir took the last verse. Liz listened, her head on one side. The parts were all right. Hedges reliable. Gattie very firm in the tenor. Lucy and Sue improving. Only the trebles were weak, almost to non-existence.

'Trebles only,' she decreed.

Her worst fears were justified. Rupert and Maurice were hardly trying. The other four were trying but were getting nowhere.

She looked at them speculatively. Maurice was red-eyed but defiant. Jim had said to her, 'I can't make nothing of him. Never known him like that before.' Rupert was whiter than usual but composed.

'What's happened to your voice, Rupert?' she said.

'I'm afraid I've got rather a sore throat,' he said politely.

'Pity,' said Liz. 'Too sore to come on the outing on Wednesday?'

'Not so sore as that,' said Rupert quickly, and the Hedges children laughed. Even Maurice looked a little happier.

'What's this outing, Mrs. Artside?' said Gattie. 'Do I qualify for it?'

'You certainly qualify if you want to come,' said Liz. 'In fact you're very welcome. I'm afraid the older members mostly regard it as something to be got out of.' She looked severely at Tim, who grinned. 'We have a joint excursion every autumn with the Bramshott and Barnboro' choirs. About thirty children and any grown-ups who can be induced to come along and give a hand.'

'Well, I'll see,' said Gattie. 'We're a hard-worked force in this area.'

'The bus leaves at nine o'clock from Barnboro' Town Hall, calls at Bramshott first, and then here. We're all going down to Belmouth. It's a bit off season, but the children like the fun fair. Incidentally, how many of you are coming. Jim?'

Too much to do myself,' said Jim, firmly.

'Lucy, you're coming aren't you? And Sue?' Sue nodded.

'Count me in too,' said Tim promptly.

'That makes four of us. Five if the sergeant can come. What about you, young Hedges?'

Four hands shot up. Maurice looked doubtful.

'What's wrong with you?' said Liz. 'Got a date with your young lady that day?'

Maurice wriggled. Liz sensed an undercurrent of something she didn't understand.

'What about you, Rupert?' she said.

'Oh, all right,' said Rupert.

Maurice's relief was patent. 'I shall be coming, Mrs. Artside,' he said.

That's all right then,' said Liz. 'Same arrangements as last year. Bring sandwiches for lunch and we'll have high tea at the Pavilion. And *don't* wear your best suits. Remember what happened last year on the dodgems. Now let's give the Anthem a run through, and see if we can't do it really well this time. On the tenth beat. A nice firm "Come".'

It wasn't bad. The thought of Belmouth seemed to have stimulated Rupert. If Rupert sang they all sang. It was one of the scant and occasional returns for months of unrewarding work that occasionally, very occasionally, a dozen ordinary-to-bad singers contrived to produce a total which was better than the sum of their individual parts.

She hoped it might be so on the great day.

After practice Tim walked home with Sue. He had a lot to tell her.

'What does it all mean?' asked Sue at the end of it.

'Search me,' said Tim. 'Some of it's clear enough but nothing like the whole picture.'

'None of it's clear to me,' said Sue. 'Who is the Captain? And his friends at this restaurant? Where do they come into it? And why did they try to beat you up? And what are the police doing about it?'

'The Captain and his boyfriends are a hardworking crowd of professional receivers of stolen goods. They specialise in jewellery, and gold and silver. They sell it abroad. The police haven't disturbed them up to date because they found it more useful to watch them and get a line on the various people who were bringing them stuff – the actual thieves. Though I rather fancy, after my spirited but incautious performance, that this phase may be over. They're about ready to gather in this little lot.'

Sue laughed. 'I should love to have seen that drunk pouring the brandy on the fire,' she said. 'What fun you do have.'

'It wasn't funny at the time,' said Tim.

'Still, I suppose a lot of your jobs are like that?'

Tim said, 'Well – as a matter of fact—'

'I know,' said Sue. 'Very hush-hush. I oughtn't to have mentioned it. But one can't help having ideas. I apologise.'

'Please don't apologise,' said Tim unhappily.

'Tell me some more about this business,' said Sue. 'There's no reason I shouldn't know about that. What have these receivers got to do with us at Brimberley?'

'That's the sixty-four dollar question,' said Tim. 'The way I see it at the moment is this. Somewhere in this district – or somehow connected with this district – I can't be any more definite than that – is a person who makes a living – a second living, because they must have some ostensible and above-board job – by occasional, well-planned raids on country houses. The country houses are scattered over the south of England. The base is here. So much seems certain. This person – this burglar—'

'Why are you being so cagey about it?' said Sue suddenly. 'You're carefully keeping off calling him a man or saying "he" or "him". Do you think it's a woman?'

'Must be unconscious caution,' said Tim. 'All right. This man works absolutely on his own. His nearest and dearest may know nothing about it. That's the pattern in these cases, you see. He may only operate on two nights in the year. He does his own reconnaissance, makes his own rules, plays his own hand. The one thing he's got to have help over is disposing of the goods. That's where the Captain comes in. He keeps a restaurant. Very handy. You go and have lunch there – perhaps only once a year. You leave a parcel with your hat and coat in the cloak room. When you've finished lunch you pick it up again. Only it isn't the same parcel. When you went in it was the proceeds of your last three robberies. When you come out it's full of pound notes. Transaction completed.'

'I see,' said Sue. 'Awkward if someone took your parcel by mistake.'

'I doubt if the attendant would let them,' said Tim. 'They're all in it. A very efficient crowd, really.'

'Go on,' said Sue. 'Let's walk as far as the first milestone and then turn back. I want to know it all. How did MacMorris come into it?'

There's no real proof about that,' said Tim. 'But I've not much doubt about it, either. He contrived to find out – probably some slip at the receiving end – the real life identity of the man who was doing these jobs. That was his meal ticket. Blackmail. Spoil the spoiler. He came down here to live on it. More comfortable than hanging round the West End stage. More dangerous, though.'

'So it was the burglar who blew him up,' said Sue thoughtfully. 'Do you know, I'm not sure I blame him.'

'Not if he'd stopped there,' said Tim. 'I didn't much like him trying to pitch my mother off her motor-bike, though, when her inquiries got too near the mark. That's the trouble with these people. As long as no one suspects them they're smooth as silk. But they'll go any length to preserve their anonymity. They'll kill to preserve it, make no mistake, you and me and the lot of us.'

'Tim,' said Sue, stopping suddenly. 'Do you know who it is?'

'Well, no,' said Tim. 'But I've got a very fair idea. That's what makes it so damned awkward,' he added.

Sue said, 'Let's go back.' She said nothing more until they got to Melliker Lane. She seemed almost afraid to speak.

They turned down into the lane, and stopped outside the gate.

Tim put his hand up to open the gate and found it on Sue's arm. He left it there for a moment. Before he could open his mouth Sue said, just as if she was concluding a conversation on a totally different subject, 'There's one thing more you ought to know. On Saturday when we were staying at Clamboys I went out for an early morning ride with Bob. He asked me to marry him.'

'Bob—' said Tim. 'Why—what—'

'I didn't have a chance to say yes or no, really,' said Sue. 'Bolo's an awful brute in the early morning and at that moment he bolted. By the time Bob got him back again the moment seemed to have passed.'

'Yes, but—' said Tim. 'I mean – would you—'

'How should I know,' said Sue crossly. 'Good night.' She stalked off up the driveway and Tim waited until he heard the door shut.

He stood for a minute or two, unmoving, in the dark. Round him the hundred noises of the night clicked and slurred and scuttered. Tim did not trouble himself about them. There were no dangerous ghosts in Melliker Lane that night.

A quarter of a mile away Constable Queen sat in his cottage parlour whilst his wife busied herself about his supper. He was a big, blond, serious young man, and at that moment his face was set into an almost terrifying concentration of thought.

It certainly scared his wife, who came back into the room at that moment, and had to put the tray she was carrying down on to the table before she spoke.

'Why, Stan,' she said, 'whatever's up?'

He turned his troubled face to her. 'If you *know* something,' he said, 'but can't tell it without getting someone else into trouble, and if you don't want to get them into trouble – it's difficult, see.'

Mrs. Queen saw nothing. She knew nothing; but being a woman did not allow this deficiency to affect her judgement.

'Eat your supper whilst it's hot,' she said. 'And stop thinking about it. It'll all come out a lot easier in the morning.'

Chapter Thirteen

THE CHOIR RELAXES

COSTARD: *'And travelling along this coast, I here am come by chance—'*

Constable Queen was not a man who thought quickly or easily. He turned things over in his mind. Scraps of what he had learned at police training school jostled with the loyalty of his class to his class; personal friendship, the dislike of interfering; and, in the last resort, that sort of fundamental honesty that you either pick up at your mother's knee or stay quit of for life.

He thought about it for all of thirty-six hours before he moved.

Wednesday was just another lovely day in that outstandingly fine autumn. Queen, who had been up and busy since five o'clock, came back to his cottage, kissed his wife, and ate his breakfast in silence. After breakfast he put a call through to Bramshott police station and found out that Inspector Luck would be in his office at ten.

Shortly afterwards he jumped on to his bicycle and pedalled off along the Bramshott road. Nobody watching him pass could have guessed that he was about to unlock mysteries which had so long confounded better brains than his.

'Well, Queen?' said Luck.

'I've been thinking, sir,' said Queen, 'that I ought to have a word with you if I could. It's not exactly in the line of duty, and yet, in a way, it is. I've been very upset about it.'

Luck sighed, but quietly. It was in just such a way that trouble started. Bribery? Women? Queen's wife? A nice girl, he had always thought, and more sensible than most.

'—on Friday night,' went on Queen. 'You know I was out with Sergeant Gattie most of the night, watching that house in Melliker Lane where they'd had the trouble.'

'I remember,' said Luck (got home unexpectedly early? cuckoo in the nest?)

'Well, we didn't.'

'Didn't what?' said the Inspector blankly.

'Didn't stand watch together. The sergeant went off. I stopped.'

'Oh,' said Luck, softly. It hadn't penetrated yet, though. 'Where did he go?'

'He drove off in the car,' said Luck. 'Said there was a girl he was courting over at Mallards Cross, and if anyone said anything, I was to say he'd been with me all night.'

Queen stopped, but Luck did not interrupt. There was more to come.

'A good deal later,' said Queen, 'I took a stroll myself. There wasn't nothing happening and I was getting cold. I went by the path – that one that goes back from the end of Melliker Lane over the hill to the old barn.'

'Fagg's barn,' said Luck.

'That's right. It's tumble-down now. Stands at the end of a bit of lane that takes you back to the road. I thought I'd go down the lane, and make the whole circuit, see. Come back to the house from the other end. When I stepped into the lane I nearly broke my shins on it.'

'On what?' said Luck with sharp suspicion.

'On the car,' said Queen softly. 'Our car.'

There was a very long and very uncomfortable silence. Then the Inspector looked at the watch on his wrist and said, 'Come along, you'd better show me the place.'

Ten minutes later they were both peering down at a patch of oil. It was the same patch that Tim had looked at two days before, still undisturbed. No-one seemed to use the lane. The tumble-down barn was quiet.

'I wonder,' said Luck. He walked across and circled the barn. Though decrepit, it proved curiously difficult to make an entry. The window spaces were filled with fallen stone and sealed with brambles. The remains of the door lay across the opening at an angle that effectively blocked it, without offering any suggestion that it could be opened. Luck shone his torch through the gap. It aroused a family of bats.

Queen called from the other side of the barn. There was a small, stone outbuilding. It might have served as a fodder store when the barn was in use.

'Been someone here more than once,' said Queen. 'They been careful too, but you can see the marks. There, and there. And the stones at the end, they've been unpiled, and piled again.'

'We'll have 'em down,' said Luck.

Together they lifted the stones which formed the end of the lean-to. They came away cleanly, without any dust or rubble between them.

'Been moved more'n once,' said Queen.

Luck said nothing. He was sweating. He shone his torch into the neat space which they had opened.

It was covered by a tarpaulin, but Luck had a sick feeling that he knew what was under it.

'Open her up carefully,' he said.

It was a motor-cycle, a newish Wolf-Ashton, fast and well cared for. The most noticeable feature was the double wicker pannier, like a dispatch rider's satchel. Luck put gloves on to open it. Rolled up in a canvas hold-all at the bottom was as neat a housebreaker's kit as Luck in his experience had ever seen. Leather loops holding an array of neat and shining implements. One pair of loops was empty. The rear loop was larger than the front one and they lay about six inches apart.

'Plenty of room for the loot, too,' said Queen, looking at the empty panniers.

'Travelling burglar's shop,' agreed Luck shortly. He was re-fastening the straps. Together they pushed the machine back and covered it. Then they built the stones back into position. It was difficult to see that anything had ever been moved.

'I don't need to tell you,' he said, 'that you keep quiet about this.'

'Quiet as the grave,' said Queen.

Luck thought about those two loops, six inches apart, one larger than the other.

'As the grave,' he agreed. Another thought was teasing him. 'Who owns this piece?' he said. 'The gate's kept locked – or meant to be. It isn't a public right of way. I had an idea—'

'I could easily find out, sir,' said Queen. 'Petch and Porter handle most of the properties round here. I could look at their estate map.'

'All right,' said Luck, 'you do that. And telephone me at the station. If I'm out, go on trying till you get me.'

Queen knew young Mr. Petch well and was shown in without delay.

'What is it this time,' said Sam Petch resignedly. 'Car on the wrong side of the road?'

'You can help me this time,' said Queen. He described the position of the barn.

'Fagg's Barn,' said Mr. Petch. 'It's still called that, though old Fagg's been dead more than fifty years. Dad just remembers him. Used to come in here every market day and drink himself unconscious in the "Farmers Glory." The landlord rolled him under the bar to sleep it off. Wonderful days. Now let me see, I don't know that I can help. We don't handle that side of the road now. Masons of Sunningdale took it over before the war. They'd know. Would you like me to telephone Fred Mason?'

Queen thought quickly.

'I'll run over and see him myself if you don't mind,' he said. 'Rather confidential. And could you forget it yourself?'

'Surely,' said Mr. Petch.

They walked down through the outer office.

On a table by the door Queen saw a pair of pigskin gloves. They were old-fashioned but good. It occurred to him that he had seen them before.

'Aren't those young Mr. Artside's?' he said.

'Nothing escapes our police,' said Mr. Petch with a chuckle. 'They are. He was in here this morning making some inquiries.' When Queen looked at him he added blandly, 'They were confidential, too, I'm afraid.'

'It's inconceivable,' said Tom Pearce.

Luck thought that it was the first time that he had ever seen his Chief Constable shaken.

'I've got his record here,' said Luck. Pearce looked angrily at the card, but hardly seemed to see it.

'Regular soldier,' said Luck. 'Then in the Palestine Gendarmerie. Then he came to us under the Special Recruitment Scheme, with his rank of sergeant. Joined us down here in 1947.'

'Which was when this crop of burglaries began.'

'That's right, sir.'

'Have you checked—'

'I haven't had time to do it carefully, sir,' said Luck. 'But I don't think he's got a shadow of an alibi for any of the other jobs. You remember that one we got tipped-off about and put out a dragnet, but missed him by inches. I've checked the duty sheets. Gattie was on leave. And another thing. One of his particular jobs was siting those checkposts.'

'Yes,' said Pearce. Like all policemen, the thought of treachery in his own force left him cold and furious.

'Have you ever had any reason to suspect him before?' he said. 'Not this, of course. But anything. Slackness, inattention to duty, petty dishonesty.'

Luck could read his superior's mind like a book. But he was unable to offer him even this salve to his feelings. 'I always found him excellent,' he said. 'A first class man, able and willing and cheerful. Exceptionally courageous, and strong as a horse.

You remember that job he did over at Ascot when the Glasshouse boys tried to throw their weight about—'

'He got a citation for that, didn't he?'

'That's right.'

'Blast,' said Pearce. 'Blast and curse him. Curse everybody. Curse everything. What the hell are we going to do?'

It wasn't a question. He didn't want advice. He wanted a miracle. He wanted the thing never to have happened. Another thought struck him.

'How old is Gattie?'

Luck looked at the card and said, 'Born 1920.'

'Well that disposes of one idea,' said Pearce. 'He couldn't have had any hand in the previous series – unless he was organising them at the age of ten.'

'Even that won't do,' said Luck. 'He's shown here as born Trinidad. I believe his father was a sugar foreman. He didn't come to this country until 1934.'

Pearce said, 'If the team idea is right, Gattie must have joined up with his predecessor somewhere about 1947. In other words, as soon as he was posted here. If he was in the regular Army – say he joined in 1938 – then the war came pretty quickly after that – then he was in Palestine. You see what I mean? He'd have been kept too busy to organise anything like this. I think he, personally, must have started from scratch in 1947. He was the hands. The other person, who had the experience and the contacts and the know-how, was the brains.'

'It could have been someone he met in the Army,' suggested Luck.

The two men looked at each other thoughtfully.

The telephone rang and Pearce hooked off the receiver.

'It's for you,' he said.

'Me, sir. Queen,' said the voice at the other end.

Luck listened, and at the end said, 'Well, that's that. It's nice to know. I'd like you to come back to the station and stand by. We look as if we may be having a busy day.'

He rang off.

'That was Queen, sir,' he said. 'He's been making some inquiries for me. Gattie's over at May Heath on an all day job. We could take him off it. I thought on the whole we'd let it run and talk to him when he gets back in the evening. Incidentally he's carrying a knife. I noticed the retaining loops in that pannier affair – about eight inches long. A commando type, probably. There was one other thing'—he spoke with studied moderation—'Queen's been looking into the question of ownership of the land where we found the motor-cycle. It's absolutely possible that Gattie was using the barn without the owner knowing anything about it, but I thought it might have given us some sort of line, you see.'

'Has it?' said Pearce.

'I hope not,' said Luck soberly. 'The land all belongs to the Clamboys estate. It was bought about twenty years ago. Most of it's let to farmers, but that piece with the barn and the lane and the spinney lies between two farms, and doesn't actually go with either of them.'

The two men looked at each other with a wild surmise.

'Mr. Cleeve,' said Inspector Luck.

'Bob Cleeve,' said the Chief Constable.

III

'Bob,' said Liz. 'I want a word with you. It's all right, Rupert, I promise we won't miss the bus. You can come back on my carrier and we'll be in plenty of time.' She looked at the large gunmetal watch that hung from a safety pin on the front of her tweed coat. 'It hasn't even left Barnboro' yet, so relax. Go and find your sandwiches or your catapult or whatever you're going to shoot your lunch with. That's right.' She added, as the door closed, 'It's no real business of mine, but that boy's not right.'

'Not right? You mean he's ill?'

'I don't think he's doctor-ill,' said Liz. 'But he's got something on his mind.'

'He hasn't been happy lately,' said Cleeve. He looked rather desperately round the big, rich, empty room. 'I thought it might be just general unhappiness, and that we'd cure it when he went to school. The good ones are all terribly full, but I've pulled some strings, and got him put down for St. Oswald's. Ought to be all right. Most of the royal family went there.'

'I think it's something more,' said Liz. 'It seemed to me to start a week or so ago, and it's been getting worse. And he's a very reserved child. That's what makes it so dangerous.'

'You're telling me,' said Cleeve. 'It's like a time-bomb. You can hear him ticking. The only question is when he's going to go off.'

'But Bob,' said Liz, 'if you think that, why not do something about it?'

'Tried a laxative,' said Cleeve. 'Worked too well. Had to give it up. Then tried cold baths. No good, either. What's next? Take him to a psychiatrist?'

'Nonsense,' said Liz. 'Psychiatrists are for old women. The only thing you've got to do is find out what's on his mind and take it off. You're the only person he'll talk to. If he won't tell you, he certainly won't tell me. But you've got to get down to it. It's important.'

She paused and both of them were silent for a space. Liz seemed to be calculating very carefully what she was going to say.

'All this trouble we've been having in the last few weeks, we don't want to let it upset our sense of values. We're most of us well on in life. I'm not being morbid, but does it really matter what happens to any of us? Any good we're going to do, we've done. A year or two more or less, it's just a matter of statistics, now—'

'My dear Liz—' said Bob.

'I'm absolutely serious,' said Liz. 'Do you know, it's Bill's birthday. If he'd lived he'd have been sixty-four today. I was lying in bed this morning, more than half asleep, and I suddenly thought, supposing some God stepped out of the Machine and offered me a choice. Bill back, in exchange for someone with all his life in front of him – I think Rupert was in my mind—'

'What an awful—'

'It's all right,' said Liz. 'I went to sleep again. When I woke up I'd forgotten all about it. It came back to me when I was talking to you. By the way, Hubert's coming over to-night. Tim and Sue are on this Belmouth jaunt with me, and they're all stopping for dinner. Would you like to make a fifth?'

Bob pulled out a fat engagement diary and looked at it.

'I'd love to' he said, 'but I daren't promise it. We've got a council of meeting this afternoon. It won't stop before six, and an Education Committee of which I'm supposed to be Chairman immediately afterwards. I'll drop in on you for coffee and pick up Rupert. Can you feed him?'

'If he eats as much as he did on the last choir outing,' said Liz, 'he won't need any supper. Quite the reverse, as the Channel passenger said to the steward. Here he is at last. Got everything?'

'Yes, thank you, Mrs. Artside,' said Rupert politely.

'Sandwiches, mackintosh, gun, dagger, knuckledusters? All right. Off we go.'

IV

Lovers of Belmouth assert that the early autumn is its best season. It is by no means empty. At Belmouth, as the advertisements tell you, you can enjoy yourself all the year round. But the crowds which throng its beaches, hotels and pleasances from June to September have thinned out. The hotel staffs find time to draw breath and attend to the wants of those discerning people who take their holidays out of season.

The dunes, which are the particular glory of Belmouth, put on their autumn heather mixture as the little bathing chalets are shut up one by one. From time to time, now, inhabitants can be seen looking forth and taking the air; like elderly tortoises, peering out from the fastness of their shells to find if summer is really gone for good.

On to this peaceful scene descended two busloads of the combined choirs.

'Now remember,' said Liz to her little contingent. 'You two tinies are to go with Miss Mallory. She's kindly promised to look after you.' The two youngest Hedges children looked rebelliously at Lucy. She didn't quite measure up to their idea of an ideal companion for a day at the seaside. 'You others'—she looked at the three elder Hedges and Rupert—'can go where you like provided you're back for tea at the Pavilion at four. We're having sausages, and I've particularly asked for them to be served first, so if you're as much as a minute late you probably won't get any. Subject to that you're free to do what you like, provided you don't break the law or get dirty or drown yourselves.'

'We've arranged to take *our* boys to a concert of music this afternoon,' said Mrs. Um.

'I've no doubt they'll be the better for it,' said Liz blandly.

She herself intended to have lunch and spend the afternoon with an old friend, the widow of General Dakers, who had come to Belmouth to die seventeen years before and had easily outlived the fondest expectations of her family and her insurance company.

'Well, that's everybody except us,' said Liz. 'I'm sorry Sergeant Gattie couldn't come. Annoying they should have found him a last-minute job today. What are you two planning to do?'

'First,' said Tim, 'we're going to the fun fair. I haven't been in a real dodgem for years. I may even throw for a coconut. After that all is in the lap of the Gods.'

The day started well. The silliest things were fun to do with Sue there gravely assisting. They had several hectic bouts in the dodgems, being crashed into from behind by Rupert and Maurice. The boys were both scarlet in the face, and seemed to have shaken off the two younger Hedges.

They ate lunch economically in the saloon bar of a small public house at the end of the front where Tim played Shove Ha'penny with an ancient lobster fisherman and lost three light ales in succession.

After lunch they strolled off the extreme end of the front and on to the dunes.

The sun looked genially down. A small but persistent wind blew in from the sea.

'What would be nice,' said Tim sleepily, 'would be to find a place in the sand which gets all the sun, but none of the wind, and lie down in it until it's time to go and eat sausages in the Pavilion.'

'Suits me,' said Sue calmly.

They walked out on to the dunes. The task they had set themselves seemed childishly easy, but, as all who have tried it will know, proved curiously difficult.

Some of the sand hollows were deep enough to be out of the wind, but into these the sun hardly penetrated. Others were full of sun, but full of wind also. When they finally thought they had found a suitable one they looked up and saw that they had come directly within view of one of the few chalets which was still occupied. Two elderly ladies were sitting in it, dressed in beach outfits, and playing a two handed game of cards. They suspended operations to stare at Tim and Sue. Tim and Sue moved on.

By now they had reached the western and most deserted tract where the cliff steepened and the dunes turned into cattle pasture.

'Let's try this one,' said Tim hopefully. 'It's got lots of sun and the wind's dropping anyway.'

'Looks all right,' said Sue. 'I don't think there's anyone in *that* monstrosity.'

She pointed to a little box of pink wooden planks. It was the last and most secluded of all the chalets and a board nailed crookedly, across an upright, announced that it was called 'The Retreat'.

'Looks as if it's been empty for some time,' agreed Tim. 'Lonely spot. We can both sit on my raincoat if I spread it out – what's the matter?'

'I don't know,' said Sue. 'I think it's all these horrible things that have been happening. Imagination, I dare say.'

'Never mind imagination,' said Tim. 'What did you think you saw?'

'It was just as you were saying how empty that place looked. I saw a face at the window.'

'Hmp,' said Tim. 'It doesn't seem possible. There's six inches of sand across the back door, and half the windows are broken. I don't think anyone can be living in it. Might be trespassers. Don't see why they should peep at us. I'll go and turn them out.'

'I'll come with you,' said Sue, hastily.

They climbed up and walked across to the hut. The boundaries of the garden had disappeared into the drifting sand which lay deep over everything. Sue pointed. Two fresh sets of tracks led up to a side door. There they got a bit mixed, as if the two owners had stood about. But there were no tracks coming away.

A thick, hot, silence lay over everything. Tim tapped on the door with his fingertips. The silence remained unbroken. He tapped a little harder. Under his pressure the door swung open.

Tim peered inside. It was a small and dust-choked lobby, with two more doors leading off it, both shut. The silence was absolute, more absolute than natural. It was the silence of held breath.

Something caught Tim's eye. He bent his head to look. Then he said to Sue, and for the first time his voice sounded serious, 'That door wasn't just forced. Someone's picked the lock, I guess. And pretty neatly, too. I really think you'd better—'

He gestured with his arm.

'Certainly not,' said Sue in an indignant whisper. 'If there's any shooting I want you right in front of me.'

'As you like,' said Tim. He moved up to the left hand door, opened it with a quick kick, and jumped in.

The room was empty. There was a little cheap beach-hut furniture; the most solid piece was a cupboard, the doors of which hung open. Tim went down on one knee and looked at the lock. 'Picked this one too,' he said. 'All skill, no force. Quite an operator.'

'The other room,' said Sue urgently.

Tim heard it too. He crossed the intervening space at a lumbering trot, kicked open the second door, and went through.

The noise they had heard was someone trying to open a window which had long been unopened.

'Good God,' said Tim.

'Rupert,' said Sue. 'Maurice. What on earth are you up to?'

Two very white faces stared up at them.

Rupert recovered first.

'We were exploring,' he said.

'All right,' said Tim. 'You were exploring. But explain just how you opened the front door – and the cupboard. You didn't do that with a bent pin.'

'I—' said Rupert.

'He—' said Maurice.

Any further explanations were cut short by the falling out from under Rupert's coat of a curious-looking instrument.

Tim picked it up.

It was about ten inches long, of bright steel. One end was formed into a sort of double handle, one fixed and one moveable. The other end was formed like a sort of flat key with two wards, rotating on a screwed thread. The wards moved independently, as the handles were turned.

'I see,' said Tim. As he did, with horrible clarity. 'Where did you pick this up?'

Rupert's mouth was a thin line.

'Rupert,' said Sue. 'It was you, then – you opened the poor-box – you did it when you went out of the room during practice—'

Rupert said nothing. He did not even bother to turn his head. Maurice started to snivel.

'And he shared it with you,' said Sue, turning on him fiercely. 'That's how you got the note. Isn't it?'

Maurice was made of softer material than Rupert.

'I never took it,' he said. 'Rupert took it.'

'Shut up,' said Rupert.

'Go on,' said Tim. 'Let's hear the truth.'

'He took it,' said Maurice. 'We went splits. He said it would be all right, see. I never touched the box. He opened it with that thing of his.'

'Where did you get that pick-lock?' said Tim.

'He got it—' said Maurice. 'He found—' He got no further. Rupert was at his throat. They went down in a cloud of dust with Tim on top of them.

It only took him a few seconds to prise them apart but Maurice was already scarlet and the marks of Rupert's fingers stood out on his neck.

'You say a word,' said Rupert, 'and I'll kill you. Understand. Kill you.'

'What on earth are we going to do,' said Sue.

'The first thing,' said Tim, twisting his hand even more firmly into Rupert's collar, 'is to find Liz.'

Chapter Fourteen

DUET – WITH TREBLE SUPPORT

BEROWNE:
'Light seeking light doth light of light beguile So ere you find where light in darkness lies
Your light grows dark by losing of your eyes.'

Liz had just arrived at the Pavilion when they got there. Luckily it was still nearly empty.

They pulled chairs up to a big corner table and told her the story.

'You mean they broke into a hut and stole.'

'There wasn't anything there to steal,' said Rupert. It was difficult to say whether he was regretful or repentant. 'We were just practising—'

'Look here,' said Tim. 'You stay with the boys, Sue.' He turned to his mother. 'Is there anywhere here we can be private? And is there a telephone?'

'I know the manageress,' said Liz. 'I think she'd let us use her office.'

The manageress was surprised but agreeable. She had known Liz for twenty years and admired her style greatly.

'It's terribly untidy,' she said.

'Never mind,' said Liz. 'It'll do splendidly. Just for five minutes. Bit of a crisis.'

'One of the boys?'

'Two of them, actually. Now Tim. What's it all about?'

Tim put his hand into his jacket pocket and pulled out the curious instrument he had taken from Rupert.

'If it had just been a matter of breaking into an empty beach hut,' he said, 'we wouldn't have worried, at least, not unduly. A bit of mischief worth a thick ear, but nothing more. This is what takes the whole thing out of the infants' class.' He nodded down at the bright piece of steel on the table.

'What is it?' Liz moved it delicately with her gloved finger tip and the steel winked back at her.

'It's a very beautiful and precise piece of craftsmanship,' said Tim, 'known as a pick-lock. You put it into the lock, like a key, and turn *that* handle until you've lifted the retaining spring – it's got a tight screw thread which will hold back even a strong spring – then you fiddle with *this* handle until the gate of the lock slides across, and there you are. Simple, quiet and effective. There are parts of London where you could get three months just for being found with one of these in your possession.'

Liz jumped a couple of squares.

'So it was Rupert who opened our poor-box—'

'I fancy so. And split the proceeds with Maurice. But that isn't the main point, is it? The question is, where did he get this jigger from? You don't buy them at ironmongers, you know.'

He handled the bright instrument lovingly. As he moved the handles the two tiny levers opened and shut like the mandibles of a Picasso crab. 'Precision work,' he said. 'Small enough to operate quite a tiny lock, but strong enough for a big one, too.'

'Does Rupert *admit* that he robbed the poor-box?'

'Maurice admits it. Rupert isn't saying a word.'

'What on earth are we going to do?' said Liz, helplessly. 'We can't just let them sit down and scoff sausages with the rest of the choir as if nothing had happened, but I don't see that we can actually lock them up until the coach goes. If only—'

'What about telephoning Bob? It wouldn't take him long to get down here in that car of his and he could take both boys straight back.'

'Bob? Yes, I suppose we could do that.' She seemed curiously unenthusiastic. 'I don't think we shall be able to get hold of him just now. He's at a council meeting.'

'Have him paged. They must be able to get at him somehow. Suppose his house was on fire.'

Liz took a deep breath, turned squarely on Tim, and said: 'I think it's about time you knew that Bob – oh, hullo. Yes, who is it?'

'Only little me,' said the manageress. 'There's a man asking for you.'

'A man?'

'A big man,' said the manageress coyly. 'Oh, here he is.'

Jim Hedges appeared. 'Finished my work,' he said. Thought I'd come and look you up. Am I in time for tea?'

'My goodness, Jim,' said Liz. 'How glad I am to see you. Have you brought your car with you? Good. Then I'll allow you five minutes for a cup of tea and you're on your way back again.'

It didn't work quite as quickly as that. Some explanations had to be given; and Big Jim, despite his preoccupation, succeeded in doing justice to a substantial tea; but within twenty minutes his old Studebaker Saloon was headed north again. In the back, both completely silent now, the two boys sat with Sue. Tim was in the front seat, beside Jim, who drove with the deceptive careful carelessness of a man who spends his life behind a steering wheel.

The sun, which had shone bravely through the day, dipped at last into a bank of cloud along the western rim of the sky. Dusk slowly coloured the fields.

'Put the clocks back soon,' said Jim, breaking a long silence. 'Then we shan't get no more of these evenings.'

He switched on his lights as they were running across Ditchley Common. Nobody spoke again until the car drew up outside the Artsides' house.

'Will I run Rupert home?' said Jim.

'No. He's staying with us until Bob comes along,' said Sue. 'Liz was 'phoning him when we left. I don't know what she's up to but we'd better do as she says. Hop out, Rupert,'

'All right,' said Rupert.

Maurice gave him a desperate look, which his ally ignored.

'I'll be going on then,' said Jim, after a pause.

'Bad business. Expect we shall see things better in the morning. You can come and sit up beside me, Morry. I'm not going to eat you.'

The car sighed off into the darkness.

A little, cold, wind had got up with the going down of the sun and Tim saw Sue shivering.

'Come on,' he said. 'Let's go in and light a fire and get a drink.'

They were half-way up the path when Rupert suddenly stopped.

'Come on,' said Tim.

'Is there anyone in your house?' said Rupert.

'Not as far as I know,' said Tim. 'It's Anna's day off.'

'What's up?' said Sue.

'I thought you might be interested,' said Rupert. 'That's all. There's someone up in your top storey. I saw a flash just as we got to the gate, and another just now. It looks like an electric torch.'

Three pairs of eyes stared at the house, which remained blind and unresponsive.

'Is this a try-on?' said Tim. He had lowered his voice.

'Try-on for what?' said Rupert. 'If I'd wanted to bunk I could have bunked ten times by now – only there's nowhere to go to.'

He sounded so desolate that Sue restrained a mad impulse to put an arm round him.

'My God, you're right,' said Tim suddenly. 'There he goes. Well played, Rupert. If you hadn't kept your eyes open we'd have walked right into it. You two – I think you'd better go back to the road and wait.'

'Think again,' said Sue.

'All right, but if you come with me you've got to do what you're told.'

His two assistants nodded dutifully.

They moved round to the back of the house. One of the French windows in the drawing-room could be opened from the outside if you knew the trick. No trick was necessary. When they got there the window was swinging on its hinges.

'Got in this way, did he,' said Tim. It started a new train of thought. 'Must be a friend of the family. Now look here, you two. You stay here. You can leave the passage door open, so you can hear what's going on, and ring up the police if I seem to be getting the worst of it.'

'All right,' said Sue.

'And if any shooting starts, lie down.'

'Ra-ther,' said Rupert.

Tim started quietly up. The front stairs were solidly built and well carpeted, and he made very little noise. The house was almost dark, but not quite. As your eyes got used to it you could see a little.

As he passed the tenth stair, just before the bend, he felt something fragile snap as his leg hit it; then a slithering, then a horribly loud clatter.

He knew at once what had happened. The man upstairs had fastened a stout piece of thread across the tread and suspended something from it – probably a brass ashtray – to give him warning of anyone trying to creep up on him.

He'd got his warning all right. Tim took the rest of the stairs fast, scuttled inside the first door, and settled down to wait.

The light they had seen had been on the top storey, which was Anna's room, the box room and the tank room. You got to it by a steep secondary staircase which was covered only by a thin drugget and had a most peculiar squeak. Tim was confident that no one, go he ever so carefully, could come down unheard.

Always supposing that he was not down already.

There could be no harm in waiting. In such blind and deadly games of hide and seek the man who waited longest usually came out best. On one such occasion—how long ago now?—in Salonika, he had sat waiting so, hour after patient hour, at the top of a ricketty flight of stairs until the old Greek below had got tired – or had persuaded himself that Tim was not there at all – and had lighted a cigarette, which was precisely the last thing he had done in his long and evil life.

If you waited long enough and sat still enough you usually heard something or saw something.

This time he heard it.

It was a tiny, but distinct, noise, somewhere right at the end of the passage.

Seemingly then, the man *had* made his way down the attic stairs whilst they were getting into the house. If so, he must have heard the ashtray drop. How long would it take him to persuade himself that it was the cat that had broken the thread?

Another tiny noise. His man was on the move.

Tim thought that he ought to shift himself. Where he stood, just inside the doorway of the bathroom, anyone coming past would see him, silhouetted against the grey of the window.

He edged out into the passage. Silence had dropped again, broken only by the bilious rumblings of the water tank.

The next door on the left was his mother's bedroom.

He won't be in there, thought Tim. The noise was further off than that. He's either at the end of the passage, or inside one of the rooms up that end. Suppose I switch the light on and rush him. No. Can't do that. He might have a gun. Better close up a bit.

He went on hands and knees along the thick carpet of the corridor. He was passing the bedroom door on his left when something stopped him.

Wait. It was gone. Try again. He had it.

It was a smell, faint but quite distinct; overriding the soapy, disinfectant smell from the bathroom and the scent and floor polish from his mother's room.

Sharp, and unmistakeable. With a tang to it – something between sweat and metal polish. He remembered smelling it before, as he had stood with MacMorris two weeks ago, outside the door of the little attic, with the water tank gurgling and whistling inside.

The difference was that this time he recognised it. He had smelled it often enough in Greece and Palestine and Italy. It was the smell of fear. Quite close to him, crouched behind the door of the bedroom, was a man who was mortally afraid.

Tim's own mouth was dry. A man who is afraid is a bad opponent.

No good stopping, thought Tim. He knows you're here. But he doesn't know, yet, that you know where he is. Move on, as if you were going past the door, then at the last moment—

Pivoting on his heel Tim hurled himself at the half-open door, in a shoulder charge. The door jarred on something soft and there was a protest of breath squeezed out of a body. Quickly Tim reversed, jerked the door open, and closed with his man.

He had him pinned into the corner behind the door. It was an awkward position for both of them. Whatever else you do, don't let go of his right arm. Cramp him. Keep him in the corner, until you can work your hand down to his right wrist.

Tim felt the man contract. Then, in a wild flurry of effort they staggered into the room. It was difficult to keep any foothold on the polished linoleum. We're going down in a minute. Must be on top after the fall.

Tim had forgotten the bed. As they went down they hit the back of it. The surprise shook them and both lost grip. The man tore himself free. No time for finesse. Tim dived after him.

He heard, more than saw, the knife blade, which said, 'whish' as it came through the air and 'kreesh' as it slit through the front thickness of his coat from lapel to pocket.

Then Tim was on top of him and they were both on the ground.

For a moment he thought he was winning, then he realised just how strong and clever his opponent was.

Unflurried by the fact that he was underneath, the man was manoeuvring, like a trained wrestler – hip – buttock – hip and in a minute he would be in position for that quick heave and roil which would reverse their positions and put Tim on the underside.

Tim put out every ounce of strength and weight he had. He heaved his body up, and came down, once, twice, three times, on the braced knees. With a sick feeling he realised that he was making no impression at all.

At that moment a lot happened at once.

The light came on; a young voice said something urgent; his opponent turned the upward thrust of his body into a sideways roil; there was a sharp crack near, but not on, Tim's head, and a sound of splintering; and the right wrist that Tim had been gripping for dear life slackened, and slipped under them.

At first Tim thought it was his own blood which was jerking out, warm and urgent, over his hand and arm.

Then the mist cleared, and he was able to pick up the details.

In front of him he saw Sue, her face very white, and Rupert, his hair on end, the remains of a china statuette in his hand.

Then he looked down at the floor, straight into the eyes of Sergeant Gattie. They were clouded, but untroubled.

'Quite a fight, Captain,' he said. 'Must have rolled on my own sticker.'

Tim knew enough not to move.

'Telephone the doctor,' he said to Sue. 'Quick as you can.' Sue fled.

'It's no go,' said Gattie. Even in that short time he was perceptibly weaker. 'And don't you try and patch me up either,' he added, with a flicker of spirit. 'It's better like this. Let it go.'

'Keep quite still,' said Tim.

What the devil was Sue doing?

'I'd like you to know something,' said Gattie at last.

'Rest easy,' said Tim. 'Don't talk. This is closing night. It's all over now.'

Gattie tried to say something more. Something urgent. Alarm flared in his eyes.

'What is it?' said Tim.

It was one word. It sounded like nothing on earth.

The door opened and Sue burst in. 'I can't make anyone hear,' she said, it's the telephone. I don't think it's working.'

'That's all right,' said Tim. He got up slowly. He was feeling terribly stiff, it's too late now. Would have been too late anyway,' he added, as he saw the look on her face.

'Did I kill him?' said Rupert.

'No,' said Tim. 'You distracted his attention. He rolled on his own knife. Give me that bedspread, will you? I'd like to clean this up before mother gets back, but I expect the police ought to see him first.'

They went out, shut the door, and went down to the hall.

Tim jiggled the telephone. It sounded quite dead.

'It's no good,' said Sue. 'I tried.'

Tim pulled the instrument, and it came away in his hand. The flex had been cut under the telephone table.

'There's a call box at the corner,' said Sue.

'You stay here with Rupert,' he said.

'I say—' said Rupert, urgently.

They looked at him.

'You know Gattie was upstairs.' They nodded. 'What was he doing, fiddling round with that torch? Was he fixing to blow this house up too?'

'Good God,' said Tim. 'I'd forgotten all about it.' He paused for a moment. It seemed curiously difficult to think. Then he said, 'You two go out into the garden – right down to the bottom. Now don't argue. You won't be any help in this. In fact, you'll be in the way.'

'Tim,' said Sue, 'You can't—'

'If we tackle it the right way,' said Tim, 'there's no danger at all. I can't explain now, but this isn't the sort of explosive which goes up at a certain time. You have to do something to start it off. If there are three of us in the house, we're three times as likely to do it.'

What doors had they opened, which must not now be shut? What lights had been turned on that must not be turned off? Or, if turned off, on no account turned on again.

Try to think.

'Off you go,' he said. 'I can't get started till you're gone.'

'Wouldn't it be better to wait for an expert—'

'I know as much about explosives,' said Tim patiently, 'as anyone within thirty miles of Brimberley tonight. If you're too obstinate to go yourself, you might think of Rupert.'

'I'm not scared.'

'Come on, Rupert,' said Sue, 'We're embarrassing the gentleman. We'll wait in the summer house till he whistles for us.'

'But I don't want—'

'Look here,' said Tim. 'If you're not gone by the time I count five, tired though I am, I'll give you, here and now, the biggest walloping you've ever had in your life.'

'If that's how you feel about it,' said Rupert, composedly, 'I'll go.'

Tim watched them off and then went slowly back through the

French window. First he must have a torch. There was one in the kitchen, he thought. Safer not to turn any more lights on, though. He got out his cigarette lighter, eased round the half-open kitchen door and started to search. In the end he found it, hanging on a nail beside the plate rack.

He came out again into the hall and walked upstairs. His search must start in the attics. If Gattie had planted the explosive anywhere else, why should he go up to the attics at all?

And it was not as if he was looking for something you could hide away just anywhere. The explosive to destroy a solid house like this would be a bulky packet – quite as big as a large suitcase.

The door to the attic stairs presented a problem. It was shut. There was no way round that. They had no ladder long enough to reach the top storey windows.

Tim tried to consider the matter logically. It was, on the whole, unlikely that this particular door had been chosen, for the simple reason that there was no certainty that any of them would use it that night. In the end he opened it. Nothing untoward happened. He wedged it open.

There were four rooms on the top storey. Two box rooms, Anna's bedroom, and the room with the cold water tank in it. All the doors were ajar.

Tim started with the tank room, which had nothing in it at all (except the tank). The window was tightly shut and had obviously not been moved for years. Next he tried Anna's room. There were a few obvious places – a hanging cupboard, a curtained recess, under the bed. None of them yielded any secrets. The window was a dormer and opened on to a steep pitch of tiled roof. Nothing could have been put or hung out of it.

One of the box rooms was used for storing apples. The whole floor space was covered with newspaper, on which the fruit lay in neat rows. Tim acquitted it at a glance.

He had kept till the last the front box room. It was the bigger of the two. Like Anna's it had a dormer window, and it was full of stuff.

It was the box room that finished him.

He was soaked with sweat; sweat that had dried on him and then sprung up again. His movements were slow and heavy as if he moved in a nightmare. Round his head, killing thought, ran an iron bracelet of tiredness. And he had to think, as never before in his life. Could he lift? Dare he probe? An endless Tantalus-torment of fatigue and dust and fear.

He lost all sense of time. He had no idea if it took him five minutes or fifty, but in the end he had done it. He walked downstairs. After the attic, the bedrooms were an anti-climax. He searched them thoroughly, but without precaution. They contained nothing that they should not.

As he reached the hall the drawing-room door opened and Sue looked in.

'Whatever have you been doing?' she said. 'Do you know you've been more than an hour? Rupert was getting worried. He said you'd fainted.'

She looked at him thoughtfully, and added, 'You look as if you could do with a wash and brush up.'

'I don't faint easy,' said Tim with a grin. 'To the best of my knowledge and belief the house is clear. I refuse to believe that Gattie had time to take up the floorboards and replace them without leaving a trace. Short of that, I've looked everywhere in the house which could contain even a modest packet of explosive.'

'Perhaps he dumped it in the garden whilst he went into the house to explore.'

That's an idea,' said Tim. 'But I'm not doing any searching to-night. Now for the call box. Hullo—'

There were footsteps in the front porch, the rattle of a key in the lock, and the front door opened and Liz came in.

Close behind her was the General.

Liz took one look at her son, another at Sue, and a third at Rupert. 'What have you been up to?' she said.

'It's a long story,' said Tim.

Then you'd better tell it quickly,' said Liz. Her voice was hard and high. 'We're up against a time limit. I telephoned Bob and asked him to come round at nine o'clock. It's nearly five to nine now.'

'All right,' said Tim. 'Only I'm going to sit down, if you don't mind.' He led the way into the drawing-room.

It did not take long. The General said nothing. Liz, who had been listening like a person who hears bad but expected news, said, 'You're certain, now, that he hasn't fixed his booby trap?'

'Pretty certain. I don't think there's any place bigger than nine inches square in this house that I haven't looked into. He can't have put it anywhere very elaborate. He wasn't here all that long.'

Liz looked at her watch.

'Rupert,' she said, 'will you go out into the kitchen and start getting yourself something to eat. Do you know how to fry an egg?'

'Rather.'

'You'll find everything you want in the larder. That's the boy. And as for you, Sue—'

'All right,' said Sue. 'If you're indicating tactfully that I'd be better out of the way, I couldn't agree more. I've less than no desire to see Bob, and I feel as if I'd crawled backwards through the corporation rubbish dump. A big hot bath is what I want.'

'There's a clean towel in the airing cupboard,' said Liz.

Something stirred, very faintly, at the back of Tim's mind, but no thought was born. He was sitting back – lying almost – in the chair and as long as no one asked him to move he thought he might get by.

The General said something quietly to Liz, who thought for a moment, then said, 'I think they're all in the cupboard in the cloakroom, just inside the front door.'

The General went out, and when he came back Tim saw that he was carrying one of his father's sporting rifles, a light twenty-bore with a dark, carved, stock and old-fashioned ejector that had been made half a century earlier but was still a very lovely gun.

The clock on the mantelshelf struck, and, as at a signal, huge headlamps swung out of the road and into the drive. The big car came quietly to a halt. The engine was cut. A click as the car door opened, and a 'tock' as it shut.

The General put the gun carefully down behind his chair.

'I'll let him in,' he said.

He went out and they heard the front door open and shut; feet in the passage; and Bob Cleeve appeared with the General just behind him.

'Come in, you bloody murderer,' said Liz, 'and shut the door.'

Chapter Fifteen

QUARTET – WITH STRINGS

DUMAS: *'Dark needs no candles now, for dark is light.'*

The three of them looked at Bob, and Bob looked back at them.

What does he say now, thought Tim, struggling against the waves of fatigue. What does anybody say, in such a situation? There was indecency in it; like a man being forced to undress in front of his friends.

The General shifted very slightly in his seat, so that the tips of his fingers rested on the steel of the shotgun.

Bob stood in the middle of the room, his feet planted square, his face a little redder than normal, his light blue eyes abstracted.

Time plays odd tricks,' went on Liz. 'I find it almost easier to forgive you what you did in Cologne in 1920 – though it cost me my husband – than what you've done to-night. Gattie's upstairs now.'

'Dead?'

'First you talk him into carrying on your stupid burglaries – because you'd got too fat or too dignified to do them yourself – then you send him to be killed. He was a nice person, too. A better person than you.'

'Not fat,' said Bob. 'I'd never allow myself to get fat. I'm as fit now as I was twenty years ago. Rupert was the trouble. If he felt lonely at night, he used to come along to make certain I was still there. Couldn't risk him finding me gone.'

He sat down carefully in the wing-backed chair beside the fire.

'By the way'—he levered himself up and looked round—'no microphones?'

'Don't be silly.'

He settled back again comfortably.

'How long have you known?' he said. 'And, incidentally, who does know?'

'Just the three of us,' said Liz.

Bob looked away. A small, cold, tremor touched the General. Exactly so had he seen the African buffalo look away. Just before it charged. He edged the gun forward into his hand.

'Well now,' said Bob. 'When did you guess?'

'When you told me,' said Liz. 'No sooner and no later. That evening at Clamboys. Do you remember? When you said that you never saw a problem in the abstract. All your difficulties were people – you actually mentioned Rupert.'

'A bit obscure.'

'It didn't register at once,' said Liz. 'But perhaps you remember, a week earlier sitting in this very room with Hubert and me. Telling us the story of Feder, the country house burglar. How he came to his downfall through being seen by a boy. It's plain now. You were rationalising your own fears. You were deadly afraid it might happen to you, so you invented it happening to someone else. Pure voodoo.'

'How do you know?'

'Don't be silly,' said Liz. 'I asked Tom Pearce, of course. Nothing like that happened to Feder at all. He was caught, all right; but nothing like that. They got at him from the receiving end. Through one of his safe deposits.'

'Did they now,' said Cleeve, amiably.

Watch him, thought the General, he's fluffing. This isn't really going home at all. He's acting. Dangerous man. Don't relax.

'It's when a thing is absolutely obvious'—went on Liz—'patent and above board and plain from beginning to end – that you don't see it. To start with, how could you possibly be so disgustingly rich, unless you were a crook? Your family never had any money, did they?'

'Not a cent.'

'And all the jobs you've ever done. Army and police and Home Office. They never paid you enough to get fat on.'

'They paid the most inadequate salaries.'

'And yet, there you were living like a—like a nabob, with an enormous house and servants and horses and cars and God knows what. And of course, when one comes to think about it, you had a top Q job at Cologne in 1920. That must have been the foundation of your family fortunes—'

'I'd pulled off a few modest coups before then, but I admit that was the beginning of the big stuff.'

'Motor-cars and tyres and petrol and Red Cross medical stuff—'

'And food,' said Cleeve, with savage good humour. 'We'd any amount of food, and the Germans were starving, remember?'

'And I suppose Bill had just about got wise to you.'

'Believe it or not,' said Bob, 'and you probably won't, because I can't possibly prove it, but that was nine tenths genuine accident. A very fortunate accident for me, I admit, but an accident just the same.'

Liz gave him a long, cold, look. The trouble is,' she said, 'that you're so corrupt that nothing you say has got very much meaning in it. It might be true. It might not. Was the blowing up of MacMorris an accident too?'

'Good heavens, no. It was a most carefully planned job. Practically the perfect crime. We couldn't be expected to guess that the little creature was going to lose his nerve at the last moment and start writing letters to himself, and roping Tim in. If it hadn't been for that, he'd have gone up and no questions asked. I'd planted one or two ideas in the official mind that he might be the country house burglar they were so interested in. Burglars handle explosives. MacMorris blew himself up. Therefore MacMorris was the burglar. *Post hoc, propter hoc.*'

'Very neat,' said Liz. 'Where did Gattie put the explosives?'

'Under the bed,' said Cleeve, a shade too quickly.

But that's a lie, thought Tim, coming suddenly to the surface. The bed would have disintegrated if the explosive had actually been under it or even near it. He's telling the truth about some things and lies about others. Why should he bother to lie about that?

'Since you're being so obliging—' said Liz.

'So damned suspiciously obliging,' said the General,

'—perhaps you wouldn't mind telling me, just as a matter of interest, why you should have tied a rope across the General's gate-post and then run into it yourself.'

'I'm afraid,' said Cleeve sadly, 'that that bit was all Gattie. He did it off his own bat. I think your activities had begun to alarm him, and he decided that it would be better for all concerned if you were laid by for a bit. I'm sure he didn't actually mean to kill you.'

'You overwhelm me,' said Liz. 'And I suppose you're telling us all this, because you know we can't prove it.'

'There's not a shred of proof in it from beginning to end. It's all the purest surmise. Intelligent assessment of probabilities. Or moonshine and wishful thinking, according to which side you see it from.'

'There's a little more to it than that,' said Liz. 'I don't know how far the police took you into their confidence, but they've been watching Brasseys and the Captain for over a year—'

'Brasseys? Oh, you mean that eating place in Sloane Square, kept by the character with side whiskers. I have been there once or twice. Got to eat somewhere when you go up to town.'

'Six times in the past twelve months.'

'You surprise me. Me and who else?'

'Oh, about five thousand other people,' agree Liz. 'It's just a tiny scrap of corroboration. Also there's a strong possibility that the police will be gathering in the Captain and his boyfriends any day now, and he may decide to purchase his own comfort by a little discreet gossiping.'

'I don't think he knows very much about me, really,' said Cleeve. 'And the worst I know of him is his post-war claret.'

'All right. Then there's the wife of Sergeant-Major Bottler.'

'Now there you have got me. I don't remember the Sergeant-Major at all.'

'No?' said Liz. 'He remembers you, though. And he took the trouble to ring up the General yesterday and tell him so.'

They both looked at the General, who shifted very slightly in his chair and said, 'That's right.' He had not taken his eyes off Cleeve for a fraction of a second since Cleeve had come into the room.

In the sudden silence they could hear, from upstairs, the faint wail and gurgle of the water tank as it filled again after Sue had finished running her bath.

The noise started off a curious train of thought in Tim's mind. It sprang from a triple coincidence of sight and sound and smell. On two different occasions he had stood, in the near darkness, outside an open door. On both occasions he had smelled the smell of a man in mortal fear. On both occasions, also – and this was the first time that it had occurred to him – he had listened to the gurgling and whistling of a water tank. What made a water tank gurgle and whistle?

'I'm still not quite clear,' said Cleeve politely, 'what it is that the Sergeant-Major, or his wife, remembers.'

'It's just one of those mad coincidences,' said Liz. 'The file that you stole, the one with all the records of the Cologne explosion, its number was M.B. 56. And the day you went there to look at it – calling yourself, with some lack of originality, Major Robinson – was Madge Bottler's fifty-sixth birthday. Therefore the Sergeant-Major happened to remember it. I'm rather looking forward to hearing that tried out on the jury. I think they might like it.'

'My dear old Liz,' said Bob, 'if you haven't got any more than you've been giving me, you won't get near a jury. You might get into court, but it'll be a civil court. Action for defamation. However—'

Watch him, thought the General. Much too pleased with himself. And why does he keep looking down at his watch. If I'm not mistaken that's twice I've caught him doing it.

'—if that really is all for the moment I must be getting along home. Rupert will be wondering what has happened to me.'

'Rupert—' began Liz. But quite suddenly there didn't seem to be anything useful to say about Rupert.

So he doesn't know Rupert's here, thought the General. Wonder what he'd say if he knew he was in the kitchen cooking himself eggs and bacon. Would it make any difference to him – supposing he has planned to do something. Better be ready for anything.

'That's quite all right, General,' said Cleeve. 'I can see the gun. But I'm quite sure you're not going to be so unkind as to use it on me.'

'Shoot you if you get difficult,' said the General. 'Not unless.'

'Then I hope you don't classify going home as "getting difficult",' said Cleeve, 'because that's what I propose to do – by all your leaves.'

He was on his feet now. Neither Liz nor the General moved.

Tim seemed fathoms deep, in abstraction. Why did water-tanks and cisterns always make such a peculiar noise when they were refilling, particularly at the moment when they were nearly full?

'You realise,' said Liz sharply, 'that there is someone who can give evidence against you. Rupert must have solved the secret of your famous priest hole; and incidentally helped himself to one of the implements you keep there – along with the explosive, and the swag, and other things you wouldn't care to leave lying about the house. You didn't by any chance lose a pick-lock? It must have been some time ago. Rupert is quite expert with it now.'

That hit him. There's his head coming round. He's going to charge.

'I don't know what you mean,' said Cleeve at last. 'But if you think that you or anyone else can make Rupert say anything he doesn't want to, I should advise you to think again. I'm fond of him, and I think he's fond of me. You'll find us a difficult combination. And now, if there's nothing further to be said—'

He was half-way to the door when they all heard it. The front door of the house opened and slammed shut; heavy and hurried footsteps in the passage, then the drawing-room door was thrown open, and the bulk of Jim Hedges filled the doorway.

In that same moment Bob Cleeve turned on his heel, ran to the French windows, thrust against them, and was gone.

His disappearance seemed to release a spring which set them all moving.

'Don't go after him,' said the General. 'Telephone Tom Pearce. They must head him off. Oh, damn, I forgot, your telephone's out of action. There's a box on the corner.'

The car outside had started, and they heard it slam into top gear as it went down the drive.

'Better be quick,' said the General. 'If he gets back to Clamboys he'll destroy all the stuff in that secret cache of his, and then he can snap his fingers at us.'

'Don't you worry, General,' said Jim. 'It's all set. That's what I came to tell you. I didn't know *he* was here. You could have knocked me down—'

They stared at him.

'Morry told it all to me. Just so soon as he was alone in the car with me, out it all came. I never heard such stuff, secret hiding places, and dynamite and burglars' kits and jewels and such. I rang up the Inspector right away, you see. Mr. Pearce was with him.'

'Did they—'

'They didn't take a lot of convincing. They almost seemed to be expecting it. They came round, and picked us both up, and Morry showed him how the thing worked – under the staircase, a real neat job. You'd hunt a month and not find it.'

'So they'll be waiting for him when he gets back.'

'That's right,' said Jim. '*If* he gets back.' They could all hear the engine rising into top pitch, as the big car, driven by an angry man, hit the long straight stretch, west out of Brimberley, on the Clamboys road.

In the silence Tim heard something else, too. It was a noise he knew well. The characteristic, expiring effort of the water cistern.

Why did *they make that peculiar noise? The water ran out, and the ball-cock dropped as the level fell. He had made a joke about it, as he stood outside the MacMorris cistern room – something about someone coming to steal the ball-cock – then, as the level rose, the arm carrying the great brass float rose too, shutting up the inlet value. Up, down, and up again.*

'My God,' said Tim, in a voice that jerked all heads round together. 'What bloody fools we are. No time to talk. Jim, get Rupert out of that kitchen and turn on the sink taps. JUMP TO IT.'

Jim jumped.

'General, take Liz out—right away—down the garden. Fast as you can. DON'T ARGUE.'

Then he was gone.

201

He took the steps in fours. There was no time even to try the bathroom door. He ran at it and slammed the sole of his foot hard, an inch below the china handle.

A smacking crack as something broke and the door burst inwards. Sue was standing just beside the bath. She gave a very faint squeak. Tim did not even spare her a glance. He was at the basin. With two rapid movements he flicked on the taps. Then the bath taps.

'Put a towel round you,' he shouted, then swept her up and was out into the passage and skidding down the stairs.

Sue said 'ouch' as a bare bit of her hit the bannisters. Then they were cascading down the hall and out into the garden.

'I think I could walk now,' she said faintly.

Tim put her down absentmindedly and she gathered the towel round her. Fortunately it was a large one.

At the bottom of the lawn they found the General with Liz, and Jim Hedges with Rupert pick-a-back on his shoulders.

'Hadn't we better get a bit further – or lie down—' said the General.

Tim let out his breath in a long, slow, sigh.

'No,' he said. 'It's all right now. But give it five minutes.'

'I got both taps on in the kitchen,' said Jim. 'And I got Rupert, too.'

'Not half, he didn't,' said Rupert. 'He nearly broke my arm when he picked me up. I say, isn't this fun. What happens next?'

'Nothing,' said Tim. 'Nothing. It's all over.'

They stood together in the dusk, listening to the cascading of the water.

EPILOGUE

'COME, YE THANKFUL PEOPLE—'

KING:

'The extreme part of time extremely forms
All causes to the purpose of his speed
And often, at his very loose, decides
That which long process could not arbitrate.'

'I could kick myself, now, for having been so stupid,' said Tim, to Tom Pearce. 'It was presented to me, on a plate, twice, and I missed it.'

'Lucky you didn't quite miss it the second time,' said Pearce, 'or we should have had a real old mystery on our hands.'

'I don't know,' said Inspector Luck, resentfully, 'that I understand it now.'

'It was the water in the main cold water cistern,' said Tim. 'However many other tanks you have, if you use any water in the house anywhere it must, ultimately, empty that tank – which fills again from the main. The whole thing is regulated by a valve, which opens and shuts by means of an arm, with a floating ball on the end. The ball goes down, the valve opens wide, the water rushes in. As the water level comes up, the ball comes up too, and shuts the valve. It's the last dying jerks of the arm letting in little spurts of water that cause the extremely odd noises most tanks make when they're almost full.'

'But—' said Luck.

'The point is,' said Tim, 'that unless *some* water has been run recently the tank won't make any noise at all. It isn't a living organism.

203

You've got to do something to set it going – pull a lavatory plug or run a basin of water. So why should the MacMorris tank have been gurgling at me when he and I were searching the house. I'd already been in the house at least half an hour – probably more. And MacMorris hadn't been out of my sight.'

'He might have just finished a bath the moment you came.'

'All right. So he might. I don't think he had, but it was just possible. But how could anything like that have happened in our house when I got back after the choir outing? It was Anna's day off. The house was – or should have been – empty since before lunch. Yet the tank was active. Meaning that someone had drawn off some water – and recently.'

'I still don't see,' said Luck. 'Where did Gattie put the explosive?'

'You're not trying,' said Tim. 'He put it in the tank, of course. A little water doesn't hurt a good modern explosive. You can immerse it for weeks. I think the sequence was this. First empty out enough water from the tank. There's usually a runaway tap up in the loft. He could use that. Tie back the valve arm so that no more runs in. Fix your detonating mechanism – a three-way switch – to the valve arm. Then untie the valve arm so that the water could run back to its proper level. That was all you had to do. The victim himself would do the rest, next time he drew off any water. If it was just a basinful, to wash his hands – which I think was all MacMorris did before he went to bed – then the tank would refill quickly and the explosion would be quick. If you emptied the tank for a smacking great hot bath, like Sue, bless her, then it would take much longer for the arm to come right up again and set the thing off.'

'And so long as you kept some water running the tank would never quite refill, and you'd be safe.'

'That's it,' said Tim. 'And if you never washed at all, you'd be safer still. Cleanliness furthest from Godliness really.'

'I see,' said Tom Pearce, 'I'll remember it next time I have a bath. That letter – I take it MacMorris probably did write that to himself.'

'I should think so, yes. Something made him suspicious. He felt they were moving in on him. Perhaps Gattie came into the house to reconnoitre and he heard him. Something like that. I think, too, though it's of no importance now, that it was MacMorris who destroyed that photograph. He wouldn't want it in evidence if the police were going to come nosing round. Too direct a lead back to his past. He was going to destroy that note about Brasseys when the explosion caught him. He already had destroyed the photograph. Probably burned it.'

'Wonder he kept it at all,' said Luck.

'He was proud of it,' said Tim. The Regiment is a bigger thing than you.'

II

'Apparently,' said the General, 'when he got back to Clamboys he spotted Luck's car – careless of Luck, that. So he turned straight round, and went back down the drive fast. Don't know what was in his mind. I expect he'd got one or two safe deposits and that sort of thing. May have hoped to skip the country. Came out into the road too fast and went straight under a ten-tonne lorry.'

'Yes,' said Liz. She sounded neither vindictive nor upset. 'Tom Pearce missed a chance there. As soon as I heard about it I suggested he took Gattie out and put him in the car beside Bob. That would have solved all their troubles.'

'He couldn't do that.'

'Why not?'

'Most irregular. You could never hush it up. Bound to come out about Bob.'

'I wasn't worrying about Bob,' said Liz. 'He did it because he enjoyed it. I told him as much. He was an Elizabethan. Piracy. Throat cutting. Love making. I wouldn't be surprised if he didn't write sonnets as well. No. All the regrets I've got are for Gattie. Thank God he wasn't married, but his mother's still living. I've spoken to her. She's a nice old girl, and she's going to get hurt by this. Rupert, too.'

'What are you doing about Rupert?'

'He's staying with me,' said Liz. 'He ought to go to school right away.'

'You can count me in on that,' said the General.

'We'll finance him jointly. He'll be a credit to us yet.'

III

'If only you'd *explained*,' said Sue.

'Well, it seemed so silly,' said Tim. 'There I was, with everyone assuming I was in the Secret Service, and all the time I was holding down a respectable job as an estate agent.'

'Was that how you knew all about Belton Park?'

'That's right. I'd inspected it the week before. I used to run round a lot of properties in the home counties. The firm lent me the car. It was rather fun.'

'Why do you say "was"? You're not giving it up, are you?'

'Well—'

'I'd much rather marry an estate agent than someone in the Secret Service.'

'That's all right then,' said Tim. He kissed her absent-mindedly. He felt no difficulty about that sort of thing now. There was a lot to be said for starting your engagement by carrying the girl, mother naked, down a flight of stairs and dumping her on the lawn.

Broke the ice, so to speak.

IV

'You *do* seem to have bad luck with your tenors,' said Mrs. Um, signalling for her bill. 'First that nice Major, and then the police sergeant.'

'I expect Tim will do the solo very nicely,' said Lucy Mallory.

'I hope so,' said Sue.

'As a matter of fact,' said Liz. 'I've had a last-minute offer—rather unexpected—I can't tell you definitely yet—'

V

Florimond had said yes. Of course he would. It would be the greatest pleasure in the world. It must be done unofficially, of course. Not a word to anyone.

Liz agreed.

Florimond no doubt meant what he said too.

But he had not calculated with his publicity man, who had no use for lights if they were hidden under bushels, and saw no reason that such a chivalrous gesture should be entirely wasted.

Nothing vulgar like newspaper publicity, of course. But if you know how to use them there are faster and better ways of spreading news than the printed word.

At midday the first of the cars started to arrive. By one o'clock the parking problem was becoming acute; and a hastily assembled fatigue party was clearing the south gallery which had not been used since it had been condemned as unsafe before the turn of the century. At two o'clock chairs from the Institute were rushed up in Jim Hedges' lorry and set outside the open west doors.

Fortunately the weather remained perfect.

The Vicar fussed round, getting in everyone's way, torn between horror at the mounting problem of accommodation and gratification at the probable size of the collection.

At two-thirty the choir squeezed their way through the extra benches in the transept and took their places.

The only perfectly composed people were Florimond himself – after some preliminary difficulty over cassocks it had been discovered that by fortunate chance, he and Liz were exactly the same size – and Rupert.

Rupert fingered from time to time a piece of paper in the breast pocket of his flannel jacket. It was the prospectus of St. Oswald's school for boys. He had no need to look at it, for he had most of it by heart. 'A fully equipped gymnasium with a whole time physical training instructor,' who also 'instructed in small-bore shooting on the 25 and 50 yard ranges.' Rupert had paced out twenty-five yards in Liz's garden that morning. He reckoned that if he could hit a moving cat at that range a stationary target should be easy meat. 'Rugby football is played in both winter terms.'

Both winter terms. If he went in January that meant he could start right in.

'We will commence,' said the Reverend Hallibone, 'with a prayer of thankfulness for the harvest.'

A strange harvest, he could not help reflecting as he glanced at the row upon row of the packed and fashionable audience. Well, never mind. Was there not a saying about spoiling the Egyptians?

'Come, ye thankful people, come.'

They were well together, thought Liz. The presence of Florimond and the pressure of the crowd were combining to raise them above themselves. It was going to be all right. It was going to be terrific. It was going to be a triumph. How Mrs. Um was going to hate her. How satisfactory everything was.

Rupert and Maurice and the other children. Tim and Sue. Lucy Mallory. Big Jim Hedges. Florimond himself, his face composed to a look of highly artificial piety.

'All is safely gathered in—' Roll on winter.

MICHAEL GILBERT

CLOSE QUARTERS

An Inspector Hazlerigg mystery

It has been more than a year since Canon Whyte fell 103 feet from the cathedral gallery, yet unease still casts a shadow over the peaceful lives of the Close's inhabitants. In an apparently separate incident, head verger Appledown is being persecuted: a spate of anonymous letters imply that he is inefficient and immoral. When Appledown is found dead, investigations suggest that someone directly connected to the cathedral is responsible, and it is up to Hazlerigg to get to the heart of the corruption.

'…brings crime into a cathedral close. Give it to the vicar, but
don't fail to read it first.' – *Daily Express*

THE DOORS OPEN

An Inspector Hazlerigg mystery

One night on a commuter train, Paddy Yeatman-Carter sees a man about to commit suicide. Intervening, he prevents the man from going through with it. However, the very next day the same man is found dead, and Paddy believes the circumstances to be extremely suspicious. Roping in his friend and lawyer, Nap Rumbold, he determines to discover the truth. They become increasingly suspicious of the dead man's employer: the Stalagmite Insurance Company, which appears to hire some very dangerous staff.

'A well-written, cleverly constructed story which combines the
unexpected with much suspicion and dirty work.'
– *Birmingham Mail*

Michael Gilbert

The Dust and the Heat

Oliver Nugent is a young Armoured Corps officer in the year 1945. Taking on a near derelict pharmaceutical firm, he determines to rebuild it and make it a success. He encounters ruthless opposition, and counteracts with some fairly unscrupulous methods of his own. It seems no one is above blackmail and all is deemed fair in big business battles. Then a threat: apparently from German sources it alludes to a time when Oliver was in charge of an SS camp, jeopardizing his company and all that he has worked for.

'Mr Gilbert is a first-rate storyteller.' – *The Guardian*

The Etruscan Net

Robert Broke runs a small gallery on the Via de Benci and is an authority on Etruscan terracotta. A man who keeps himself to himself, he is the last person to become mixed up in anything risky. But when two men arrive in Florence, Broke's world turns upside down as he becomes involved in a ring of spies, the Mafiosi, and fraud involving Etruscan antiques. When he finds himself in prison on a charge of manslaughter, the net appears to be tightening, and Broke must fight for his innocence and his life.

'Neat plotting, impeccable expertize and the usual shapeliness combine to make this one of Mr Gilbert's best.'
– *The Sunday Times*

MICHAEL GILBERT

FLASH POINT

Will Dylan is an electoral favourite – intelligent, sharp and good-looking, he is the government's new golden boy.

Jonas Killey is a small-time solicitor – single-minded, uncompromising and obsessed, he is hounding Dylan in the hope of bringing him into disrepute.

Believing he has information that can connect Dylan with an illegal procedure during a trade union merger, he starts to spread the word, provoking a top-level fluttering. At the crucial time of a general election, Jonas finds himself pursued by those who are determined to keep him quiet.

'Michael Gilbert tells a story almost better than anyone else.'
– *The Times Literary Supplement*

THE NIGHT OF THE TWELFTH

Two children have been murdered. When a third is discovered – the tortured body of ten-year-old Ted Lister – the Home Counties police are compelled to escalate their search for the killer, and Operation Huntsman is intensified.

Meanwhile, a new master arrives at Trenchard House School. Kenneth Manifold, a man with a penchant for discipline, keeps a close eye on the boys, particularly Jared Sacher, son of the Israeli ambassador...

'One of the best detective writers to appear
since the war.' – BBC